ALL OR NOTHING

Miranda Sapphire

For all my fellow monster fuckers, who look at weird shit and think, "hell yeah I want to fuck that."

And for the big girls who think no one will ever want them. I'm sorry, but you're just wrong.

About

<u>Joss</u>

As far as I'm concerned, hell is being stuck at a soul-sucking retail job while your mom insists you go to nursing school and get back with your toxic ex. All I want to do is write about people falling in love and nurse my poor broken heart in peace. I definitely need a vacation…but getting abducted by aliens wasn't what I had in mind. Although, when a smoking-hot green dude with horns buys me to set me free, I realize that maybe this is my chance to turn this catastrophe into a blast-trophe and live out my own alien romance…

<u>Xollen</u>

I can't take it anymore—I'm so lonely and miserable that I'm willing to break every hygiene law on Billieu to hire some company for the night. But I should have known I was too stupid to handle even that. Instead, I find myself the sweaty, anxious owner of five female slaves, my entire savings account cleared out to rescue them from a fate worse than death. All I wanted was to free them, but when the soft, gentle human in the group asks to stay with me and help me get back on my feet, I can't say no…

Joss and Xollen have a lot of work to do to get their new life as roommates up and running smoothly. There's getting Joss set up as a citizen of an alien civilization, finding a new place to live, navigating how to work together, dodging Xollen's terrible parents, and figuring out if the attraction they feel for each other is just that…or something more.

Will finding each other prove to be a dream come true, or a nightmare they can't wake up from?

Content Warnings: slavery, abduction, mentions of fatphobia and racism, internalized fatphobia, narcissistic parents, toxic relationships, manipulation and emotional abuse, mention of homelessness and housing insecurity, discussion of poverty, graphic sex scenes.

Tropes: alien abductions, human women facing enslavement by aliens, alien peen/"what that dick do?", MMC with anxiety, "get your ass to therapy" (and he does!), culture shock/fish out of water, hygiene laws, roommates.

Chapter One
First Contact

JOSS

I sighed, snuggling deeper into my pile of warm and cozy blankets as I pulled up *Silent Love* on my e-reader. I was pretty sure that the sexy but surgically muted alien assassin was about to bone down on the human woman he'd rescued from slavery, and I'd been waiting all day long to dive back into this juicy piece of sci-fi smut. It had been a long day too—we were approaching Valentine's Day, and it meant my life was shittier for a couple of different reasons.

I worked as a cashier in a big box retail store, and so any time a gift-giving holiday approached I was treated to the absolute worst parts of humanity every time I clocked in. Valentine's was better than Christmas at least, but there was still an awful lot of entitlement and screaming in my face. And the *mess*—oh my god why did people have to leave shit *literally* anywhere but where it belonged? It meant my closing shifts took forever, and I'd been late to my nursing classes more than once in the last few weeks.

It wasn't like I really minded though; I hated getting chewed out by my professors, but I wasn't really interested in the classes, or the degree, and was really just taking them to keep my mom off my back. She and her sister, my aunt, were both nurses, and she was determined for me to follow in the family footsteps and enter the medical field as well. But whenever I had the energy I engaged in my true passion—writing.

The energy was definitely not there tonight, so I was consoling my aching body and soul with someone else's words.

Just as I'd gotten comfortable I felt my phone buzz by my elbow. I glanced down at the screen and groaned when I saw it was my mom calling. *Motherfucker.* I set aside my e-reader with a longing glance at its screen and picked up the call.

"Hey, mom," I answered, trying to sound chipper. If I let my fatigue leak into my voice she'd get snippy with me and accuse me of giving her attitude.

"Joslyn," she sighed, and I wished I could let out a sigh of my own. I knew that tone: she was going to lecture me. "Have you talked to Alex recently?"

My heart sank. He'd broken up with me months ago, but my mom still asked about him like she didn't even know we were done. "Nope!" I trilled, swallowing down the bitter grief creeping up my throat. "He hasn't talked to me since he asked for that hoodie back."

My mother tutted, fabric rustling on her end of the call. "Such a shame, I loved Alex. He was such a sweetheart. And so *handsome.*"

Of course my mother had loved him—he was just like her. Putting on a kind face for the world, but as soon as the doors closed he'd been mean and hypercritical of me, tearing me down in the hopes that I'd rebuild myself just how he liked. Sure, he *had* been handsome, and pretty fit thanks to being a gym bro, but even though it still hurt it was definitely good that he wasn't in my life anymore.

But I didn't say any of that. I'd been talking it over a lot with my therapist Dr. Jackson, and we agreed that it was time for me to start withdrawing from my mother. She wasn't listening to me or respecting my boundaries, and I was working too hard on myself, on fixing the wounds that my mother had gifted me, to deal with her anymore. It wasn't an easy decision by any means, and had been years in the making, but in moments like this it was obvious that it was the right choice.

"He really wasn't nice at all," I said for the millionth time, bracing myself for her to reject my words. "He was pretty emotionally abusive."

My mom sighed, and I could practically hear her roll her eyes over the phone. "Well, Joslyn," she insisted, and I rankled at that—not only did she invalidate my abuse, but she refused to call me Joss like I preferred. "I know how sensitive you are, and I can't help thinking that maybe you just took his helpful advice the wrong way..."

She was still talking, but the blood was rushing too loudly in my ears for me to hear her. How fucking *dare* she?! This was one of her favorite attacks, and I knew it well, but in that moment it came crashing in on me, how awful it was that she kept doing this, and how much *more* awful it was that I kept letting her do it.

I didn't know if it was because I was so tired, or if I really was done and had reached my breaking point, but before I could stop it I was speaking again, interrupting her.

"Fuck you," I spat, "just leave me alone." I stabbed at my phone screen to end the call and blocked her number before she could call me back.

I stared at my phone, now dark and too heavy in my shaking hand, and felt a wave of tingling heat sweep all through my body as what I'd done hit me. My gut instinct was to unblock her and beg for forgiveness, the people-pleaser in me still so strong even after all the years I'd been in therapy. But I took a deep breath, then another, my eyes sliding closed, and tried to get control of my thoughts.

After several long minutes, my eyes started prickling, and then a laugh bubbled up into my throat, and I wasn't sure how much of what my body was doing was crying and how much was laughing—all I knew was that it felt like a dam had broken inside me and all of the emotion that had been trapped behind it surged out into my chest with so much power it was squeezing my heart and lungs. I was gasping for breath, tears and snot dribbling down my face, but I realized I wasn't regretting it—I was scared of having made such a big decision out of the blue, I was scared of her finding a way to punish me, but I didn't regret telling her off and blocking her. It was way overdue, for a lot of reasons.

I didn't know how long it was before I managed to calm down, but the tears and unhinged laughter did eventually die out, and I slipped out of my bed and into the bathroom to clean my face.

I was completely beat now, I realized bitterly, so when I flopped back into my blanket nest and saw my e-reader darkened to its lock screen I put it back on my nightstand and turned off the lamp, rolling onto my side and drifting off to sleep.

I woke up in an unfamiliar place, my bare skin shivering with cold. It felt like I was naked and lying on a slab of icy metal, but my body was so heavy I couldn't seem to move it aside from opening my eyes. Blindingly bright lights seared into my tear-swollen eyes. I winced, squinting, and was surprised to realize I wasn't alone. I was surrounded by weird sparkly jellomen, and said jellomen were hovering over me with some pretty intense tech clutched in their shiny, translucent hands. They seemed to be speaking, though not in English or even Spanish (which I didn't actually know, anyway, since mom was white and my Puerto Rican dad died when I was two), and were gesturing at me. I found myself staring hard at them, entranced by the translucent brightness of their flesh, at the way it seemed to sparkle and shift as little lights blinked off and on from within their bodies like tiny fireflies. The jellomen were human-like in shape but had random spiky bits all over, and no faces I could see on their heads aside from their two big black eyes. One was bright red, one orange, and one yellow, and I found myself calling them Cherry, Orange, and Lemon in my head. Cherry seemed like he was in charge; he had the fanciest-looking tool and seemed to be doing the most talking. But without mouths, it was hard to tell who was saying what.

This is a weird fucking dream, I thought hazily, studying them as best I could while half-blind from the bright lights. But maybe it would get better and I'd get to have some saucy fun, like in my alien romances.

After a while of them gesturing and talking they seemed to realize I was watching them, and Cherry make a high whistling kind of noise that sounded surprised. They started jabbering louder and faster, almost like they were alarmed, and because I was certain I was dreaming I started laughing.

"Listen, guys, this is fun and all but you're making me hungry and I'm getting pretty cold over here, so if you're going to do something to me can we get on with it? I probably gotta get up soon so, y'know, let's hurry this along already. Especially if it's going to get sexy."

All three fruity flavors froze, flinching back from me as I spoke. I laughed again, wiggling my eyebrows and winking at them. In real life I was still struggling with loving myself, with seeing my body for what it was instead of my enemy, but in my dreams I was free of that and able to be bold. I mean if you couldn't be your authentic self in your dreams, then when *could* you be?

My three new friends jabbered some more, and then Cherry took a gun-like implement from Lemon and twisted a dial on the barrel.

"Ah, so we're not getting sexy, then. That's a real shame, boys," I sighed, though really I wasn't all that disappointed by this development. I was into some weird shit, sure, but I wasn't ready to find out I was into fucking food tonight.

Cherry leaned down, holding the icy barrel to my bare neck and making me hiss and flinch. There was a click, a prick, and then things faded to black.

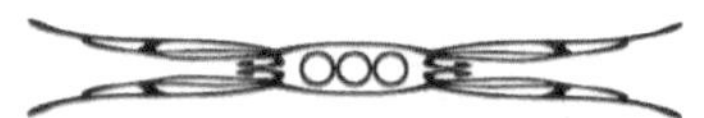

When I next woke up I was laid out on a thin, upsettingly gritty cot in a cold, bare room that looked an awful lot like a cell. My mouth was cottony and tasted foul, and my head pounded with a nasty headache that had my eyes feeling swollen and hot. My ears were also really bothering me; they felt tender and a little swollen, almost like I was fighting off a double ear infection. I wasn't naked anymore, I didn't think, and when I finally got the strength to lift my head I saw I was back in my pajamas—a ratty old t-shirt and flannel shorts. No bra. Very old panties. A terrible look for being out in public. While I had my head up I looked around and was startled to see I wasn't alone. In the dim yellow light I could see there were four other cots on the floor in here with people passed out on them. My head slammed back down when my weakened muscles gave out, but I managed to roll onto my side and prop my head back up on my hand, being careful of my sore ear, so I could keep looking around.

My heart was pounding so hard it felt like it was trying to jump up into my throat and choke me, but I forced myself to take deep breaths and calm myself down. I didn't know what was going on, but it didn't look good, and I'd probably need to keep my cool. My stomach still gave an ominous gurgle though, and I prayed nothing was going to come shooting out of me unexpectedly because I did *not* see a toilet.

Once I'd calmed down a little I started taking stock of the room I was in: I was at one end of the plain rectangular room, with the other cots spaced about four feet away from each other. My nearest neighbor was lying on their side facing away from me and looked like they were wearing a fur coat. They moaned and rolled over onto their back, and I was startled to see that they were dressed like they were auditioning for *Cats*. The fur coat was actually a full-body suit, their face totally transformed by what had to be some really high-quality prosthetics to give an extremely cat-like face. *If they would have used this person as a model for that creepy CGI movie it probably would have actually taken off*, I thought. I even saw sharp fangs glittering from their sleep-slackened mouth, and the shine of long claws tipping their furry hands in the gloom.

Beyond the cat person was someone huge who looked a lot like an orc with an extra eye in the middle of their forehead. They, too, were asleep, but facing toward me on their side, and unlike me, they were wearing proper clothes that looked like some kind of armor.

I realized that it probably wasn't a person in a cat suit, now that I'd seen the orc. I swallowed, beginning to sweat with nerves, my efforts at calming down going out the window. Beyond the orc-person, it was too dark to make out much detail about the last two figures, except that one was very small and had either a really long scarf or a tail, and the person on the opposite end of the room was about my size.

"Fuck," I cursed, dots starting to connect. "I better not be about to get asked if I want to play a game," I muttered, lowering myself back down and curling into a ball. Humor had gotten me through a lot of tough times, but something was telling me I was in for something that would take an unprecedented amount of jokes to slog through. After all, I'd seen this before, if only in the filthy alien romances that featured abducted women getting rescued and wooed by sexy aliens. I wasn't stupid: I knew that in real life that scenario was going to be far from flirty and fun. I swallowed, curling in on myself tighter. *Okay, since it's just me I'll let myself have a little freakout. As a treat. And then I'll get my shit together and try and figure this out. I can do this. I'm strong and capable. Would someone who just told their abusive mother to go fuck herself give up in the face of alien abduction? I think not.*

With no clocks or windows, there was no way for me to tell how much time had passed, but it seemed like it was probably close to an hour before my fellow cellmates started waking up. I was still scared as fuck, but I'd gotten some control over myself and no longer felt like I was on the verge of a panic attack.

The next person to groan to life was the three-eyed orc, who took one look around and swore, rolling to their feet and struggling into a crouch. They patted themselves down, clearly looking for something, then swore again, more violently.

"Fucking Veldar's tits," they hissed, and though the voice was rough and gravelly I thought there was something feminine about it overall. "Anyone else awake?" they called softly.

I raised my hand, sitting back up. "Yo. I think you and me are the first ones, though."

The orc nodded, their eyes darting around the room. Keeping to their crouch, they crept around the perimeter of the room, giving each of the sleeping figures a once-over when they got close. "Any idea where we are?" they growled as they finished their recon. This person *screamed* military.

"Nope!" I responded cheerily, trying to lighten the mood. "And my name is Joss, by the way. Or Joslyn if you're feeling fancy." I didn't trust my legs to hold my weight to go over and try and shake their hand, but I'd read enough alien romances with slave tropes to know that I probably wasn't on Earth anymore, that I might have been the only human in this room, and that for all I knew a handshake was a declaration of war to this person. So I settled for a smile and a wave. *Shit, hopefully that's nothing dirty either.* The heroines in monster romances made this stuff seem so easy. But now that someone else was up and seemed a lot more capable of handling shit, I *was* feeling a less overwhelming flavor of panic.

The orc grunted and lifted their chin in one of those cool half-nods I'd never been able to pull off. "I am Uraka. Have you seen any others while you have been here?"

"Yeah, I thought it was a dream at the time but I guess not, huh? When I first woke up there were these three spikey guys that looked like they were made of jello but with blinking lights all through them. I didn't know what they were saying but there was a red one, an orange one, and a yellow one."

Uraka sat down hard and wiped their hand down their face. "You are female?" they asked.

"Yeah. Uh…are you?"

"Yes. And this felican between us is female. I am certain we are all female, and headed to the stocks as pleasure slaves."

"Oh," I squeaked, feeling hot and queasy all of a sudden. "What makes you think that?"

"I do not know what this 'jello' is, but from your description, I would bet good credits that those were th'rak slavers." At my blank expression, Uraka sighed and elaborated. "They specialize in female sex slaves and exotic black market meats."

I swallowed, panic starting to make me feel sick. I did wonder, though, just how a whole race of people wound up specializing in something like that. "So since we're all female we're probably going to be slaves? Not meat?"

Uraka shrugged. "In my mind, either way we are to be meat."

Bile surged in my throat, though I was able to swallow it back down and keep that much of my dignity, at least. Uraka didn't look like she was panicking; she was just incredibly pissed, and it gave me a kind of hope. Surely someone as large and capable as her would have some sort of plan? And then I'd have something to do, something I could actually tackle, to make me feel better: help Uraka kick whatever ass she was planning to kick.

"Do…do you think we could try and escape?" I asked in a whisper, my eyes darting around the plain concrete room.

Uraka shrugged again. "We can always try, but they would just kill us instead. Slavers always protect against resistance well, especially the th'rak. Maybe if I had all my gear, or if everyone here had combat training we would have a chance. But tell me, Joss—are you combat-ready?"

I huffed, frowning. "No," I admitted, crossing my arms over my free-hanging breasts that felt too prominent and heavy. Man, I *really* wished I was wearing better clothes. Or at least better underwear.

But I hadn't spent the last five years with Dr. Jackson working on my self-esteem just to forget all she taught me at the first real test. *"You are so strong, Joss,"* I could hear her reminding me in her smooth, soothing voice. *"You deserve good things happening to you, and you owe it to yourself to make those good things happen."*

Man, I missed Dr. Jackson right about now. But thinking about her, about how she wouldn't want me to give up, made me not want to give up either. Maybe I was being *como una cabra,* as my abuelita liked to say whenever I did something kind of dumb, but I thought I could trust Uraka. She radiated safety and seemed to be making an effort to be kind to me, even if she was tense and upset about the situation.

"Well, how combat-ready do you think you can make me before they come for us?" I asked the she-orc, uncurling the rest of the way from my panic ball. I was scared shitless and if I thought about the situation too closely I felt screams bubbling up my throat, but I wasn't going to just sit here when I could be helping, could be doing something.

One of her thick eyebrows arched at me, followed by a decidedly wicked grin spreading over her olive green face and pulling her lips taut against her small tusks. The look in her three golden eyes said she approved of my question. "Let us see."

Chapter Two
El Lonely Boy

<u>XOLLEN</u>

My console lit up with another notification about an incoming comm from my best friend, Derris. Yet again, I silenced it and focused on the autopilot's route to Quellor Station as if I could understand any of what I was seeing. I didn't want to ignore him, of course, especially when this was the first time he'd reached out to me since he had mated to Gesea five lunars ago. But if he knew what I was up to way out here there was no way he'd let it stand.

What was it about best friends and their terrible timing? Lunars upon lunars with almost no word from him and as soon as I was about to do something stupid he was suddenly determined to talk to me.

I sighed, scrubbing my hand down my face and contemplating my life yet again. It was both a blessing and a curse that I couldn't pinpoint any one decision that had tipped everything one way versus another. On the one hand, it helped me to not beat myself up over it too much, but on the other, it meant I had no way to stop it from happening again.

I had had a decent relationship with a beautiful and high-class woman, I had been in university studying to take over my parents' media empire, and I had been feeling pretty good. I never felt *truly* good, but I had felt well enough. And then Verilla had left me, saying I was too sensitive and hideous for her to stomach me despite my family's reputation and wealth, and I was failing all my classes, and I was feeling very far from good.

Loud blaring startled me from my rankling thoughts, making me jump and yelp. What in the name of the Goddess was *that?*

"Xollen Me'Tirri Be'Faan, why are you avoiding me?" Derris's voice snapped, making my bowels feel slightly liquid.

"D-Derr?" I called tentatively, whipping around to try and find him.

"I sent the comm as an SOS. Now you *have* to talk to me, you piece of *vrakaash.*"

I winced. "I wasn't avoiding you," I tried. "I was…in the hygiene room?"

He snorted, the sound of a chair creaking in the background. "Xoll, I've known you since we were five orbits. I know when you're hiding." He cleared his throat, and when he spoke next his tone had softened. "Listen, I know I've been kind of…absent since me and Gesea made it official, and I'm sorry for that. I hope you know it wasn't on purpose."

I was torn. I wanted to be mad at him, to make sure he knew my hurt, but this was *Derris.* The male who'd stood up for me against bullies, who'd made sure I had a fun birthday when my parents forgot or made it miserable, who was the only one who thought my art was worth spending my time on. I sighed, slumping back into my chair. "I know," I told him quietly.

I could hear the smile in his voice when he spoke. "I missed you, Xoll. It's been too long."

"I missed you too, you *vrakaashaad,*" I grumbled, a smile of my own twitching the corner of my lips.

He chuckled. "So why are you avoiding me?" he pressed.

"I was hoping you'd forgotten about that."

"Not a chance. My 'Xollen is up to something' alarm has been blaring all day. What is it?"

I squirmed. "I-I can't tell you, Derr. It's…"

"Illegal?"

I jolted. How in the name of the Goddess did he *know?* I neither confirmed nor denied it, my tail lashing the air behind me.

He sighed, and I could just picture his copper eyes squeezing closed, his mouth pressing into a hard line in exasperation. "Xoll…" he said in a warning tone.

"I just—I have to do something, Derr." I waved my hand in the air as if he could see the gesture. "I don't want to talk about it but I promise I've thought about it a lot and I'm—I'm sure."

He was quiet for several minutes. "Is this about Verilla?" he asked quietly.

I tensed, spine snapping straight. "Not really," I hedged. It wasn't about her per se, but she was a piece of the equation. With my people's extremely strict hygiene laws, physical intimacy between unmated partners was illegal, punishable by life in prison, and mating rights being taken away. But I was the only person I knew my age who was still unmated without any prospects whatsoever.

I wanted to be touched so badly I ached. At this point, it wasn't even about sex—although if I could get it I wouldn't be upset. I just wanted to hold and be held. To feel someone's skin against mine, their body heat seeping into me, without any PPE between us.

I could feel Derris's piercing look across the comm and several planets' worth of distance. "Just be careful, Xollen," he said at last, and I loosed a breath in relief. I really did love Derris, he was a good male and a better friend. Gesea was a lucky female. "If you need someone to bail you out call me last," he teased.

We chatted for a bit longer, then ended the comm, with me promising to call him once I got back home.

It was good to hear from my oldest and best friend, but it hadn't helped my nerves to be reminded of just how risky all this was. But I felt…trapped. Desperate. I'd gotten a letter from my university saying I'd been dropped from my program, and on top of what had happened with Verilla, and Derris mating Gesea, and all the other matings that my parents were constantly shoving in my face, it had just gotten to be too much.

I needed close physical contact. I was going to do one of the worst things a citizen of Billieu could do…I was going to hire a sex worker. I might just spend the hour cuddling them, but that was plenty deviant all on its own.

This is why I was heading to Quellor Station: this particular rotting hulk of space trash had a reputation for catering towards billieuan clientèle, offering extremely discreet accommodations and certified clean workers. Not just of sexually transmitted infections, but of *all* illnesses. Given Billieu's tragic history with disease, it was a necessary precaution to regulate physical contact so tightly—you never knew when a hug or a kiss would lead to the next Drowning Flu, after all— but it made for a miserable and touch-starved populace.

I was snapped from my brooding by another alarm, this one from my shuttle's AI informing me we were on approach to Quellor so that I could strap in and prepare myself. The AI would handle the docking and clearance with the station's systems while I got myself ready.

I headed to my quarters, where my private decontamination stall was located, to get sterilized and don my PPE. I didn't particularly like the tight glass container and the astringent mist it filled with, but I did like how much safer I felt after I'd done it. Right outside the stall was the PPE dispenser, allowing me to don my mask, gloves, booties, and safety goggles as soon as I was sterilized. The faint odor of the mask and the papery scrape of the booties against the magsteel floors was a comfort, taking the edge off my nerves as it hit me that I was really doing this, I was really going to Quellor to try and slake my desire for touch with a stranger.

I made it back to the control console, limbs trembling and my tail wound tight around my leg to try and soothe my nerves. I strapped into the captain's chair and accepted the docking bay the station AI had assigned to my ship.

I took several deep breaths and tried to calm myself. I could still change my mind once I got there and head home, I reasoned. No one knew I was doing this but me, and if I turned tail then so what? But it didn't make sense to come all this way and not at least check it out.

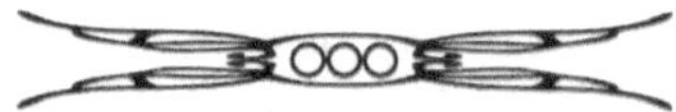

As I stepped from my private shuttle onto the filthy docks of Quellor Station—intensely grateful for the layers of protection covering me—I was struck by a glaring flaw in my plan: I had no idea where to find what I was looking for. Were there actual establishments I was meant to pick up a companion from? Did I need to make a reservation? What sorts of processes and decorum was I meant to observe? A wash of panic flowed through me as I realized just how many things I didn't know, how much could go wrong.

Would I be alright searching the station's nexus access point for this information? Sex work was generally legal now but was it legal here? Was it only legal sometimes? Would I get picked up just for running that search on Quellor's access hub because I was billieuan? Would my government be able to track that search and use it to arrest me? My hands were getting uncomfortably sweaty in my gloves.

I spun on my paper- clad heel, ready to retreat and call this trip a bust when I heard a snippet of conversation flit past me.

"…bay 13, I think. Real fresh cargo, untouched."

Their companion whistled low, barking a laugh. "You ever have pussy that fresh, Gart?"

"*Pfft*, hell no. With this ugly mug I'm lucky to get any at all…" the two males slipped out of my hearing range, and I found myself compelled to go to docking bay 13. Perhaps it was nothing, but then again, perhaps it was a lead I wouldn't need to incriminate myself to get. Worst case scenario, it was nothing I was interested in and I would go on my way.

Before I could think too much about what I was doing I scrambled over to the information desk for a map. I was tragically far from docking bay 13, I discovered, but if I shelled out for station transports I'd make it there in five minutes, give or take.

What's the rush, really? I found myself thinking. *You're just going down there to take a peek. More to satisfy curiosity than anything.* I took several deep breaths to try and fortify myself, my tail still wound soothingly around my leg. But I couldn't ignore the way my heart was pounding, the way something I couldn't name was tugging at me deep in my belly. As if something big was about to happen.

Chapter Three
Crazy Orcs Make the Best Friends

<u>JOSS</u>

I decided that if the jellomen didn't kill me, Uraka would be able to handle the job nicely. My muscles were weak and rubbery from what felt like hours of lessons on basic self-defense. I appreciated what Uraka was doing for me, truly, but also I definitely hated her and would gladly have ripped her smug face clean off her skull.

"Come on, Joss! Really come for me, put some spirit into it!" she called, bouncing easily on the balls of her feet. I was so tired, and so sweaty, and seeing her there looking fresh and spry and oh-so-dry had me wanting to weep.

"I don't know how much more spirit is left in my body," I wheezed, hating the whine I heard in my own voice. "I'm not as strong as you," I admitted quietly, almost without meaning to. Like many bigger girls, I tried my best to love my body, to appreciate it and fill myself with confidence, but a lifetime of being told I was lazy, weak, gluttonous, and pathetic because of my weight was hard to drop. And whenever my confidence faltered, whenever I felt vulnerable or too visible…well, that old insecurity would hit me like a freight train. And seeing how weak and ineffectual I was next to Uraka on top of this being a stressful and scary ass situation…well, it was definitely rearing its ugly head. All I seemed to be able to think was that I'd never be able to do this.

But Uraka just snorted. "Strength is nothing, little one. What is strength worth if you don't know how to use it? Stop thinking about what you cannot do and focus on what you *can*. This is what I have been trying to teach you!"

I wanted to believe her, I really did, but my emotions were just running too high, and to my eternal shame I found tears pricking at my eyes. My can-do attitude had finally run out, it seemed. "But what if I can't do anything?" I asked softly, my gaze falling to the dirty floor. I mean, look at my track record: I couldn't finish my degree, couldn't land a partner, couldn't lose the weight, couldn't figure out what I wanted for a career, couldn't even keep my damn cactus alive (RIP Prickly Pete). Uraka meant well, but I couldn't shake the feeling that she only thought so highly of me because she didn't really *know* me.

Uraka's three eyes softened, the third in the middle closing. "You have been told this before, that you can't do things?"

I nodded, sniffling pathetically. Uraka abandoned her fighting stance and crossed the space we'd cleared to grip my shoulders in her huge calloused hands. "Many people have told me this as well. 'Uraka, you are too dainty the join the vanguard', 'Uraka, your tusks are much too small to hope to rip out a veshtun's throat', 'Uraka, that knife will never be able to pierce my tough hide'…" Okay, so this orc lady might have been a little more insane than I first realized. But I couldn't deny that the hands on my arms were comforting. "It makes it all the sweeter when you prove them wrong and do all the things they said that you could not, and more.

"You are doing well for your first lesson, I promise you. But what I do not teach you now I may not be able to teach you later, yes? I am going as hard as I can because I do not know how much time we have. So tell me: can you find more spirit for me? Can you find that spirit for *you?*"

Goddamn, this crazy orc was going to make me cry. Dr. Jackson would love Uraka, I decided. I straightened my shoulders and wiped away the lone tear falling from my eye, nodding. She was right; I didn't know how much time we had, so we had to make it count. Self-pity time was over.

By now the other three sleeping women were awake, and while the felican, whose name was Djelani, was watching us closely—especially Uraka, I thought, and if I wasn't mistaken Uraka was flexing and showing off *just* a little under Djelani's appreciative green gaze—I was the only person interested in Uraka's hasty self-defense lessons.

The small figure with a tail was named Wren, and she looked so much like the Pokémon Mew that it had me wondering if maybe the guys over at Gamefreak had somehow gotten a photo of one of her people. The only thing that was missing was that Wren couldn't float, and wasn't psychic…maybe. I hadn't been able to figure out where the hell she'd been talking out of yet, since she didn't seem to have a mouth. At least, not one where I'd expect it. The last woman and the only other human in the group was Ghena. She was strikingly gorgeous, with large doe-like eyes, full pouting lips, high razor-sharp cheekbones, and a lithe, delicate frame. Perfectly mussed auburn hair and a light dusting of freckles all over her tawny skin completed the picture, and if it weren't for our situation I'd've probably been a little jealous of her.

But what did prettiness have to do with where we were going, wherever the hell that might be? We weren't on Earth anymore, and might never be ever again. It hit me all at one, like I'd been dunked into an icy tank of water: I was *free*.

Not literally, obviously, but in terms of the insecurities that I'd been struggling with my whole life, in terms of the judgment of others that had tricked me into thinking that there was something wrong with me and my body just because it tended toward squishiness...I *was* free. I stood up straighter, realizing that this was what Dr. Jackson had been trying to get me to see when she'd said that my body wasn't good or bad, it just *was*. And even if I wasn't as strong as Uraka, I was still strong enough to keep up with her. I'd been the first one to wake up, and whatever they'd used to knock me out wasn't hitting me as hard as it was Djelani, Wren, and Ghena—and wasn't that a *good* thing?

I'd been giving myself a hard time for so long, telling myself in one moment that I was beautiful and good and worthy and then letting myself undo that in the next. But I wasn't on Earth anymore. I had been abducted by aliens and would be fighting for my life, and having more weight to throw around was going to come in handy. Being able to resist drugs that knocked me out was going to be valuable.

Fuck, had my body been *good* this whole time, and I'd just been too well programmed by my culture's fatphobia to see it?

Uraka put her hands up, palms out, so I could keep practicing my punches. "Twist from the hips and shoulders, little one," she coached, her gold eyes watching me move. "You generate more force this way, putting your body weight behind it. Picture someone you hate; it helps put fire in your spirit."

Easy: I pictured Alex's smug face twisted in distaste, telling me I shouldn't wear a form-fitting dress or that I'd look so much more put together if I was blonde. I pictured my mom and the way her mouth would purse any time I'd eat anything other than salad or chicken breast in front of her. I thought of my classmates, giggling and making comments about my big butt and jiggly thighs. I pictured my doctor telling me over and over again that I must be lying about how much I was eating and exercising because I was still fat despite everything. And I pictured the little girl I'd been, crying her heart out in her room because everyone who looked at her saw too much and not enough at the same time.

I managed to hit Uraka's palm hard enough that she staggered back a step, her muscles jumping under her olive-green skin to absorb the impact.

"Good, Joss," she urged me, grinning. "I will make a warrior out of you yet." Despite my lingering fears and frustrations about my situation, I beamed with pride. "Again," she barked, getting back into position. Nodding, I returned to the stance she'd shown me.

After what felt like another hour, I was officially too tired to stand, flopping onto my abandoned cot. "You guys sure you're good? It's a great workout, really takes your mind off of things," I called out to the other three females in the room with me who'd declined self-defense lessons earlier.

"Um…maybe I could try?" Ghena said in her soft rasping voice, her hands gripping the hem of her oversized sweatshirt and twisting it. She bit her full rosy lips, clearly nervous. "Um, that is, if you don't mind."

"Certainly!" Uraka crowed, waving her up. "Were you watching what I was doing with Joss?" At her nod, Uraka smiled. "Good, then show me what you have learned."

Chapter Four
Meat Market

XOLLEN

I had really, truly stepped in *vrakaash* now.

This wasn't a bordello. This wasn't any sort of establishment where one could hire a sex worker, in fact.

This was a meat market. The three gentlemen standing before me in front of a glowing holoscreen with privacy filters engaged were th'rakkans, and they were selling slaves. A pair of mean-looking yvrenii males were leaning down towards the screen and dragging the pads of their fingers along the serrated edges of their tusks.

"They're guaranteed untouched?" one asked, crossing his thick arms over his broad chest. "How do you know?"

"We contracted top investigators to seek out these targets. Their every communication, their medical history, and our own scans have verified this. We are honest traders, sirs," the red th'rakkan assured his potential customers.

The orange th'rak peeled himself away from the group and approached me, bowing his translucent head in greeting. "Are you interested in our wares, *sir*?" he hissed, his tone making it clear that if I wasn't shopping I wasn't welcome. He seemed very skeptical of me, his black eyes narrowed. I supposed he probably didn't see many billieuans in his line of work.

I barely suppressed a shudder, disgusted at the thought of there being slaves here, and was torn about what to do about it. I could contact the authorities and hope that Quellor Station wasn't being bribed by these three and would actually respond, and quickly. This was unlikely, if Quellor was anything like any other station I'd ever been on. I could just walk away, turn tail and leave the knowledge of this behind me like the not-my-business I could argue it was.

Unbidden, an image flashed through my mind of the poor souls being held in captivity, my mind conjuring the faces of my loved ones in their place, since I hadn't seen the slaves' faces yet. I pictured their faces twisted, haunted, warped with fear and agony, at the whims of monsters.

I couldn't do it. I couldn't just walk away.

But what *could* I do? Like most people from Billieu, I avoided physical confrontation because of its high bacterium transfer risk, but it also scared me and was something I knew I was in no way equipped to handle. I was tall and had some muscle from keeping to a fitness regimen, but I had no real strength, and even less coordination.

What if…what if I *bought* them? I had inherited 1.5 million credits two solars ago from my uncle when he passed. I was up to a little over 3 million now with interest and the rest of my savings. It was all the money I had in the world, since I didn't work and my parents had cut me off when I was ejected from the business program, but surely I'd be able to figure something out. Could I really leave those females behind when I had the means to help them?

"I am interested. What do you have for sale?" I heard myself say, my tail squeezing my leg harder.

The orange th'rak seemed to look me over, assessing my net worth, perhaps. I wasn't dressed extravagantly—I had wanted to blend in while I was here, after all—but the quality of my clothing and the jewelry I wore in my ears and draped over my horns was unquestionably fine, if simple. Seemingly satisfied, the orange th'rak led me to the screen and tapped a button on his wristcom to allow me to see what was on it. The two yvrenii had moved on, and it was just me and the th'rak now.

On the screen, five portraits of sleeping females were displayed along the top, with a live feed of a cell with the same five females up and moving around. There wasn't any sound, but it looked like the massive yvrenii female was fighting a much smaller one of a species I'd never seen before. But no—they weren't fighting, the movements were too slow and controlled for that, and the yvrenii was gesturing, clearly demonstrating to the other female how to perform a grappling maneuver.

"What is that smaller one that the yvrenii is fighting?" I asked, curious. I couldn't tear my eyes from her, from the sensual curves of her exposed flesh, the gritted determination plastered on her little face that gave way to shocked delight as I watched her land the move the yvrenii was showing her. It was doing very odd things to my chest.

"Human, from Earth. A planet in restricted space, very rare. Especially at this price." One of the th'rakkans clicked a button on his wristcom and prices appeared beneath the portraits.

I whistled low, my eyebrows shooting up towards my horns. Heavenly mercy, but that was a lot of credits. Each of the three women whose races I recognized were listed at 250,000. But the humans were over 1 million each.

I had just barely enough to buy all five of them.

Wait, what am I thinking, here? I could buy all five of these poor souls from these slavers and then set them free. But I wouldn't be able to support them once I freed them; I'd be completely broke. I'd be on public care. I'd have to *work* for the fine things I'd grown accustomed to. I'd never had to work before, and had only recently moved out of my parent's palatial estate to try and find my own way after they'd stopped supporting me. I was borderline helpless, with no practical skills, and would probably be dead without my credit reserves to smooth my way.

It would be beyond stupid to do this, no matter how good my intentions were. I mean, what if I was caught with them? The authorities would never believe I had purchased five females being sold as bed warmers out of the goodness of my heart.

But if I didn't, what would happen to these five helpless beings? The yvrenii might be alright, but the others? Especially that tiny, soft-looking human—what would happen to her? What would happen to that smile she'd given so freely to her companion? I felt sick to my stomach thinking about what those two yvrenii males would have done to someone like her.

"I'll take them," I heard myself saying with horror. But with pride as well. I was being reckless, foolish, impulsive beyond sense—but I was *doing* something. And I realized in a flash that I didn't think I'd ever been able to say that before. All my life, I'd gone along with what other people wanted for me and just forced myself to like it. I didn't know what it said about me that *this* was the situation in which I'd finally found my backbone, but oh well.

"Which one?" the red th'rak said, pulling a tablet from an unseen spot on his person.

"All of them," I managed to reply, switching on my wristcom to initiate a transfer. It wasn't real yet, what was happening. It felt like I was still stuck in the time several minutes ago when I was just watching this screen and thinking about what I could possibly do to help instead of doing this insane thing.

All three th'rakkans froze, regarding me, their postures wary and tense. "All…five? Are you certain? You have the credits?" the red one asked after a moment.

I nodded, flashing him the screen strapped to my wrist that was displaying my account balance.

It would be a tight squeeze, fitting five extra passengers on my little shuttle, especially when one of them was an yvrenii warrior. But I was committed now. If I backed out these three would probably kill me and try to steal the credits. They might even be planning on doing so anyhow.

But after a moment the red th'rak bobbed his head and pulled up a transfer screen on his tablet. I held out my wrist and authorized the credit transfer. A cold stone sank in my gut as I watched the display flicker, then stop at "128 credits". I gulped. Thank the mercies of fate that I'd just refueled my ship and paid my rent before this. That 128 credits was going to have to last a very, *very* long time.

But I was now the queasy, sweaty owner of five female slaves.

"We will pack your purchases and return shortly," the red th'rakkan said, gesturing for the yellow one to follow him. I had no idea what that could entail, but the orange slaver left standing with me didn't seem concerned—although I had to admit, th'rakkans were very hard to read. My orange companion disconnected the monitor and folded it up, tucking it into a pouch he produced seemingly from thin air. *Where are these people storing all these things?* Not one was wearing clothing, and with the translucence of their bodies, there wasn't anywhere something could hide. Presumably.

I was starting to get extremely nervous and faint. I was horrified at what I'd done—both the fact that I'd spent that many credits, and even more so that I'd spent it on buying *slaves*. Yes, I fully intended to release them and get them whatever help I could, but it still felt unspeakably, horrifically wrong, and I just wanted to be done with it already.

I just had *to come to Quellor today*, I thought, my skin feeling slick and feverish. *I just couldn't wait one more day, huh?*

After both the longest and shortest twenty minutes of my life, the other two th'rakkans returned with a large crate hovering between them. The yellow one keyed something into his wristcom, and the crate floated over to me, likely keyed to the ID chip I'd used for the transfer.

Vrakaash, can the police use that to track me? I should have encrypted that better. I...am stunningly stupid.

It was too late to fix it now. I waved meekly at the slavers and retreated, the crate looming behind me. I was certain that there was no way I'd make it all the way back to my ship with this. Surely such an obviously person-sized crate would get flagged. I'd be stopped, arrested, and thrown into the deepest darkest pit the nearest prison had to offer, my entire family's name tarnished beyond saving.

I swallowed thickly, my mouth bone-dry and the bitter acidity of bile flirting with my tongue. Spots danced on the fringes of my vision, and it was all I could do to keep my legs moving and to keep my body upright. The death grip my tail had on my one leg was cutting off the circulation and hurting, but I couldn't ease up for the life of me.

I didn't notice anyone paying particular attention to me on the eternal walk back to my docking bay, but I felt eyes on me all the same. It was nightmarish, but with the crate and my newly depleted credits, I had no choice but to slog through every step.

By the time I stepped into the hangar housing my ship, I was soaked in sweat and feeling really, truly faint. I hurried on board, wedging the enormous crate into the tiny cargo bay, and summoned the AI to plot me home.

I strapped myself in, then knew no more.

Chapter Five
Into the (Sexy?) Unknown

<u>JOSS</u>

When the slavers had come into our cell, all the sass and bravado I'd been working up sparring with Uraka fled like it had never been there. My limbs immediately went weak and numb, my heart ratcheting up into my throat to choke me. Desperate for something to ground me, I'd locked my eyes with Uraka. If this was our chance, I had no doubt that Uraka would lead the charge. But she shook her head in a barely-perceptible *no* and stepped closer to me, her stance widening as she looked down her impressive nose at Cherry and Lemon.

When the two jellomen spoke, I found that I could understand them now; did that mean that I'd been fitted with some sort of translator? It would explain the head- and earache I'd had when I woke up, and the fact that I could understand all my cellmates.

"Why don't you go grab the crate while I round them up," Cherry said, translucent red fingers darting and flicking at something on his wrist.

Lemon nodded, turning and leaving us alone with Cherry.

My pulse started quickening again; surely with just the one, now was our time? I stared hard at Uraka, trying to will her to give me a sign, when a wave of dizziness started to sweep over me. What the hell? Was this nerves?

But I realized that Uraka was swaying as if she was also not feeling well, and when I looked around at my cell mates I saw they were all slumping forward, unconscious.

Pinche Cabrones, I thought drowsily, my knees buckling. I had the random thought that my abuelita would be so disappointed that most of the Spanish that had managed to stick were swear words. Then I was out once again.

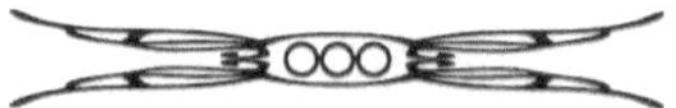

When I came to it was pitch black and stuffy verging on hot even with how little I was wearing. I felt the press of bodies up against me and thought I felt fur brushing my shin. Djelani, maybe?

The wall of flesh to my right let out a now-familiar sounding grunt, and I reached out blindly, seeking the source of that grunt. I got a handful of what had to be orc-boob.

I snatched my hand back and patted the arm I found, hoping she hadn't noticed. "Uraka?" I whispered.

"Joss," she responded, her own hand finding my shoulder in the dark. "I think we have all been bought together. I have felt the others in here with us."

I nodded, forgetting Uraka wouldn't be able to see it. "Yeah, it's really cramped in here so I'd believe it." I hugged my arms to my chest, biting my lip as I considered some questions. "Hey, so I was wondering…why didn't you try to rush him back there? When it was just Cherr—er, the red guy by himself?"

Uraka grunted, the rustle of fabric telling me she was trying to move. "They implanted control chips while we were out. I found the incision site shortly after I woke up. I did not think any of us would get more than a few steps before they would have activated the chips and put us down. With our new owner, we might have a chance to catch them off guard before they can do this. We can pretend we are asleep still when the crate opens and make our move if they get in close."

I bit my lip, tears threatening at the back of my throat. "That makes sense," I said softly, thinking about just how sucky and unfair the situation was. Had I been bored and lonely in my life back on Earth and throwing myself into fantasy after fantasy to make it through the day without spiraling into dark places? Absolutely. Did I spend my days constantly wishing that I was a romance heroine, whisked away to a new life full of excitement and love so beautiful and deep it shattered you only to rebuild you into something more? You betcha. But did I think I would be able to handle that situation or survive for more than a couple of minutes if it actually happened to me?

Big no. This was not sexy. This was not exciting. This was not full of promise or adventure. None of the aliens had been hot and desperate to eat me out so far, and that might have been the greatest tragedy of all. I had been abducted by aliens in my sleep and sold into slavery… and it fucking sucked. It sucked ass. It sucked big, stinky ass.

I sniffled, the sound pathetic and overloud in the dark, and I felt Uraka shift again beside me, her big callused hand settling on my shoulder and squeezing, then lifting to honk my boob.

I jolted, too shocked even to swat at her or cry out, but it was over as quickly as it had come, leaving me very confused. It hadn't been sexual, I was pretty sure—had Uraka thought my earlier faux pas was intentional? I decided not to say anything since she'd been so nice to me this whole time when she hadn't needed to be. Or maybe I'd stumbled on a three-eyed orc cultural thing without realizing it. Wouldn't that just be my luck?

"Is it just us awake again?" I asked, realizing I hadn't heard anything from the other three ladies yet.

"I think so. Most tranquilizers do not work well on yvrenii. My people," she added helpfully. "Perhaps it is the same for you?"

Interesting. "When I woke up the first time they did seem shocked that I was awake. But Ghena's just as affected as the other two, so I don't think it's all humans."

"Interesting. I have never seen your kind before, so I thought perhaps they simply misdosed from lack of experience."

Of course humans would be rare out here. Weird that alien romances had gotten so much right. "You've never seen another human before?" I asked, just to be polite.

"No. That is what you are? From what sector?"

"I don't know. Uh…the Milky Way galaxy? Planet Earth?"

"This means nothing to me. Perhaps it is restricted space. Are your people space-faring yet?"

"Not really," I said, shifting my weight from foot to foot to try and calm my nerves. "I mean we got to the moon like fifty years ago but people think that was fake. And sometimes billionaires like to stick their dick in outer space just to say they can. But we haven't even made it to another planet yet, really." After thinking for a second I felt compelled to add, "But we got some robots on Mars. They're very good little guys."

"That sounds like it would be in restricted space. I hope you were not overly fond of Earf, my new friend Joss. Because I do not know that you will be able to see it again."

Ouch. Thanks for that, Uraka. "It's Earth, with a -th. And because we're friends I feel like I can tell you that aside from the fact that I wasn't a sex slave back home I can't say I'll miss it too much." I shifted, the hard surface beneath me digging into my butt uncomfortably. I tried not to think of my mom and way I'd left things with her. "What about you? What did you leave behind?"

Uraka grunted, her leather boots creaking faintly as she shifted her weight. "Also not much. I spent my youth in the vanguard, hopping around the Galthus sector from warfront to warfront as our chief needed. But I…have retired now. I was thinking of trying bounty hunting, or perhaps private security next. No kin, no friends still living. I think this is probably intentional. These th'rak slavers know what they're doing," Uraka admitted grudgingly.

I was starting to feel very hollow and cold now. It was gradually settling in just how fucked I was, crammed in this crate with four strangers, probably billions of light-years from anything I'd ever known, waiting for a fate that might be nightmarish.

I could feel my heart racing faster and faster, my skin going clammy and tingling, the air thinning in my lungs. *Oh god I'm going to have a panic attack, I'm going to die, I'm going to—no, no I'm not. I'm going to BREATHE, I am going to remind myself that I don't know what's coming and that I am strong and capable and I have a huge, absolutely jacked new friend who's looking out for me. It's not over yet…*It was hard to say whether or not it was helping, but I thought I felt a little less weepy, at least.

"I haven't felt us moving at all," I mused out loud once I'd managed to get calmer, flattening my hand to the side of the crate that was behind me; there was a faint vibration coming through the material, but I couldn't feel anything else, or hear anything beyond the breathing and snuffling of my cratemates.

"You are right, little Joss," Uraka agreed. "Perhaps we are already on board our purchaser's ship?"

I swallowed, sweat beginning to run in tickling rivulets from under my breasts and down my back. I was potentially in space. On a goddamn spaceship. There was already basically no hope of escape, but if we were already out in open space…

I let my tears fall in the dark. It would be my little secret, this moment of weakness and fear. I didn't want to be the first one to freak out and start everyone else off; Uraka didn't need that in her life. But in the dark no one would know but me if I cried a little.

As hard as it had been to tell time in the cell, it was a thousand times harder to tell in the crate. It was like a sensory deprivation chamber, and after a while my brain was so starved for some action that it started making shit up. I was moments away from screaming until I passed out when I heard what might have been an actual sound from outside the crate. I froze, my hallucinating still-aching ears straining for more. Uraka's hand found mine and squeezed.

"I think I hear movement, little one," she breathed, leaning closer to me. "Pretend to be unconscious when the crate is opened. Follow my lead, and remember your training."

"Okay," I managed, my voice so small, even to my own ears. I could be about to die, if this went badly. And even if it didn't, I'd be trapped on a spaceship with who knows how many big baddies waiting just around the corner to make my shitpile of a life even shittier. But Uraka's steadiness settled something in me, gave me a kind of…well not courage, but a sort of stillness, a calm.

Her words from earlier came back to me: *In my mind, either way we are to be meat.* If I was meat, then I decided I was going to be the toughest and most unpleasant meant the assholes who'd done this to me had ever encountered.

I squeezed her large rough hand one more time, then slumped back against the side of the crate, trying my best to look like I was unconscious. On the opposite side of the crate, I heard something creak, then a rush of cool fresh air slid in with a faint hiss, cracks of light flaring blindingly beyond my closed eyelids. Heart hammering, I waited, the light growing brighter. I heard a sigh and some jingling.

"What was I thinking?" a male voice muttered, and I had to fight hard to keep my breathing deep and even. I heard more rustling, more movement, and intermittent beeps. I felt the new stranger coming closer, a spicy-sweet scent beginning to wrap around me. Cologne?

Before he could get any closer, Uraka sprung her trap: I felt her heave herself up and over to where the sounds had been coming from, my eyes flying open to take in the situation. Uraka was already on top of the guy, her thick corded forearm pinned over his throat and her knee pressing into his hand, rendering it useless. A flash of silver caught my eye and I lunged for it, hoping it was a weapon.

The new stranger—I refused to think of him as my "master"—was sputtering and gasping, possibly trying to say something, but Uraka was relentless. "Joss, can you detect anyone else beyond the crate?" Uraka growled, scanning the area she could see. I hopped over Djelani and Wren, peeking around the edge of the crate. Seeing no one, I crept out a little further, brandishing the little silver rod I'd found like it would do me some good in a firefight. I mean they do say that confidence is key, right?

It was a little gloomy in the far corners of the cramped room we were in, but I didn't see anyone. I didn't even see anywhere that would make a good hiding spot: it was just a plain rectangular room made of dull metal. Where the hell *were* we?

"I don't see anyone else," I called to Uraka, scurrying back over to the crate. "There's no one in here besides us."

Uraka eased up enough on her captive's throat to allow him to suck in great gasps of air. "Who are you? Who else is on this vessel?" she growled. "Where are we headed?"

Her prisoner coughed, his skull banging into the floor of the crate with the force of it. He had horns, I realized, that were also hitting the floor and gouging into it.

"Xollen...Billieu...please..."

"Why did you purchase us? Are you some sort of deviant?"

The new stranger—Xollen, or maybe Billieu depending on what order he had answered Uraka—sputtered and hacked some more.

"No! I saw...th'rakkans. Couldn't...leave you there. You're... free..."

That got my attention. He'd bought us to free us? Maybe it was just a cruel trick to help this guy get his rocks off, but there was a chance, however small, that he meant that. I started shuffling to the side, trying to get a better look at the guy.

Uraka was clearly thinking the same thing about the guy's claim that I was; she leaned more of her weight onto her knees, grinding her captive's hands into the floor and causing him to gurgle and scream. I had to admit, I was kind of feeling bad for the guy. Uraka unleashed was scary as hell.

I finished inching around to get a good look at our master-turned-captive, and I couldn't stop the little gasp that wrenched out of me.

"Oh no, he's hot," I breathed, hopefully too quietly for anyone to hear. I hated how immediate and powerful my attraction to the guy was —but then, there was a small chance he wasn't actually a slaver, so maybe it wasn't quite *so* wrong to be mesmerized by him. He was wearing an off-white medical mask, but the papery material did little to hide his chiseled jaw and large eyes the color of blooming violets. Something that looked like safety glasses were on the floor a few feet away from his head, and I also noticed her was wearing gloves and booties. Was he a sexy germaphobe? His build was slim and tall and his skin was a delicious minty kind of color. Thick horns swept back from his temples and were crusted with glittering jewelry. I could just see a sickly green bruise marring his wide, flat nose from Uraka's attack peeking out of the top of his mask, but aside from that his complexion was enviously clear and smooth, like he'd been digitally altered.

"Uraka? What are you doing?" a small voice called out groggily from inside the crate. A moment later Djelani stumbled out to meet us, blinking hard and squinting in the dim light.

Uraka stilled, her expression growing a hair softer. "Djelani? Are you alright?"

"Yes. Who is this that you're torturing?"

"The pipe scum who purchased us."

"For…free…dom!"

Djelani cocked her head, crossing her arms over her chest. "He wants to free us? Then why are you strangling him?"

Uraka turned a bit to make eye contact with Djelani over her shoulder. "He could be lying. I would say it is even *likely* he is lying. Who buys five slaves worth at least a million credits just to let them go? No one is *that* foolish"

"Hey," Hot Alien Guy wheezed, managing to look offended despite his position. Something about that completely ridiculous indignation decided something in me: I was going to believe that he was telling the truth. I mean sure, I was as ignorant as it got about just about everything having to do with the situation, but there was something to be said for a man who managed to give off a good vibe, right?

"Does he have a weapon on him, Uraka?" I asked. Both Uraka and Hot Alien Guy turned to look at me, and I was struck again by just how beautiful his eyes were. They weren't like a human's eyes: there was no white part, it was just swirly deep purple with a pale blue pupil that looked almost like it was glowing. And of *course* they were ringed by the thickest, curliest lashes I had ever seen, black as the silky tresses growing from his head. But I figured if he hadn't bothered bringing a weapon, that might give his story more credit.

Uraka looked embarrassed for a moment, then turned around to pat Hot Alien Guy down. She pulled a box of something that rattled out of one of his pockets and ripped a little smartwatch-looking device from his wrist, then gave one of her signature grunts. "No weapons." Uraka turned to me and nodded her chin at the silver tube in my hands. "Let me see that," she asked.

I walked closer, holding the tube out to her eye level.

"A multitool," Uraka muttered. She sighed heavily and looked back at Djelani again, who clearly disapproved. Uraka got to her feet, glaring at Hot Alien Guy all the while.

"If you make any moves I don't like," she growled at him, "then I will rip your head from your shoulders before you can blink."

Hot Alien Guy swallowed, nodding enthusiastically. "Y-yes ma'am. Of course. I really don't mean you any harm."

Chapter Six
Ragrets

There was no way these females were going to believe me, I realized.

Today had taught me that I was hopelessly stupid and naive when it came to anything real, anything that mattered. The big one—Uraka seemed to be her name—had been embarrassingly correct in her assessment of me. What could I do to convince them of the truth? Did the truth even matter here?

There was a very real chance, I was quickly realizing, that my intentions in buying these females didn't matter. That the only thing that mattered was the plain fact that I had purchased five sentient beings as if they were trinkets in a vendor stall. And that that may be all I ever did for them, since I was destitute now, and didn't have the sorts of connections that would be of any help to these female refugees.

I swallowed as best I could with the incredible weight of the yvrenii female on my throat, my eyes darting around from face to face. I realized I'd lost my goggles at some point in the fray, and I was starting to feel faint again.

"Come on, Uraka…let him go," the strange one said softly, tucking a strand of her pale gold hair behind a small rounded ear. The gentleness of her voice made me feel strange: still and level, like I was at peace and…wait, was this *calm* I was feeling?

I had spent years and years on emotional regulators to try and help me find calm. And with a handful of words from a strange alien, I was finding it. My eyes locked on her face, urgently trying to drink in the sight of her.

The name of her people escaped me. Hue-something. She was much smaller than Uraka but plush and soft in a way that made my fingers itch to touch her, to pull her close and feel that softness against me. In the dim lights of the cargo bay it was hard to tell what color her eyes were, but they were curious rather than horrified, white all along the edges and some sort of darkish color in the center. Her skin was a pale tan color, with a fine down visible along her mostly bare legs. Her clothes seemed thin and ragged, and she hugged herself as if she was cold.

After a pause to consider, Uraka heaved a sigh and hauled herself off of me. I rolled onto my side, coughing, then pushed myself into a sitting position.

"What's your name?" the soft one asked, offering me a smile. My hearts clenched in my chest. She was quite lovely, despite how different she looked.

"Xollen Me'Tirri Be'Faan," I replied, my voice hoarse in my ears. I coughed again. "And can I ask your name? Er—all of your names?"

The soft one's smile brightened. "That's a mouthful. You ever go by anything else?"

"Just Xollen is acceptable."

"Well, alright then. Nice to meet you, Xollen. I'm Joss. Short for Joslyn Aceveda. But I like just Joss." She uncrossed her arms, revealing the heavy roundness of her breasts and peaked nipples. I had to clench my jaw to keep myself from groaning at the sight. Joss gestured beside her at the yvrenii. "This is Uraka, and that's Djelani—" she pointed at the felican, "and Wren and Ghena are still unconscious in the crate."

"We should check them out in your medbay, slaver," Uraka growled, glaring at me with all three of her golden eyes, a very unusual color for an yvrenii. "I do not like how long they have been unconscious."

My immediate reaction was to try and protest that I wasn't a slaver, but the words caught in my throat. I *had* bought them. If I was being objective and honest with myself I'd participated in the system and given 3 million credits to terrible people who would likely use those credits to do terrible things. I swallowed.

"Of course. Help yourselves to whatever you'd like. I really do mean to help," I said, trying to pour the earnestness with which I felt those words into my eyes. I scrambled to my feet, brushing dirt from my pants and tunic and adjusting my mask to it sat more flush against my face. I winced when the bridge pressed into where Uraka had punched me in the face.

Uraka grunted. "Who else is on the ship with us?" she asked.

"It's just us. Everything else is bots and AI."

She raised a thick honey-brown brow, scrunching her third eye on that side. "Full auto on a shuttle? You really are loaded, slaver."

"Was," I grumbled, hating the whining note I heard in my voice. "I only have 128 credits to my name, now."

Uraka ignored me and went back inside the crate, emerging with the unconscious myauanni female cradled in her muscular arms. "You can grab Ghena, make yourself useful."

I nodded, shuffling into the dark confines of the crate and carefully lifting the remaining female's limp, delicate form from off the floor. Even with my paltry strength I was able to lift her easily; likely Uraka had realized just how unfit I was and done this on purpose. As I passed Joss on my way out she offered me a shy smile. "Hey, um—thanks, by the way. For saving us. I know Uraka's being a hardass about it but I really appreciate that." I returned her smile, feeling a little better. I wasn't sure what she meant by "hardass" but perhaps that was a strange saying of her people.

I led the way to my shuttle's tiny medbay, feeling Uraka's three eyes on my back like daggers the whole time. Opening the door with a voice command, I gently placed Ghena on the only exam table and pulled the bioscanner from its charging port on the wall. I was struck by just how different Joss looked compared to Ghena when the two females were the same species. Ghena looked nice enough, but I was not drawn to her like I was Joss.

"It's just the one bed I'm afraid," I apologized, my grip on the scanner tightening.

Uraka grunted. "I will hold Wren while you scan Ghena. Be quick about it, slaver."

I swallowed my protest and nodded. From behind Uraka, I spotted a flash of gold hair and wide brown eyes. Joss elbowed the yvrenii in the side and hissed at her to be nicer before she turned to me with a smile. It was so warm, so sweet, that little smile, and it made me feel like maybe I hadn't completely ruined my life today.

Maybe I'd somehow find a friend despite all this.

I turned to Ghena and turned on the scanner, tapping my foot as the device slowly went through its boot processes.

After a short eternity, the scanner beeped and announced its findings: "Mild dehydration and malnutrition present. No detected communicable diseases. Female human aged twenty-one SIY. Unconscious."

I loaded the injector gun with subcutaneous fluids and a nutrient blend the scanner indicated and fired into her slim arm. She flinched when the needle entered her tawny skin but remained unconscious.

I lifted her off of the bed and nodded at it with my chin, letting Uraka know she could place Wren there now. She laid her gently on the padded surface, snatching up the bioscanner from the little built-in table I'd left it on, and performed a scan.

"Mild dehydration present. No detected communicable diseases. Female myauanni aged eighty-two SIY. Unconscious," the scanner chirped, and Uraka injected fluids per the instructions.

Djelani stepped closer, her movements graceful and fluid, even more so than usual for a felican. She placed one softly-furred hand on Uraka's thick olive-green forearm. "See?" she said soothingly, rubbing the yvrenii female's arm. "They're alright. We should all get checked out though, just in case."

"I'm shocked Wren's that old," Joss piped up from the other side of Uraka. "Eighty-two? She looks *good*."

"Myauanni are very long-lived," Djelani offered, smiling at Joss. "She is still young by her people's standards."

"That's fucking nuts," Joss breathed. "Eighty-two is pretty old for humans. Living into your nineties is considered long-lived, and if you make it to one hundred I'm pretty sure they give you a prize or something."

The three conscious females took turns scanning each other and administering the correct doses of hydration and nutritional supplements. Now that all of my guests had been cleared of communicable disease I ripped off my battered mask, breathing in the stale recycled air instead of the papery chemical smell of the mask for the first time in what felt like hours. I wiped the moisture from wearing the mask for so long from my lower face and saw Joss looking at me intently, her soft lips slightly parted. I felt my face flame; likely she was alarmed by my facial defect and couldn't help staring. At least she wasn't saying anything about it, or looking at me with pity.

Once everyone was taken care of, I led them to the small rec room where we could lay the two unconscious members of the group onto the soft couch, then led them to the mess hall and told them to help themselves to whatever they wanted.

"Here, small one: let me show you how these synthesizers work," Uraka rumbled gently, giving Joss a quick tour of the machine and helping her select some food. The yvrenii seemed content to ignore me now and I was perfectly fine with letting her. She was *frightening*.

"Why don't you sit with us, Xollen?" sweet little Joss asked, offering me a shy smile. "It'll be nice to talk things through and get everyone on the same page, right?"

Uraka sneered and growled, but settled into a tense glower under Djelani's disapproval.

I gulped, considering fleeing to my chambers and locking myself inside, but it did seem like a good idea to talk things out. "A-alright," I managed, my throat painfully tight. I pulled some water from the beverage dispenser, then took a seat across from the three females, who'd clustered together all on one side of the single table, sharing the bench there. "W-what would you like to know?"

Chapter Seven
Introductions

<u>JOSS</u>

I was having a hard time ignoring the way my body was reacting to Xollen and focusing on what he was saying. He'd been hot with the mask on, but once it was off he was next-level: he'd been hiding some sinfully plump lips under there, a thin silver ring bisecting the bottom one and a strong, slightly pointed chin. He was *gorgeous*, and I couldn't stop staring at him.

"What would you like to know?" he asked as he sat down, the muscles of his long mint-colored throat working.

"Where are you taking us?" Uraka demanded as she shoved most of an animal limb into her mouth and stripped it to the bone. Man, I loved that crazy bitch.

"Billieu," Xollen answered her, transfixed by how she was tearing into the meat on her plate and getting paler as he watched her. "I-I can take you to an embassy once you're there. Or—or a shelter for victims of trafficking. I'll let you pick. But I'm wiped out, I can't help beyond that."

"You could give us this shuttle," Uraka mused, using a claw-like nail to pick gristle from her teeth, flashing her sharp fangs and tusks. "Give us all of your valuables and then go take a swim with a pocketful of rocks." I gasped but was too stunned to make a sound.

Luckily Djelani had no such compunctions. "*Uraka!*" she cried, looking furious. "He has said he is helping us, and you need to calm down and get that through your thick skull," the slim felican shouted, her hackles rising visibly. "Or do you need to step out into the hall while the rest of us adults have a conversation?"

The change was instant in Uraka: gone was the bristling, furious female, to be replaced with someone who looked every inch the well-chastised child. Uraka said nothing, just picked at her food, and I almost felt bad for her. Almost: I was also pretty pissed at her for picking on Xollen so much. Sure, he hadn't been perfect, but he'd saved us, and she was being a big 'ole poo about it.

"I think that sounds lovely, Xollen," Djelani continued, her fur smoothing as she calmed down. "How long do you think we have before we land on Billieu?"

"Uh—the computer was estimating three days. Standard."

"Excellent. That'll give us plenty of time to rest and recover." She took a delicate nibble of the spicy, fishy-smelling stew she was eating. "*Some* of us might not know how to show gratitude, but I know I am glad that you did what you did," she said, shooting a sour look at Uraka.

Face dark and stormy, Uraka shoved back from the table and stomped out of the mess hall. Djelani watched her go with a pained expression that she quickly hid. Then she also got up and followed her out of the mess hall, leaving me and Xollen alone.

"I don't know why she's being so awful," I piped up, wanting to break the tension and get his swirling purple gaze to land on me again. His eyes snapped to mine, heat creeping into my face. "I'm sorry for how she's acting. You saved us all though and…and I know I'm really, really thankful for you. For your doing that." I found myself smiling, praying there wasn't anything stuck in my teeth.

But then I had a thought. "Will I be able to get home? Would humans have an embassy?"

Xollen cleared his throat, gulping water only to choke and sputter on it. Once he'd managed to suck some air into his lungs, his face flushing an interesting taupe kind of color, he spoke: "I think you'll have to go to the shelter," he wheezed. "The th'rakkans said your planet was in restricted space, meaning it's illegal for anyone to take you there. I'm…I'm sorry."

My heart dropped like a stone. "So I can't go home? I can never go back to Earth?"

Xollen looked just as heartbroken as I felt, like he wished he could tell me something else. His glove-clad hand inched across the table until he was patting my forearm awkwardly. "I…I don't think so," he said quietly. "I'm so sorry, Joss."

Shit. The last thing I'd ever say to my mom was "fuck you". I'd never see my friends. I'd have to get used to a whole new planet, a new society, a new culture, where I didn't know anyone.

It was terrifying...but also exciting. For every good thing I was leaving behind there were at least two bad ones. I'd never have to worry about bumping into Alex and his fucking goons. I'd never have to worry about paying off my student loans. And I could even get *really* lucky and Billieu could have like, no fatphobia or racism making my very existence something I had to constantly validate. They might just let me be fat and Latina in peace. I'd miss my mom, but we hadn't been close for a while; losing my Dad had torn her up inside, and we'd butted heads my whole life. Abuelita had been gone for three years now—that was my Dad's mom—and while I worried what my mom would do with me gone, I also thought that maybe she'd finally be able to move on from Dad's death without me around constantly reminding her of what she'd lost.

And of course, there was also the very real possibility of being able to get closer to Xollen. There was something about the way he was looking at me that made me think that he liked what he saw at least a little.

I bit my lip, fear making the air feel thin in my lungs.

"A-actually," I blurted out, my hands tugging and wringing the hem of my thin nightshirt. "If it's all the same to you, I'd like to stay. With you. Maybe I can help you get back on your feet or something?"

Xollen blinked at me, looking shocked. "Stay with me?" he asked.

I nodded, my face growing hot. "If that's okay."

"I don't know," he answered, his perfect brows lowering. Now that we were in better lighting I could see that his hair wasn't actually black, it was a stunning shade of blue so dark it *looked* black. "Can I ask why?"

I shrugged, my eyes locking on his full, pouty lips. *Because you're fucking hot and I'm lonely? Because I have the chance to have an honest-to-god adventure with a sexy alien man and I'm gonna take it?* "Because you seem nice. Kind of...innocent, maybe? But nice. And it's not like I can go home, Earth's off-limits. So...why not? I'd rather crash with you than throw myself at the mercy of strangers." Okay, so maybe that was crazy and dumb, but the longer I sat here, the more I felt myself just wanting to *go* for it and try some new shit. Back on Earth I never did anything fun or risky, because I didn't want to upset or disappoint anyone.

Xollen blinked some more, his head tilting ever so slightly to the side. There really was something about him that was kind of naïve. But it made him endearing. And the fact that I was a sucker for a jaw sharp enough to cut didn't factor into that.

The mess hall doors opened again with a *whoosh*, and Uraka and Djelani re-joined us, both looking calmer. They re-took their seats and resumed eating.

"I can't provide much for you," Xollen said slowly, studying my face with those breathtaking violet eyes of his. "As I said, I'm bankrupt now."

I smiled. "I know, and that's why I want to help. You rescued us —" Uraka tried to interject, but Djelani laid a delicate hand on her forearm and Uraka's mouth snapped shut, her eyes riveted to that hand on her arm. "You rescued us," I continued louder, "and I want to help you get back on your feet." I crossed my arms over my free-swinging breasts again, hating how exposed I felt being in public bra-less.

Xollen looked thoughtful, the quiet stretching on until I was sure he'd turn me down and I'd have to figure something else out.

But then he nodded. "Alright," he agreed. "It won't hurt to try it out and see how it works. I will need—I would certainly appreciate the help, Joss." The way he said my name had me feeling *gooey*. He had no business being so damn sexy.

I beamed across the table at him, then decided to throw caution to the wind and jumped to my feet to come around to his side of the table and give him a hug. *New Joss is bold,* I decided. *This is an adventure.*

Xollen stiffened when I threw my arms around his neck in an awkward half-hug, but one arm did come up to pat my shoulder awkwardly. When I pulled back he gave me a puzzled smile. "What was that?" he asked.

"A human thing. It's called a hug."

"What is it for?"

"For showing affection. Do…do aliens not hug? Was that weird? Or inappropriate?"

Xollen shook his head. "No I-I liked it. It was just a shock. My people do not engage in physical contact casually. We have a complicated history with disease."

Fuck, the mask and booties! The gloves! My hands flew to my face, my skin going hot. "Oh god, so it *was* inappropriate! I basically just spit in your face, didn't I?" I'd only been in a partnership with the guy for a single minute and I'd already managed to commit a war crime.

But Xollen shook his head. "No, that was fine. Though please do not ever spit in my face, that sounds awful. I'm just not used to it. Please don't worry, Joss."

"Okay," I squeaked, backing away from him and sliding into my seat. I crossed my arms again, my whole face on fire. This was going *great*.

Uraka was smirking, shooting me a saucy look, but Djelani looked more sympathetic. I saw her hand slide up Uraka's arm until she was grabbing her elbow, tugging the much larger woman to her feet and dragging her out of the mess hall.

"We'll just go check in on Wren and Ghena," she trilled, smiling at us. "We'll be in the rec room if you need anything!" Uraka looked like she was ready to protest, but Djelani smoothed her palm over Uraka's bulging bicep and the grumpy she-orc melted like butter.

Then it was just me, Xollen, and tension thick enough to cut left in the room.

Chapter Eight
Teaming Up

I couldn't decide if my hearts or my cock were throbbing harder.

First Joss had declared that she wished to stay with me, and that had been wonderful enough. But then she had done that human gesture, that *hug*, as she had called it, and after that I thought I might faint from just how much blood had rushed to my groin. I could feel her softness pressing into me, the globes of her breasts perilously close to my chest and her delicious sweet scent wrapped all around me. It had taken every drop of my willpower to avoid moaning out loud.

But as pleased as I was with the way things were working out with Joss, I was equally afraid of what Uraka would do to me. I had no doubt that if it wasn't for the felican female, Djelani, I'd already be a faint smear on my cargo hold floor. I just couldn't understand it—yvrenii were a very battle-lusty race, but I offered her no challenge, no glory, so why had she decided I was such an attractive target? It felt very personal and to be honest, it really hurt my feelings.

Joss was flushed and avoiding my eyes across the table, picking nervously at her food. I felt heat creep up my own neck as I realized I'd said something to make her uncomfortable. Why did the Goddess refuse to show me mercy and make even just *one* social interaction go smoothly? I cleared my throat, attempting to drink from my now-empty water glass.

"Um, so Joss," I rasped, "what sorts of things do you think you can

"

help me with?"

Her eyes crept up until they met mine hesitantly. "I guess I don't know. What sorts of things do you think you'll need help with?"

I felt my blush deepen. "Will you think less of me if I say everything?"

She smiled at me, her soft brown eyes calming me a little. "Well it's pretty broad so it's not all that helpful," she said, crossing her arms over her ample chest. "I guess just tell me about yourself then. Maybe we'll both figure some stuff out that way."

I nodded, thinking. "Well...I'm an only child. My parents own and run Se'Tirraan Entertainment. It's a media company that manages talent for holo-programming in Billieu's capital city of Escheva. We're a wealthy family, but I've recently had a falling out with them." I paused, trying to read her strange face. No—it wasn't strange, it was just so different from the billieuan faces I was used to. It looked a lot more like mine, now that I thought about it, with my facial deformity that had prevented the graceful facial cleft from properly forming in the womb. As soon as I realized this though, it confused me; how could I find her lovely if I thought myself hideous? What about Joss made this feature that I had loathed my whole life suddenly...good? I couldn't dwell on that, though; it very much felt like a train of thought that would send me spiraling.

I cleared my throat and continued. "I was supposed to follow in their footsteps, take over the business, but I...well, I had a difficult time with my business classes and got kicked out of the program. And I didn't want to try another one." Joss's eyebrows drew together, and she placed one dainty hand on my forearm.

"I'm so sorry, Xollen," she said quietly, offering me another of her soft smiles. "I know how hard it is to struggle to get your parents to accept you for who you are. My mom did the same thing, wanted me to be a nurse like her and my aunt, but I always wanted to do other stuff."

I couldn't help the smile that broke over my face. "Really?" I had felt so alone in this, seeing all of my peers—including Derris—following their paths in life with no issues, no resistance. They all seemed to just settle into where they were meant to without any of the angst and confusion I was rife with. But here was Joss, telling me that she'd felt the exact same thing. It warmed my hearts.

She nodded. "Can I ask what it is you felt like doing instead of business?"

I pursed my lips. Was it wise to confess something that personal so soon after meeting someone? Derris was the only person I trusted this with. I cleared my throat, swiping my long hair over one shoulder to get it off of my neck, which was getting uncomfortably warm.

"I, um—I like drawing. Not painting, that gets tedious to me. But just quick sketches. I like to try and tell a story with the pictures." Goddess, it sounded so foolish and silly when I said it out loud like that. I felt my face get even hotter.

"Oh wow, that's so cool!" Joss exclaimed, her eyes sparkling as she beamed at me. "So like a kommick, then? I've always wanted to try teaming up with an artist to do a web-kommick. Oh, I'm a writer— that's my thing," she blurted, color seeping into her own face.

"Oh. Um, I don't know what that is," I admitted. "What is a kommick?"

She cocked an eyebrow. "Maybe that's a translation error. A kommick. You know, like you have a bunch of panels with drawings and speech bubbles and they tell a story."

My brow furrowed in confusion. "I'm sorry, but that still doesn't sound familiar to me."

She frowned. "Interesting. Maybe I'm not explaining it right. Do you have something I can sketch on?"

I nodded, standing to retrieve a tablet from the charging bank over the food synth. I opened it to a note-taking app that allowed for handwriting and passed it to her.

She took it from me, concentrating as she moved her finger quickly over the screen, drawing something out. She had it in her hands and angled towards her face, so from my seat across from her I couldn't see what she was doing. I was buzzing with excitement though. There was a name for what I wanted to do with my vision, meaning I wasn't so misguided as others had led me to believe.

After a few minutes she put the tablet down flat on the table and pushed it forward. "I'm not much of an artist," she said apologetically, pointing at what she'd drawn. I looked down, following her finger with its blunt delicate nail pointing out what she'd done as she explained it. "So, this is a kommick. See how it's telling the story of this little doggie finding a big bone and deciding to give it to his friend the kitten?"

I blinked down at the image, flabbergasted. "I-I've never seen something like this before." I picked up the tablet, caressing the screen with trembling, reverent fingers. "This is *amazing*," I breathed.

Confusion settled heavily on her delicate features. "What? No, it's a *kommick*, it's nothing special."

I shook my head, insistent. "No, Joss, I'm telling you—I've never seen something like this in all my 26 solars. But this is what I think I want to do, to tell a story with pictures that lasts longer than what can be told in just one image."

"Do you mean to tell me that you people have mastered *intergalactic space travel* but you haven't stumbled on *kommicks?!*" she burst out, her voice getting high and squeaky with disbelief.

I shrugged. "I think so? How do you spell it, I will try searching for it on the nexus."

She carefully scrawled out C-O-M-I-C on the tablet screen, and I typed it into my browser. When it turned up nothing I flipped the screen around to show her. Her brow wrinkled.

"Try just searching for different illustrative art forms, or animation," she demanded, coming over to sit next to me. I couldn't decide if I liked this sudden shift to bossiness from her, but I definitely liked her sitting so close to my side.

I did, and none of the encyclopedia entries I found looked anything like what she'd drawn for me.

"This is impossible!" she cried, snatching the tablet from my hands and standing up. "I'm going to show the girls and get to the bottom of this."

I got up and followed her out the door, admiring the swing of her hips and the way her smooth flesh shivered with her angry steps as she stomped down the hall to seek out the other females in my small rec room.

She held out the tablet to each female, showing them her little comic (as I now knew it was spelled) about the Earth animals that she'd drawn for me.

Uraka squinted at the screen with her two parallel eyes. "I am sorry, Joss, but I have never seen this before. It is cute though, did you make it?"

Joss huffed a thanks, then shoved the screen at Djelani. "Anything?" she demanded.

Djelani shook her head, grinning sheepishly. "No, I can't say I've seen anything like it."

A frustrated growl tore from Joss's throat as she also showed a very groggy Wren, who also answered in the negative.

"I'm sorry, but this is *impossible,*" she fumed, spinning around towards me again. "How in the actual *fuck* does that even happen?!"

I held up my hands, palm out, in what I hoped was a placating gesture. "Calm please, Joss. I don't know why you are letting yourself get so worked up by this. It must be an Earth-only media."

"B-But...*how?*" Joss sputtered, her eyes roving over all of us. "I'm sorry, this is just such a common thing on Earth I'm having a lot of trouble believing it's not out here, too." Her arm holding the tablet sagged down against her side and she shook her head, making an incredulous sound.

"I have to admit, it is very difficult to wrap my head around," Ghena interjected softly from beside Wren. "But it does make a certain kind of sense. Just because it's old and common back home doesn't mean it would be everywhere."

Joss blinked, shaking her head in disbelief. "No, you're right. Just… wow, y'know?" She pushed her hair back out of her face and sighed. "Alright, well, thanks for your input, everyone. I don't know why this is the thing that's breaking my brain but man, it really is. Shit."

Uraka chuckled, leaning forward and resting her forearms on her spread knees. "It is alright, little one. It is a shock to encounter the wider universe for the first time."

Joss smiled at the grinning yvrenii female before turning back to me. "Well, I guess that's that. I'm just going to have to learn how to live with this information." Then she was turning and heading back to the ship's tiny mess hall, chuckling and shaking her head as she went along.

Once we'd sat back down—Joss across from me once more, I noted with a pang of loss—she handed the tablet back to me. "Well, I guess if no one else has ever done it then we can invent it out here. Which is completely insane to me, but kind of cool at the same time." Some of her words were translating oddly, and I assumed it was some sort of alien slang gumming up the works. It would likely take time for my translator to pick up all of her uses and allow me to understand her fully, and I found myself excited and delighted to realize we would have plenty of time together for that to happen: Joss was staying with me, she was going to help me.

In a stunning upset, I was excited about the future.

"Anyway, so you were describing comics as being something you'd like creating, and I think that's amazing. If you need help writing the story I'd love to pitch in. Like I said, I like writing a lot and have done a fair amount of it." She paused, then frowned at me, looking wary. "You guys *do* have writing, right? Like, books and short stories and poems and shit?"

In a good mood and surprisingly calm for being me, I pretended I was confused again. "A book? What is that? What do you mean by writing?" A look of incredulous horror spread over her face, making me sputter with laughter.

Joss rolled her eyes and slapped my hand on the table gently. "You jerk, were you messing with me?"

I nodded. "Yes, I was only teasing. We have written forms of entertainment."

"*Anyway*," she said sternly, trying to hide a smile of her own, "that's a great thing to aspire to, starting up a comic. But you'll still need a day job to pay for rent and groceries and stuff, so what sorts of job skills do you have?"

I cocked my head. "To pay for rent and food? Why would you have to pay for that?"

Joss smirked. "Well if you've only ever lived with your parents I guess it might not be obvious that you have to pay for those things. But yeah, you have to pay for the roof over your head and the food that you eat, and other stuff like electricity and medical care and all that good stuff."

"Oh, you mean with taxes?"

"What?" Joss's smooth golden brow scrunched again with confusion. "I mean I guess a little, but most stuff you have to pay for separately, or else you'll wind up homeless or starving."

"That is *awful*," I breathed, pity for Joss and her primitive planet washing through me. "On Billieu that doesn't happen."

She blinked. "You don't have homeless people?"

I shook my head, making my horn ornaments tinkle. "No, if you cannot afford a private dwelling you simply move into the public dorms. Then they give you stipends for food and whatever else you need."

Joss sagged, wonder filling her wide brown eyes. "You're socialized. You live in a goddamn socialist utopia," she breathed, her eyes growing glassy and wet with tears. "No one—" her voice cracked, and she swallowed thickly. Without thinking, I took one of her hands and held it on the table. She didn't react except to squeeze my hand back. "No one is homeless?" she finished with a rasp.

"This is correct," I assured her gently. "Are you alright?"

She nodded, snatching her hand back to swipe at her eyes. "Yeah, I'm okay," she said. "It's just that I was homeless for a little while when I was younger." I made a noise of shock in my throat. Her people had let her live without a home? On the *streets? As a child?!*

"I'm so sorry," I told her. "Is there not enough room for everyone on your planet?"

She shook her head, her laugh bitter. "No, that's the really shitty thing. They have empty houses, I'm pretty sure, that just sit there rotting away because someone couldn't afford them anymore and no one else can or wants to buy them." She shook her head. "Our systems on Earth are just way more fucked. We…we don't really take care of each other. People think if you're homeless it's because you did something to like, earn it. You fucked up in a big way and now you're getting what you deserve."

I wanted to be sick, to fly to her home planet and shake some sense into those people. How could they think that someone *earns* misfortune? Even if someone spends all their credits on drugs or gambling it is not their fault, they are simply sick and in need of help. If anything those are the people who should be getting the *most* attention and care. A society is only as strong as its most vulnerable people.

"That...is horrible." I swallowed down the bitter taste at the back of my tongue. "I am so sorry that you have had to endure that. I can't even imagine what it must have been like. And you said you were just a child when this happened?"

She nodded, hugging herself. "Yeah, I was...maybe ten?"

"And no one would even help *you*, an innocent child?"

She nodded, more tears spilling from her eyes. "Yeah, no one did. They—they actually teased me, the other kids, because I was dirty all the time and got free lunch."

It felt like my hearts were breaking in my chest, shattering into dust from how unfair that was. To think that she had gone through something so senseless and cruel and was still kind enough to help me, despite my not having any excuse to need help. I was in no danger of living like that. I was just going to have to move and get rid of many of my things.

They were nice things, but compared to having nothing, I could make that sacrifice. Meeting these females, seeing the harsher realities of life in the wider universe, was putting a lot of things into perspective for me. I was realizing just how sheltered and—and *privileged* I'd been. It was hard to sit with.

"That is...unbelievable," I murmured. "That will not happen again, especially if we get you Billieuan citizenship. There is always a safety net." Her lip wobbled, but she managed a faint smile.

"That's so good to hear. It'll make it much easier to get you on your feet, if you have room and board already covered." She took a deep breath and squared her shoulders. "So what *doesn't* the government cover?"

"Entertainment expenses. Most leisure activities you have to pay for with credits, and for any clothing beyond the government-issued jumpsuits. I'm sure there's more, but I haven't had to look into it before so I can't remember." I felt myself flush again. "Sorry," I added lamely.

She shook her head again. "No, that's fine! We can always look it up, I'm sure." She twisted her mouth to the side and hummed a few discordant notes. "I guess then I'll help you figure out how to live on your own, and we can work on getting you a job to pay for all of that other stuff, since that's still important. You've got to have a fun budget!"

I nodded, smiling at her shyly. "Yes, that sounds wonderful. Thank you so much for helping me, Joss."

She smiled back, her tears already drying from her sweet face.

Chapter Nine
Skeletons in the Closet

JOSS

I was still reeling from what I'd learned about Xollen and his world, Billy-ooh (or however it was spelled; I'd probably have to figure that out soon, huh?). No comics but these guys had interstellar travel *and* had a successful socialist society?! Screw Earth, I wanted a big 'ole slice of that. No more breaking my back and stifling my soul just to scrape by, no more panic attacks when I looked at my bank account, no more boring nursing classes to make my mom happy. And no more Alex lurking around, trying to shove his skinny new girlfriend in my face.

Xollen himself was a pretty nice perk, too. He'd been really hurt on my behalf after I'd accidentally spilled all about my past, and he wasn't ogling my free-swinging tits at all. I couldn't say that about most of the men I interacted with in a day back on Earth. And boy was he hot, I mean like, *seriously*. Whoo-mama.

Now that we'd gotten to know each other a little bit better I felt comfortable asking him for some stuff. If I had to sit around in ratty old pajamas for one more minute I might scream.

"Hey, Xollen?" I asked during a lull in our conversation. "Do you think you have any spare clothes that would fit me that I can borrow?"

His violet eyes widened, the colors swirling slightly faster. I'd noticed that happening earlier, too: it seemed like whenever his emotions got stronger the swirling also got faster. Except when he'd gotten sad for me—then they'd basically ground to a halt. It made his eyes so expressive and interesting to look at.

"Oh *vrakaash*, of course, Joss. I'm not sure if I will though…" a part of me braced, waiting for him to call attention to my size, "…because you are so much smaller than me," he finished.

I wanted to snort. He'd called me *small*. I guess compared to him though, I *was* pretty short.

"Would you like to go through my spare clothing in my quarters and look for something?" He put his hands up. "I will leave you alone to do this, I'm not trying to do anything inappropriate!"

I smiled, softening towards him even more. "Yeah, that sounds great. Thanks so much, Xollen."

He smiled back, his cute little fangs glinting in the ship's bright light. We stood and he led me down the short hallway I'd taken earlier to get to the rec room, but in the opposite direction. Thanks to my translator implant I could read the signs, I realized, though it was really trippy: if I just focused on how the signs looked, it was obvious they weren't in English, and all I could see was the alien lettering. But if I looked at them like I was trying to read them, I could understand them. It hurt my brain so I tried not to think about reading signs and other text too much.

Man, they had fucking brain manipulating universal translators but they didn't have *comic books*? This end of the universe was weird as fuck.

The hallway ended in a little cul-de-sac kind of thing with three doors. One was marked "Maintenance", another "Cargo", and the third "Quarters". Xollen approached the third one, the door opening with a faint scrape at his approach.

"It's keyed to my ID chip," he explained as he led me through. "So I have to let you in but you can leave on your own." He stepped aside, ushering me into his quarters. He pressed a button on a wall panel and the door stayed open. I felt a rush of gratitude for his thoughtfulness. I wasn't afraid that he'd try anything, but it meant a lot to me that he'd realized I might not like being shut up in a room alone with a guy I didn't know that well.

The next time I saw Uraka I was going to punch her in the tit for being so mean to him. He really was so thoughtful and kind when he didn't have to be.

It was a small room, only about half as big as my bedroom back home, but it was nice. Everything was clean and neat, the colors all soft neutrals: dove gray walls, beige upholstery, and black and steel fixtures. The only spot of color was a drawing of a gorgeous alien flower stuck to the wall above the bed. I gasped when I saw it, heading for it without thinking.

"Oh my god, Xollen, did you draw this?" I asked, just barely resisting the urge to reach out and run my fingertips over the drawing. It was even prettier up close: bright, detailed, but highly textured in a stylized kind of way that made me want to pet it. I looked over my shoulder at him and saw that he was blushing, his eyes swirling.

"Yes, I did. You…you like it?"

"I *love* it," I beamed at him. "You're seriously so talented, oh my god."

He smiled, blushing harder. "Thank you. It's really nothing though, it barely qualifies as art."

I snorted, rolling my eyes. "Oh please," I told him, putting my hands on my hips. "You have it pinned up above your bed so you have to think it's *something*, dude. You're good at this, own it!"

He ducked his head, making all of the jewelry he wore on his horns jingle softly. I bet he could get a pretty penny for that stuff if he sold it, now that I was thinking of it. If he had more stuff like that at his house then he'd probably be alright for a while, even without a job.

He thanked me again, his voice sounding a little tight, then led me over to a panel that he said was for storing personal effects.

"I don't have much on me, I'm afraid," he was telling me as he swiped up on a little pad in the wall. "Since I was just—running an errand on Quellor, I didn't bother bringing many clothes." The panel slid up smoothly, revealing a tightly-packed wall of fabric. It looked ready to burst.

I cocked an eyebrow at him, giggling. "Oh, just a couple of outfits, then?" I asked sarcastically. Xollen blushed again.

"It looks like more than it is!" he insisted, his slim tail with its tufted tip whipping through the air behind his legs like an irritated cat's. "These things are always weirdly shaped and hard to get stuff into."

"Suuure," I agreed, giving him a great big wink.

He chuckled, smiling at me shyly before turning and making his exit. He told he'd be in the control room if I needed him. Then I was alone in Xollen's bedroom.

I immediately went to his bed, burying my face in his pillow and breathing in his spicy-sweet smell. God, he smelled *incredible*. I didn't know if it was his cologne or what, but I couldn't seem to get enough of it. It didn't smell exactly like anything I'd encountered on Earth, but it reminded me of walking into a coffee shop on a chilly autumn evening, the smell of coffee and cinnamon mixing with the smell of the rain outside. I seriously needed to figure out a way to bottle that smell.

Eventually I tore myself away from his neatly-made bed and

started picking through his closet. There were a lot of frilly shirts, which surprised me since what he was wearing right now was pretty normal-looking: a black long-sleeved shirt with a collar that was somewhere between a crew neck and a turtleneck, and olive green pants with a bunch of extra pockets that hugged his long legs. But there was stuff in this closet that had crazy patterns, ruffles, dangly bits, even a kind of glitter on some of them. *Okay, so he's a bit of a peacock*, I thought with a smile, letting a metallic silky-smooth sleeve slip through my fingers. *He's used to being rich so I guess that makes sense.*

I pulled out a ruffly coral shirt that felt like it had some stretch and decided to try it on.

I stripped off my ratty old shirt, wincing at the huge hole in the armpit, and carefully slipped my arms into Xollen's shirt, hoping I wouldn't feel the telltale resistance that meant it wasn't going to fit, but even if it wasn't the most comfortable thing it fit just fine. It made a cute shirt dress, coming down to my mid-thighs. The fabric carried more of his addictive smell, and I took a minute to picture him wearing it, the flowy fabric skimming over the long lean lines of his body, the coral color popping against his mint-colored skin. He'd look *delicious*.

I kept digging through the closet, hoping to find something that I could use as pants. It was a little chilly on the ship, and I wanted to be able to sit without worrying about flashing anyone.

All of the bottoms were full-length pants, and too tight besides, not quite making it over my womanly hips, but there was so much leg to the couple of pairs I tried that I didn't think I'd be able to wear them anyway. There was only so much you could cuff, and I didn't want to mutilate Xollen's nice clothes. However, just when I was ready to give up, I spotted something that looked like a maxi skirt. I grabbed it, yanking it out of the tightly-packed closet, and saw that it was more like harem pants, with super wide and flowy legs. Very 2000's. I snorted, taking them off the hanger and slipping them on under the shirt. I let out a deep sigh of relief when they fit. I had to pull them up above my hips in order for the band to not dig into me, but overall they were comfortable.

I also found thick tube socks rolled up on a shelf above the bar that the clothes hung off of, and I snagged two and rolled them onto my freezing cold feet. I felt bad about getting the pristine white fabric dirty with my disgusting feet (I hadn't had any footwear this entire time), but it was so nice to not be barefoot anymore.

Pleased, I closed the closet and scooped up my pajamas and started heading out of his room. But just before I got to the panel with the button that would let me out I paused. I *was* all alone in here. Would it really hurt anything to poke around a little before I left?

I hesitated, biting my bottom lip. I mean, he'd been so nice, rescuing us and giving us food and medicine and whatnot. And he'd let me in here and given me free rein, trusting me with his personal space. It wasn't right to snoop. But if I just walked around, looking at what was already out, was that still snooping? I mean, if he left it out knowing I'd be in here, that must mean it wasn't private, right?

I clutched my pajamas to my chest in a loose bundle, walking carefully around the perimeter of the small room, taking in the details. It was clear that he didn't live here full-time; it was nice, but there wasn't much to it, the walls bare except for the flower drawing and no shelves anywhere with personal stuff on them. I tried not to be disappointed by that. There was a desk though, with a tablet resting on the top, the screen dark. I noticed paper peeking out from under the tablet, and I carefully lifted it, memorizing where it had lain so I could put it back exactly where I left it.

I gasped at the drawing that emerged. It was a woman, probably alien, her face in profile as she gazed out a window she was seated in front of. She had the same horns as Xollen, though hers were much smaller, and the lean lines of her body could have been a feminine version of his as well, making me think she was the same kind of alien as him. It was a simple sketch, but drawn with such tenderness and care that it felt…intimate. The paper looked worn, the edges soft and curling without the weight of the tablet on them, and my heart sank as I realized this was probably his girlfriend. Maybe even his wife. Or mate? I wondered if aliens actually had mates or if that was something that was just from the books. *Of course he'd have someone waiting for him back on Billy-ooh*, I thought bitterly. *He's so gorgeous and sweet.* I sighed, trying to let go of my disappointment. It wasn't like I ever really had a chance with him, anyway.

I wanted to groan when I realized then that I'd been thinking some bad thoughts about myself just now, and I put the tablet back over the sketch, standing straighter. I sucked in a breath and shook out my tangled, bleach-fried hair. Who was to say that I didn't have a chance with Xollen? He was an alien, and it wasn't like I was hideous. So what if I was fat? No one so far had made me feel bad about that, and it wasn't like it was an objectively bad thing in the first place. I'd been *made* to feel bad about it, but it wasn't bad, it just *was*.

Without Dr. Jackson here to help me I'd have to make sure I kept on top of myself with that kind of thing. It was crazy that even after five years with her I still caught myself doing that shit: ragging on myself, tearing myself down, bullying myself inside my own head. It was loads better than it had been before, but it still happened a lot, and I was impatient for it to go away.

You've got to be patient with yourself, Joss, I could hear her telling me, a soft smile on her dark brown face. *It didn't start happening all at once and it's not going to get better all at once. So just focus on catching it and correcting it when it happens, and never mind how long it takes.* I nodded as if she was here, as if she could see me, then turned and headed out of Xollen's room to meet him back in the control room.

Chapter Ten
Xollen Makes a Friend?!

<u>XOLLEN</u>

When Joss finally joined me on the bridge I was a little calmer, my mind turning over the things she'd told me. She'd been through a lot of hardships in her life, and while my hearts hurt for her, I was also a strange kind of glad. It meant that she would probably be able to better understand me. Even Derris, as much as I knew he cared for me, didn't quite understand what it was like to be on the outside looking in, and I was desperate for someone to finally *get* it. And I felt like Joss did—she had already said she understood how I felt about my art, and she hadn't flinched in the slightest at the fact that I'd been kicked out of my program. She hadn't gently suggested, like Derris sometimes did, that maybe I should just do what my parents wanted to keep the peace. And possibly most exciting of all, she looked upon my hideously deformed face with fondness, as if she *liked* looking at it, beyond just tolerating it.

She glided in with a shy smile on her round face, her hands smoothing the front of her borrowed shirt. She'd chosen my coral Hevetta shirt and some Ishta wide-leg pants, filling them out far better than I ever had. I felt my mouth begin to water at the sight of her, all full curves and feminine softness in my clothes—a fact that had me wanting to growl and sweep her into my arms possessively. I had the sudden perverted urge to put my mouth on her, to taste her golden-brown skin and sink my teeth into her delicate softness. My cock twitched in my pants, growing heavier with a tingling rush. I swallowed, shifting nervously in my seat, shocked by my reaction. I'd never had that happen before, not even with Verilla, a stunningly beautiful billieuan by all rights. But while Verilla was attractive, she'd never caused me to…*awaken*, like Joss was doing. She was lighting me up just at the sight of her.

"Does it look okay?" she asked me. I mentally shook myself and smiled at her, swallowing desperately in an attempt to get moisture into my dry throat.

"You look fantastic," I managed, my voice cracking at the end in a way that made me wince. "I'm glad you were able to find something that wasn't too big on you."

She looked at me strangely, one eyebrow lifting, before breaking into another smile. "Yeah. Sure. Thanks again for letting me borrow this. Um, so what are you up to in here?"

The truth was that I was hiding from Uraka and the rest of the females I'd rescued, but I didn't want to admit that to Joss. I wanted her to think I was brave and capable. For her to turn to me for protection and comfort. "Just checking up on the autopilot and making adjustments," I lied smoothly, flicking through screens on the console at random. I had no idea what I was looking at.

"Cool," Joss said, sitting in the co-pilot's chair beside mine. "How's it looking?"

"Everything looks good; we should get to Billieu without incident. Do you have a mate, Joss?" I blurted, feeling my neck and face flame. Where had *that* come from?

She blinked at me, looking surprised, before twisting her mouth into an odd smile. "Nope!" she declared, grinning at me and pulling her pale gold hair over her shoulder to comb through it with her fingers. "Do you?" she asked me, her voice quiet and unsure.

"No, I have no one," I assured her quickly. For some reason, it felt vital that I tell her that as soon as possible. For the first time in several lunars I was *glad* that Verilla had cut me loose. It meant my path to Joss was clear. If she would want me.

She chuckled, color staining her cheeks. "Well, that's good to know, then. Um—because if you had someone, then obviously that would change the dynamic of how I'd help you. Of course."

"Yes. Certainly." I cleared my throat, my fingers tingling with the urge to smack her hands away and take over combing her hair for her. But I resisted; now was not the time to start courting her, not when she was fresh off of a traumatic experience and about to have to rebuild her whole life. I may have been an idiot, but I knew that much. Though

I couldn't stop myself from staring at her face, drinking her in.

Beyond just being beautiful, what I liked about Joss was how *kind* she looked. There was no hard edge to her glances, no daggers hiding in her smiles, and I found that almost as attractive as the sparkle of her brown eyes or the plump bow of her lips. She made me feel...safe.

I wanted to know everything about her, but when it came to it, my brain stuttered to a halt and refused to supply me with anything. The only question that would float to the surface was "what does your cunt taste like?" and obviously—*obviously*—that was about as far from appropriate as you could get.

Goddess be blessed, Joss spoke first, saving me from myself yet again. "So what sorts of things are there to do on the shuttle for fun?"

I shrugged, trying to think of just one of the things that I usually did that sounded impressive. "I spend some of the time drawing. But unfortunately there isn't much to do on a vessel this size when so much of it is automated."

"You don't have any games or anything?"

"A few, but most of them require more than one player. And usually I am alone—" I snapped my mouth shut, not wanting to sound pathetic. But the truth of it was that I was alone most of the time.

Joss tilted her head, then smiled warmly and swept out her arm. "Well lookee here, you've got someone you can play a game with right now!" She leaned closer to me, her voice dropping. "I'm not very good at games, but so long as you promise not to laugh at how bad I am I'm down to play something."

My throat tightened, lightness suffusing my limbs. I was too moved to speak for several seconds. "Oh, um, yes I think that would be a lot of fun! Let me just grab my personal tablet from my quarters—it has all the games on it." Technically this shuttle was my parents', but they hardly used it and I often borrowed it for quick trips. Still more technically, now that they'd cut me off my borrowing this craft probably counted as theft, but it wasn't like I'd been able to ask permission to use it.

I hurried to my quarters and snatched my tablet off my desk. Underneath it was one of my drawings of Verilla, possibly my favorite sketch of her because of how I'd managed to capture the lighting and the fabric of her dress, and seeing it there made me pause. I'd been hung up on her for a while now—she'd been far out of my league and I'd been devastated to find that our relationship was entirely one-sided, but truth be told I didn't really miss *her.* I missed having a companion, I missed having her on my arm and showing her off, proof that I wasn't unlovable, but Verilla hadn't been what I'd missed this whole time.

Now that I'd met Joss it was so obvious.

I held the well-worn paper in my hand, staring at what had once been my most cherished drawing, and was shocked to realize that for the first time in a long time, what I felt when I looked at it was… nothing. After a moment of hesitation, I folded the drawing up and tossed it into the recycler. My hearts clenched for a moment, and I braced like somehow Verilla would know what I'd done and try to punish me, but nothing happened, and I turned to rejoin Joss in the command room, smiling a strange little smile.

Once I was back in the pilot's chair, I showed her several games that two people could easily play on one tablet (since the tablets that came with the ship all had the download function disabled), and we settled on one called Hunters, which had caused several fights between me and Derris in our youth, but which we'd had a lot of fun with nonetheless.

"It sounds kind of like *Battleship* mixed with checkers," Joss mused as it booted up. Since I'd played it before I went first, holding the tablet so she couldn't see it and setting the starting locations of my herd. Then, as the hunter, Joss would try and sniff out where the six different creatures in my herd were hiding in a field and stop them. But if I managed to get more than half the creatures from one side to the other then I'd win.

I took my time setting down the starting positions of my creatures, trying to keep them spread out but not too much, in case she tried a scattershot approach to start. Satisfied, I handed the tablet to her so she could take her first turn, and the game was on.

On the first turn, the hunter chose three spots along the starting edge of the field to inspect, and if any of them revealed one of the spaces my creatures occupied (with some of the larger ones taking multiple spaces) then she got another chance to inspect to try and flush the creature out.

Somehow, Joss managed to find one of my creatures on her first guess.

"You peeked!" I cried, forgetting for a moment that I wasn't playing with Derris this time. I snapped my mouth shut, slouching back in my chair. "I'm sorry," I hurried to add. My anxiety started to spike, my breaths growing faster and my palms going clammy as my vision went the littlest bit spotty on the edges. I'd only just met this female, had barely agreed to live and work together with her when we got back to Billieu, and I just had to go and ruin it. *Stupid, Xollen. Stupid, stupid, stupid…*

Joss looked a little shocked for a second, but she recovered quickly, smirking at me. "Listen, it's not my fault your strategy is terrible," she quipped, smirking at me in a way that made my stomach flutter. "If you don't want people to figure out everything on the first turn then you'll just have to, as we say on Earth, 'get good'." Then she giggled, putting her hand on my arm with a warmth I wasn't expecting. "It's alright," she said, her eyes going soft. "If we're going to be living together we have to get comfortable with each other, right? Become friends? And what better way to get close than to trash-talk each other over a video game?"

Some of her words didn't translate well, but they still soothed me. I took a shuddering breath, then another, before managing a weak smile. "No, of course you're right. I suppose I was just…not expecting you to dive right into it." Merciful goddess, this *female*.

I lost soundly, but somehow still had more fun than I'd had in years, so I was reluctant to let it end even after we'd had our fill of Hunters. To my surprise, Joss didn't seem to want to stop talking to me either— my brain was certain she was already sick of me and ready to slip away and join her more normal companions in the rec room, but after her third straight victory she merely put down the tablet and turned to me with a question that should not have made me as happy as it did.

"So," she began with a clap of her small golden-brown hands, "what do you want to do now? Watch a movie?"

I cocked my head. "What is a movie? My translator didn't catch that one."

She smiled, looking bashful. "Oh, sure. Um…it's like a story that you watch other people act out…from a…recording?"

I nodded, understanding dawning. "Oh, yes, a holo! Certainly, we can watch one." I opened the appropriate folder on my tablet and handed it to her to browse. "You go ahead and pick something, I'll be just a moment." I shot her a smile and then slipped out to use the hygiene room.

When I returned, I was horrified to find that Joss had found my collection of sappy, dramatic holos that I had been hiding from absolutely everyone my entire life. All it had taken was one encounter with my parents when I was six solars where they teased me and lamented my poor taste to get the message that it was unacceptable for a male to like such dramatic drivel, but I hadn't quite been able to stay away from it. When I felt lonely or sad there was something about them that perked me up and gave me hope. But I'd hidden my collection carefully on my personal tablet. Or so I'd thought.

"Oh! Um, not those—" I sputtered, trying to reach for my tablet before she could see any more. My hearts hammered, panic sweeping through me in a too-bright wave.

Joss looked up at me, her brow furrowed. "Oh, I'm sorry, are these private? I just thought they looked really good. Especially this one, *'Til I Die*."

That was my favorite one of the bunch, an epic fantasy where a hero went on a journey for selfish reasons and wound up finding himself and his true love instead. My hearts surged painfully in my chest; she wasn't making fun of me for liking what I liked. She was just as interested in it as I was. "It...is one of my favorites," I heard myself admitting with horror. "We—we can watch it if you'd like."

"You're sure?" she asked, watching me carefully. "We don't have to if they really are private. I don't want you to be uncomfortable."

Sweet glory of the Goddess, the things this female was doing to me. Tears threatened at the backs of my eyes, and I swallowed hard and blinked to try and keep them from falling and embarrassing myself further. "No, we will watch it. I...I want you to see it." I smiled at her, then took the tablet from her so I could queue it up on the spare holoscreen here in the control room.

I was damp with sweat, hearts pounding and stomach churning, but it felt good, it felt *right*, to be showing this to Joss. And if she responded poorly to it, if she made fun of me after all, then it was better to know now, when it was still early into our agreement, when I knew it would be easier to send her on her way. Even if the thought of losing her *did* leave me cold.

I didn't pay attention to a single second of *'Til I Die*, my attention riveted to the fascinating female beside me. I was nervous that she wouldn't like it, or that she'd grow disgusted with me once she'd seen it because of what it would say about me that I liked it. I kept peeking at her out of the corner of my eye, hung on her every expression, watching to see if she laughed when I laughed, if she gasped when I gasped, if she found herself unable to keep the sappy smile off of her face when Callai and Destev finally admitted their feelings for each other.

When I realized that she was moved to tears by the holo, it felt like she'd reached into my chest and cracked both my hearts open. Warmth and feeling so intense it hurt suffused me, igniting me and making me feel alive in a way that scared me. Watching such a sweet and lovely female fall to pieces over the things that I'd only ever allowed myself to love in secret made me feel vulnerable and almost too hopeful.

As the credits rolled Joss turned to me, her eyelashes dark and clumping with the remnants of her tears. "Oh my god, Xollen," she sighed dreamily, smiling wide, "that was amazing! I haven't seen a movie that good in a while. What else do you have? I want to see all of it!"

I melted.

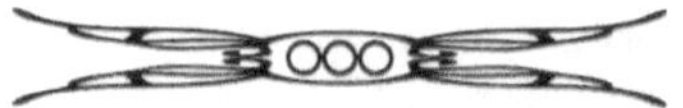

I was pretty sure Uraka was planning on killing me, and the only reason she hadn't yet was because Joss and Djelani were so determined to keep me alive. Any time she had something sharp in her hands, she crowded close to me. Every time she looked at me her eyes were full of cold fury. I guessed I couldn't blame her, given how we'd met, but it still frustrated and annoyed me. I was *really* trying to put her at ease and prove I meant them no harm.

I turned the rec room into an impromptu dorm for them, grabbing every blanket and spare cushion I could find and dumping them in there for their use. No one except Joss wanted clothes, so I turned all my other spares into pillows by stuffing them into clean linens. It wasn't a great solution, but they only needed to endure it until we docked at Escheva in three days. Everyone except Uraka seemed happy or at least content, but she seemed…very upset.

Luckily, most of my time was spent with Joss during the long three days standard. We talked a lot about what we might get up to once we landed. I did my best to prepare her for what might come next: we'd report the th'rak slavers at the trafficking shelter, after which they'd all have to give statements to the authorities. Then they'd guide us through the process of getting Joss citizenship and helping the others get home. Once she was in the system, we'd tackle my finances and living situation.

"You'll probably want to get rid of a lot of stuff," Joss was telling me as we shared another meal. "Moving sucks ass and the more stuff you have the worse it is. Plus, you can probably sell a lot of it off for cash—sorry, credits—which will soften the blow of going to the public dorms."

I nodded, spooning more of my vish'tal stew into my mouth. "I suppose that makes sense," I muttered, but I was not feeling as calm about it as I was letting on. Truthfully, I was devastated and more than a little cranky about the whole thing. I had spent a lifetime acquiring those things, and a lot of them were important to me. Wasn't it enough that I'd given all of my money? Should I really have to give up all of my favorite things along with my home? It didn't seem fair to me, that my reward for a good deed should be to lose everything about my current life that I enjoyed.

"You okay, Xoll?" Joss asked, looking at me with concern. I bristled, not wanting to deal with her judging me. Luckily I was saved by an incoming comm call from Derris. I swiped at my wristcom, letting him know I'd pick up in a minute and sending the call to my quarters.

"You'll have to excuse me," I told her, standing and dumping the rest of my stew into the recycler. "This is an important call, I've got to take it." Then before she could say anything I was leaving the mess hall and jogging to my room.

I finally accepted the call once I was alone in my locked room. "Derris, to what do I owe the pleasure?" Now that I was within a daycycle of Billieu the call was able to come through with video. The broad, gentle face of my best friend filled the little screen set into the wall above my desk.

"Hey, Xoll. Just checking in. You were acting very strange the last time I talked to you, and you know how I worry."

I snorted, crossing my arms and leaning back in my chair. "You're worse than my mother," I teased him with a pang. My mother seldom worried about me, truth be told, unless it was to worry I was going to mess something up for her.

Derris grinned, white teeth flashing and copper eyes swirling warmly. "Can't help it, Xoll. Maybe if you didn't get into trouble so much..."

I sputtered, glaring at him through the screen. "*Me,* get in trouble? I'm sorry, have you met yourself? If I remember correctly, you were the one who put eggs in our school's ventilation ducts so that they'd rot and stink up the whole complex and got suspended for an entire lunar."

Derris laughed. "Yeah, but you didn't try and stop me."

"Slander! I absolutely did tell you not to do it."

"Sure, sure, whatever Xoll." Derris's face sobered, and he searched my face carefully. "Seriously, Xollen. What's going on? Are you in trouble? Are you okay?"

I was tempted to give in and tell him what I'd done, but then I'd have to admit what I was even doing on Quellor to begin with. And there was always the chance that the comms were being monitored, and anything I told Derris would incriminate me.

But I didn't want to lie to him, either. "I'm fine. I'm not in trouble, but I can't go into more detail than that right now. When I dock in Escheva tomorrow I'll call you up and we can get together and talk. Alright?" He studied my face carefully, his eyes narrowing, before pursing his lips and giving me a tight nod. I loosed a shaky breath. "Please be safe, Xoll," he told me.

We chatted more casually after that, Derris telling me all about what he and Gesea had been up to in the last several lunars. "You promise you'll fill me in once you're back?" Derris asked after we'd agreed to disconnect.

"Yes, I will reach out as soon as I can and catch you up on what's been going on. But, Derris?" I swallowed thickly, nervous. "Please... please don't judge me, when I tell you, okay?"

He frowned, looking ready to protest, but something in my face must have changed his mind. "Alright, Xoll," he sighed, tugging on the end of a horn in a nervous gesture he'd had as long as I'd known him. "Be careful, okay? Take care of yourself. Goddess guide you."

"Goddess guide you," I responded, disconnecting the call. I leaned back in my desk chair, trying to stretch out the tension in my neck. I decided to make a cup of tea; perhaps that would help soothe me. I stood from my desk and strode to the door, which slid open at my approach.

Rather than the empty hallway I was expecting, a large, bulky form was lounging in the doorway, arms crossed over her chest and leaning her shoulder against one side of the door jamb. I was so startled to see her there that I froze, staring at her as if in doing so I could make her appearance make sense.

But Uraka was not so slow to act. She put a large hand on my chest and shoved me back inside my room, following me so that the door shut behind her.

"I would like to talk, Xollen," she said in a deadly quiet voice. The tone of her voice put my control over my bladder into question. It was possibly the first time I'd ever heard her willingly use my actual name, and I did not think it was a good sign.

"What do you want, Uraka?" I asked breathlessly, hating how I was trembling.

"Just to talk," she said slowly, a small blade—Goddess only knew where she got it from—appearing in her hand. She used it to clean under her nails, but the threat was clear. "I have noticed you getting very close to our sweet Joslyn. She plans to live with you, even. To help the male who bought her like she was just a thing, because her heart is so sweet and tender.

"I have seen what males do to females when they get their filthy hands on them. I rescued them often when I was still in the vanguard. That will not happen to Joss. I will be keeping a close eye on her when we land in Escheva, checking in on her, making sure she does not become a victim of her kindness."

I swallowed, sweat sliding down my back in a river. "I-I understand, Uraka. And I *swear*, on all that I own, on the Goddess

Herself, that I will not hurt her. I don't *want* to hurt her. I'm an idiot, but I'm not cruel. I don't know what I can say to make you believe me —"

"You cannot say anything. I must see it. So if you are as good as your word, you have nothing to worry about." She finished cleaning her nails, the small blade disappearing as quickly as it had come. "But I do not bluff, Xollen. I do not threaten idly." Goddess save me, but I had no trouble believing her. Uraka oozed threat and menace, making it easy to picture her covered in blood, soaked in it, and cackling in delight. She hadn't asked me a question, but I found myself nodding anyway.

Uraka grinned, her lips pulling taut over her tusks, before turning and sauntering out of my room. "If anyone asks, we did not have this conversation," she threw over her shoulder as she left, making me shudder.

"S-sure," I managed to spit out. She nodded once more and then closed the door behind her, leaving me alone to sag into a puddle on the floor. My tail was wrapped so tightly around my leg my foot was falling asleep, and it was hard to breathe. She hadn't killed me though, and she hadn't sounded like she was going to murder me just for fun. Maybe she'd even leave me alone, so long as I kept Joss happy. And why wouldn't I want to keep Joss happy? She was all those good things that Uraka had said and more; I'd have to be a monster to want to let any harm come to her. I'd spent 3 million credits on *stopping* that from happening, I huffed to myself, my pulse settling as I thought of Joss.

Maybe Uraka would come around. Maybe she just needed time to see that I wasn't what she thought, that I only wanted the best for all of them...but especially for Joss.

Chapter Eleven
Home Away from Home

<u>JOSS</u>

Usually I wasn't the most social person, but when Xollen got weird and ran off to his room I decided it was a good time to hang out with the girls.

With so little to do on the shuttle, we'd wound up watching a *lot* of holos in the two days we'd been flying through space on the way to Billieu. I'd shown the others the amazing holo I'd seen with Xollen, *'Til I Die*, though no one was as into it as I was. Uraka fell asleep on Djelani's shoulder immediately, and by the midway point Djelani was just as passed out, her cheek smooshed into the top of Uraka's head. Wren and Ghena had been a little more into it, but I was the only one moved to tears by the ending.

"It is a nice holo," Wren had intoned in her deep, flat voice. "But I took many issues with the logic of it. Why do they not simply leave? Why let themselves be torn apart from each other?"

"Um, yeah I thought that as well," Ghena had added, smiling gratefully at Wren. The two of them had formed a close bond, though I didn't think there was anything romantic happening there like there was between Djelani and Uraka. They were both quiet and soft-spoken, and whenever I dragged myself away from Xollen to hang out in here the two of them were usually talking quietly in the corner.

Today when I walked into the rec room, Ghena was seated cross-legged on the floor in front of Wren, who was carefully braiding

Ghena's shoulder-length auburn hair back into french-braided pigtails.

"How's it going, ladies?" I asked as I joined Uraka and Djelani on the one couch. There was really only room for two on the narrow seat, but with Djelani curled up in Uraka's lap I was able to squeeze in.

"I am well, though bored out of my skull," Uraka told me, idly scratching behind Djelani's ears. "These have been the longest two and a half days of my life, I think." She chuckled, a hard edge entering her three golden eyes. "And I was once held as a prisoner of war for over a month."

I gasped, covering my mouth with my hand. "Oh my god, seriously?! I'm so sorry."

Uraka shrugged, her arm tightening around Djelani's shoulder. "Eh, it was many years ago now. And I was able to unleash Veldar's wrath upon those *vrakaashaad*. They paid for their crimes." Djelani, purring softly, rubbed her cheek against Uraka's face in a very catlike gesture that made me smile.

"Man, Uraka, you are an absolute badass. I wish I could be half as tough and cool as you," I told her.

She waved a hand dismissively. "Bah. Everyone should be who they are. You are a good and kind person, little Joss. You are patient and fair. These are things that I wish I could be."

"And you're brave," Ghena interjected. "You weren't going to just let those—those bad aliens hurt us. You're more badass than you think."

My eyes burned with unshed tears. "Thanks, Ghena. You guys are the best." I sniffled, smiling at all of them. "If I had to get abducted by slavers I'm glad I at least got kidnapped with such a great group of people."

It still didn't feel totally real, that I'd been abducted by aliens, almost sold into slavery, and rescued by a different alien hottie all in the space of what was probably just a couple of days (it was hard to say how much time had passed while I was unconscious, though). I was having a little trouble sleeping because of it, nightmares about waking up strapped back into that freezing cold medical table while Cherry, Orange, and Lemon talked about all of the things they were going to do to hurt me. It had taken a while to fall back asleep each time it had happened, my arms hugging myself tight and wishing I had someone to turn to, to soothe my nightmares away. But with how much I tossed and turned in my sleep the others had learned pretty quickly that giving me a wide berth once I lay down was smartest.

"What do you guys think you're going to do when we get to Billieu?" Ghena asked softly, turning to face us now that Wren was done with her hair.

"Yeah, what are you all going to do?" I asked, suddenly nervous about losing the group. Everyone but Ghena and me probably had a life and family and friends that they would want to get back to, meaning we might be scattered all over the universe by the time all was said and done. Once we docked in Escheva in less than 24 hours I might never see any of them again. The thought made my throat feel too tight.

"Djelani and I will most likely stay on Billieu," Uraka offered, grinning at the felican woman still curled up in her lap. "I have no living family and I do not wish to return to Exodia, the planet of my birth, without any kin there to hold my roots. And now that I have found... Djelani, I go where she goes, and she has also expressed a desire to stay."

Djelani's pointed ears twitched, her fine white whiskers pushing forward; I got the impression it might have been the cat equivalent of a blush. "Yes, well, I always wanted to visit Billieu for its unparalleled art and culture museums, and when Ura expressed she wanted to be able to stay close to you, Joss, I thought it was a nice idea. I don't have any real ties to Tunnalah, my own homeworld, anyway."

I beamed at them, touched that Uraka was so protective of me. "What about you, Ghena?" I asked, turning my smile on the dainty person who was the only other human besides me around for who even knew how many light years.

She shrugged, pulling her knees up to her chest and hugging them. "I don't know," she admitted, biting her lip. "I guess I haven't wanted to think about it. It's not like I had much going on back home, but I don't know that I want to stay on Billieu either. Xollen is nice but..." she trailed off, shifting uncomfortably. "I-I don't want to be a freak. Someone who stands out. Anyone who sees me is going to know I got there by being abducted a-and—"

Wren reached out and put a hand on Ghena's shoulder, making the woman smile in thanks. "You can come with me to Mon II," she intoned. "None will think to judge you, or call attention to your misfortunes. My people do not have time to meddle in the business of others."

Ghena's eyes widened, her big brown doe eyes brimming with hope. "Really? You'd want me to go with you?"

"Of course," Wren nodded, "we are friends, are we not? There is plenty of room at my domicile to house you in addition to myself."

Ghena's tawny brow furrowed. "But...what will I do there? For money?"

Wren waved a fuzzy pink paw dismissively. "We will have time to discover that. All you need to worry about is where you would like to go."

Wren and Ghena would be leaving? I was glad that sweet, delicate Ghena would have someone looking out for her, and it made sense that Wren would want to go home, but it still hurt knowing our little group was going to be broken up. "How far away is Mon II from Billieu, do you know?"

Wren cocked her head, thinking. "Only about four daycycles, I'd think. Visiting and communications will be quite simple. There is no need to fret, Joss." Okay, maybe Wren really *was* some kind of psychic.

I swallowed, forcing a smile. "Yeah, okay, that's really great. I don't want to lose touch with you guys." Djelani and Uraka reached out to me and I clasped their hands tight, then went over to Wren and Ghena and did the same. Hugging wasn't super common, I'd been told, but the hand clasping was the alien alternative.

After a moment, Djelani cleared her throat delicately and inspected her claws a little too innocently. "So…you and Xollen, eh?" she asked, Uraka going stiff under her.

I sighed, rolling my eyes but unable to stop the smile twisting up my lips. "Yeah, I know. But he's so *nice*. And you gotta admit he's hot as fuck; can you blame me?" Ghena giggled, hiding her face in her hands. "See, Ghena gets it."

Uraka's eyes hardened as she turned her burning gold eyes on me. "I do not trust him," she growled.

I slapped my hands onto my cheeks and made my mouth into a big O. "*No!*" I said in exaggerated surprise. "You don't like Xollen? Really?!"

Djelani snorted and kissed Uraka on the cheek. "Yes, I know I have made no secret of how I feel," the large yvrenii woman said. "But I have seen the blood that can flow from trust placed poorly too many times in my life. I only want you to be safe, Joss. To be careful."

"I know," I sighed, crossing my arms over my chest. "And I don't want to get hurt either. But he hasn't done anything shady. Does he really seem dangerous to you?"

She twisted her mouth, her tusks jutting out. "I…suppose not," she allowed, squirming before surging to her feet and gently depositing Djelani onto the couch. She crouched down in front of me, putting her heavy hands on my shoulders. "You are an adult, and no fool. But you and I will strike a bargain, here and now, that if anything happens, you will call on me. *Anything.* Do you understand, little one?"

"Yeah," I said, my voice soft yet rough with emotion. This crazy she-orc was so kind, so protective of little old me. I felt better-taken care of in her presence than I ever had with my mom. "If anything goes wrong you'll be the first to know," I promised.

Uraka nodded, getting back to her feet and turning to leave, saying she needed to use the hygiene room.

"Does it feel real to any of you?" I found myself asking quietly, my hands tangling together in my lap."

Djelani cocked her head. "Does what feel real, Joss?"

I shrugged, my eyes sweeping over the room. "This. Being here. The fact that we got abducted and almost wound up—" I couldn't get the word "slaves" out. "We were almost in a really bad situation," I said instead. "I mean, up until a couple of days ago I didn't even know that there really were aliens, and now…"

Ghena nodded, hugging her knees tighter, but remained silent. Wren seemed to drift just a little bit closer to her, her tail curling around Ghena's back.

"I suppose it doesn't," Djelani admitted. "It feels like one minute I was coming home from rehearsals, and the next I was waking up in a cell with four strangers." Her eyes drifted to the doorway that Uraka had left through, and a small smile tugged at her lips.

"I'm sure it will catch up to us in time," Wren said, "we are likely still in shock from our experiences." Wren was always so logical and calm; I could see why Ghena gravitated toward her. For someone nervous that kind of confidence was appealing. "You are not bothered that Ghena has not chosen to remain with you, are you, Joss?" she asked unexpectedly, startling me out of my thoughts.

Ghena blushed, shooting Wren a look I couldn't read from where I was sitting. "Uh, no. I mean I'll miss her, I'll miss all of you, but I don't hold it against her or anything." My brow furrowed in confusion. "Should I be?…"

"No! No, it's all good," Ghena blurted, giving me a tight smile. "Um, so does anyone want to watch a movie? I saw one that looked good when we were browsing last time…" Ghena sprang to her feet and dashed to the holoscreen, turning it on and flicking through the selection of holos available. *Super fucking weird, but okay*, I thought, settling back into the couch just as Uraka returned looking refreshed.

The holo finished loading, silence settling on our strange little group. But I wasn't able to focus, my thoughts swirling around and around.

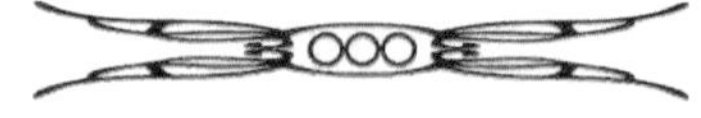

I guess I was expecting Escheva to look like a cool sci-fi city, all gleaming towers and scuzzy neon bars in a designated underbelly. I figured there'd be hover cars everywhere, in invisible traffic lanes stretching from the ground to the top of the tallest skyscrapers, with aliens snarling at newcomers. But it was just a city, not too different from Chicago, honestly. The biggest differences were the green sky and blue-tinged plants decorating the buildings and walkways. There were aliens, but they just ignored us, walking quickly with their heads down. The few who did notice us really only looked at me and Wren, who were the two rarer species, and even that was more of a curious once-over before going back to ignoring us. There were some hovercars, but most of the vehicles I saw were more like hoverbikes, and the rest of the time people were walking or taking one of the many buses or trains I saw everywhere. Skyscrapers were a thing, but they weren't all soulless towers looming over a seedy underground; there were some really lovely ones, with interesting architecture and gorgeous decorative edifices covered in intricate carvings and sculptures. There were trees and flowers and grass. There were murals and ornate trashcans. There were public restroom booths with water and nutrition tabs scattered all over that were totally free.

I wanted to start crying, it was all so great. I'd never felt so safe in a big city. These people really believed in taking care of each other, and that was just so beautiful to me.

Landing and docking had been…interesting. Xollen's ship was in no way designed for six passengers, and there were only two seats with harnesses for passengers to strap into for landing, so we had to get creative. Xollen tore up some of his linens and tied Ghena to his cot in his room and Wren and Djelani to the seats in the rec room. Uraka insisted I get the co-pilot's chair because, in her words, I'd "pop like an overripe fruit" otherwise because of my soft skin and bones (like she knew anything about human bones!) and she said she'd brace herself in the shower stall—sorry, the *sanitation booth*. I'd have to get used to all the new terminology.

The solution was sloppy and risky, but by some miracle it worked: we landed without anyone getting injured or killed. Even Uraka was barely disheveled when she emerged from the hygiene room.

I was nervous when we disembarked, knowing the next step was going to be talking to cops and bureaucrats for the next eternity, but I was also kind of exciting. As much as it sucked to have to leave everything I'd ever known behind, this was a once-in-a-lifetime chance to completely reinvent myself. I could be bold, I could be confident, I could pursue writing without worrying about winding up on the streets again—the possibilities were intoxicatingly endless. It was like starting up at a new school turned up to eleven.

I was expecting the worst from talking to cops, but I should have known that a society as advanced as Billieu's would also have law enforcement figured out. They talked to me and the rest of the girls, getting our statements and whatever information we could on the three th'rak slavers who'd abducted us. I was worried they'd try to arrest Xollen if they found out that he'd bought us initially, but since all of us— even Uraka, to my surprise—corroborated that he'd freed us immediately they just slapped him with some fines and left it at that.

He looked sick when he was told he'd be responsible for 10,000 credits, but I threaded my arm through his and squeezed it against my side, since I'd noticed that when he got upset his tail tended to wrap around one of his legs and squeeze the shit out of it. "It'll be okay, Xoll," I promised, smiling up at him gently. "We'll find the money." I bet he could sell off just the jewelry he was currently wearing and get pretty damn close, if not more than enough to pay the fines.

He smiled weakly down at me, leaning into my touch, and my heart did little flips in my chest at the sight. He really was so damn handsome. I jumped a little when I felt something slither up my calf, but it was just his tail grabbing onto me and pinning me next to him. I had a feeling that I'd be doing a lot of comforting in the coming days as I helped this pampered rich boy figure out how to live like the rest of us.

Once we were done with the cops, ambassadors and counselors from the trafficking shelter swooped in to take care of us. I was completely blown away when a small older human woman in a smart pantsuit strode in among the other various aliens. She walked up to me, her hand out and a terse smile on her face.

"Welcome to Billieu, Miss Aceveda," she said, her voice raspy as if she spent a lot of time screaming. "I'm Rita Benson, feel free to call me Rita. I wish you were here under happier circumstances, of course, but I'm sure you'll find plenty to love here or wherever you choose to settle."

I nodded, smiling politely. Now it was my turn to cling to Xollen, nervous now that I was around another human—which was weird, right? Being around someone of my own kind should have put me at ease, but as soon as Rita Benson had walked up to me I'd felt the old compulsion to pose carefully and suck in my gut, to suppress my little bit of an accent, hoping it wasn't too obvious that I wasn't wearing a bra and feeling embarrassed about my clothes and hair. I felt his tail tighten around my lower leg, the tufted tip flicking against the back of my knee soothingly, even if it also tickled.

"I think I'm actually going to stay here. With Xollen," I gestured at the gorgeous tree of a male whose arm I was still clinging to. "He's the one who rescued us all," I added, wanting to explain myself.

Rita smiled stiffly, her eyes darting from me to Xollen quickly, and I could practically hear her thoughts: *he's way out of her league. What does she think she's doing with him?* I tried to sag away from Xollen, trying to prevent those thoughts from getting any worse, but he held onto me firmly, not letting me squirm away. It gave me some courage.

"So then you'll be staying on Billieu? Do you plan on becoming a citizen, Miss Aceveda?"

I nodded. "Yes, I'd like to get that process started as soon as possible, actually."

Rita smiled again, pulling a small tablet from her shoulder bag and gesturing her silent companion forward from where they'd been lingering several feet away. "This is Trista Me'Hessa Be'Yeveh, an ambassador for Billieu. She'll be able to guide you through the process of acquiring citizenship. I assume you will be sponsoring her, Mr. Me'Tirri Be'Faan?" Xollen nodded, then dipped his head as if he was trying to hide his face from the ambassador who'd finally joined our little huddle. I hadn't paid her much attention before now, since she was off to the side and all my attention had been on Rita and Xollen, but now that she was in front of me it was taking everything I had not to burst out laughing.

She was like Xollen…but not. She had the same long, lean build, the same horns and pin-straight hair, the same thin tufted tail and swirling eyes, but her face—

It looked like a butt. Where Xollen's face was roughly human-shaped, if with slightly different proportions of things, this woman's face had a deep cleft running from her hairline all the way down to her chin, forcing the two halves of her face to curve gently forward towards each other. "Greetings, Joslyn Aceveda," she greeted me, bowing her head and making the delicate chains she wore on her horns tinkle. "Welcome to Billieu. I look forward to guiding you on your journey to becoming a citizen of this great planet." She bowed again, looking at Xollen quickly with a look that turned me sour on her and had me itching for a fight. It was like…she was grossed out by him or something. Xollen, who looked like a fucking model, was grossing her *out*?

I looked around at the other Billieu ambassadors talking to the rest of the girls and their counselors, and I realized that all of the others billieuans I could see had the cleft. I almost gasped with the shock of realizing that if that cleft was standard, then Xollen might be considered deformed by the other members of his species. That they might even see him as *ugly*. Was that why he was trying so hard to hide his face, why he was clinging to me again like he was drowning and needed me to save him?

Man, perspective really was everything.

The ambassador gathered herself quickly, pasting a smile on her strange face. "Did I hear correctly? You are Me'Tirri Be'Faan? Any relation to Se'Tirraan Entertainment?" At Xollen's hesitant nod her smile grew wider. "How exciting! I adore their Super Soldiers franchise of holos! I cannot even imagine how exciting it must be to be a part of such a prestigious family." Poor Xollen looked like he was being forced to swallow a hedgehog, his tail and hand clutching at me with something like desperation.

"I-it's certainly int-teresting," he allowed, clearing his throat. "So, um, Ambassador Me'Hessa Be'Yeveh, what will you need me to do as Joss's sponsor for citizenship?"

She blinked, her eyes swirling slowly in shades of bronze. "Oh! Not much, no need to worry! Most of your burden will be in additional paperwork. And of course, if Ms. Aceveda ever finds herself…in trouble, you will have additional responsibilities."

"Of course. Shall we begin, then?" he asked, sweeping his free hand towards one of the empty tables they'd set up for us to work at when we were brought into this meeting room at the city records office.

Trista nodded, and we made our way over, Rita handing me the tablet she'd pulled out and telling me that it was mine to keep, as a welcome gift; I just had to register it under my name and ID number, once I got it. In the meantime I could still use it, but if I lost it they probably wouldn't be able to get it back for me. I was touched, glad that I had something that was all mine at last. I'd have to get my own smartwatch thingy—I think Xollen had called it a wristcom?—but it was still a really great feeling.

The next three hours were an exhausting slog of paperwork. Form after form had to be filled out, most of them duplicated across me and Xollen because he was sponsoring me, and even though Rita and Trista were watching us fill out each form, they still insisted on checking each page before I hit submit. By the end of it, me and Xollen were both so bored that his tail had finally loosened up and dropped away behind him, lazily flicking against the mosaic tile floor.

At long last, Trista clapped her hands together and declared our preliminary paperwork done—an ominous statement that threatened more down the road. She and Rita bowed at me, then Rita shook my hand, giving me a tired smile and congratulating me on my pending citizenship. Our group was the last to leave, the other women already being citizens of the Collective and so needing much less paperwork, and I was so tired and worn out that it barely registered when Xollen guided me out of the records office and out into bustling Escheva, picking up his luggage from security on the way out, and over to the nearby train hub.

I was expecting something like the L, but the Escheva trains were nothing like that. They didn't smell even a little bit like piss or rank shoes and looked more like the high-speed bullet trains I'd seen talked about in places like Japan. The station was a little crowded, shops mingling with service kiosks to clutter up the otherwise clean and open space, but once we'd managed to squeeze past the station traffic to the platform it got a lot easier to make our way through. As soon as we'd entered the station Xollen had taken my hand, squeezing lightly. "Don't want you to get separated from me," he'd told me with a blush. "It should be safe for you here, but it's better not to take chances." Hey, you weren't going to see *me* complaining about getting to hold his big warm hand. I hadn't noticed it before, but he had one less finger than me, and he felt almost feverishly warm compared to my own body temp. But I liked the way holding his hand felt. I liked it a *lot*.

We were able to find two seats open next to each other fairly easily, Xollen giving me the window seat so I could sit and gawk at Escheva as it blasted past us—not that I could see much, with how fast the train was moving. But what little I could make out was really nice, just as green and warm as what I'd seen already. I kept expecting Xollen to drop my hand now that we were on the train, since there wasn't much of a chance that I'd get separated from him now, but he didn't, and after a while I shifted our hands, threading my fingers through his. Despite being short a finger it felt so...right. Nicer than holding anyone else's hand had ever been. I felt him stiffen beside me when I first did it, but after a second he relaxed and shifted a little closer to me, his thumb tracing lightly over my skin in a way that was making me shivery and breathless.

It seemed like we'd just gotten on the train before it was time to get off again.

"From this station, we'll take a bus down to my apartment," he explained as we carefully disembarked, our hands still linked. "If it's alright with you, I'd prefer to leave all the hard work ahead of us for tomorrow."

"Oh, no, totally," I agreed, smiling up at him. I could *feel* the bags under my eyes. "I'm exhausted. I'd love to just take it easy the rest of the day." He smiled down at me, his thumb still tracing the back of my hand in soft, slow strokes.

"Good. Oh—there's the bus we need!" he exclaimed, pulling me into a light jog, his luggage hovering close behind us.

Chapter Twelve
The Man Cave

<u>XOLLEN</u>

The whole ride over I'd been agonizing over what Joss would think of my home. I'd been proud of the lavish penthouse apartment when I'd started renting it, but now that I'd talked to Joss about her own struggles with money and how little she'd had back on Earth, I worried it would be…too much. It was larger than I needed and full of things that cost more than the Earth equivalent of Joss's nursing classes, most of which I didn't truly need. I enjoyed them, and liked having them in my life, but my life would be no harder than it was now if I lost it all.

Which might happen; I'd been fined 10,000 credits for my hand in the five females' enslavement, and with my savings depleted that meant I'd be forced to sell things instead. I'd never had to do that before, and I was finding that it made me feel sour and sullen. Sure, my parents had paid for most of it, but was it my fault that I had been born into a wealthy family? My life still hadn't been easy, had even been miserable a lot of the time. My collection of horn jewelry brought me joy. My nice clothes made me feel better about myself, especially on days when my facial deformity bothered me. I couldn't fix my face—countless doctors had assured me that surgery was too risky—but I could make myself look nice in other ways. Did I really deserve to have all of my creature comforts torn from me? Especially when the reason I'd lost everything was in the service of helping others?

But now was not the time to let myself get carried away with my thoughts. I needed to get Joss settled in and comfortable first.

I greeted the attendant at the front desk of my building with a curt nod, the hidden scanners confirming my identity. I signed Joss into the guest log, then guided her over to the bank of elevators along the far wall. She was quiet, her energy not quite what it had been before. Once we were alone on the elevator I turned to her, studying her face.

Despite how different her species from mine, I felt like I found something new to like about her appearance every time I looked at her. This time it was noticing the way her ears curved and swirled against the side of her head, reminding me of delicate *issta* cookies. She had several pieces of jewelry embedded in the tender flesh, highlighting the shape in a way that drew attention to certain lines by interrupting them, enhancing the natural shape rather than disrupting it. It was mesmerizing, and I wondered if I might not try doing something similar. Maybe once I was no longer destitute. I liked the double hoops I had going through each ear lobe, but suddenly I was interested in…more.

She looked tired, I thought, her posture slouched and the shadows of her face seeming more pronounced. No doubt this had been a long and difficult day for her. I shifted my weight closer to her, encouraging her to press against my arm. She turned to look at me, her big brown eyes losing some of their dullness as she smiled.

"We're almost there, now. You'll be able to rest soon."

"I can't wait. I feel like I haven't really slept in weeks. No offense but it's not exactly comfortable sleeping on a space couch—" she stopped talking when the elevator doors parted, revealing my penthouse apartment. Her mouth went slack with shock, her eyes bugging out of their sockets.

"Is something the matter?" I asked, pulling away from her and exiting the elevator car.

She shook herself. "Uh, no—sorry. I guess I was just surprised. I don't know what I was expecting but…wow. It's so nice." She followed me off the elevator car, her eyes wide and drinking in all of the details. It was a very open space, full of bright light from the many windows and decorated in tasteful neutrals. All of the furniture was simple, with the clean angular lines that were so in style right now, but had cost a hefty amount of credits despite its simplicity. Apparently, it cost a lot of money to make furniture that understated. I had painted many of the art pieces hanging on the stark white walls, the paintings in the more public rooms uncomplicated things like landscapes and still-lifes, but in my bedroom and studio I had several more…personal pieces. A self-portrait where I painted in a cleft down the center of my face. A scene from a novel I'd particularly enjoyed, of the novel's hero finding his love in a crowd just when he thinks he's lost her for good, the people of the crowd loud and raucous and blurred, but the two lovers utterly still, utterly silent.

I cleared my throat, my tail winding around my leg as the silence stretched on and grew awkward. "I'll show you to your room," I told her, setting my luggage to return to its docking bay in my bedroom and leading her through the wide open space of the living room/kitchen/dining room at the center of the space, to the guest wing of the penthouse. Everything was clean and orderly, thanks to the maid I had come twice a week, and I decided to give her one of the corner suites, which had attached hygiene rooms and the best views of the city spread out below us. This wasn't the tallest building in Escheva, but it was one of the tallest in the immediate area.

"Oh my god, Xollen. Is—is this *my* room?!" She stepped forward as if in a dream, her clothing fluttering gently with her movements. It drew my attention to the rolling sway of her wide hips, the way her flesh trembled ever so slightly with the rhythm of her steps, making it harder for me to breathe. With the late afternoon light streaming into the windows gilding her, setting her pale gold hair aflame and making her already golden skin glow, she was a vision. It hit me then that she was *here*, in my home, settling in to live with me, possibly for quite some time. *Maybe forever.*

But no—that was crazy. Why would she want to stay with me that long? She was just helping me get back on my feet to thank me, then she'd sail off on her own and leave me to figure out the shape of my life without her.

Goddess, but I must have been more tired than I realized—it wasn't like me to be so…poetic.

"It is," I finally answered her, my tail flicking in irritation behind me. "My rooms are on the other side of the main section we walked through, so you'll have plenty of privacy. If you wanted you could take all three of the guest rooms," I chuckled. She spun to beam at me, her eyes sparkling with joy and something else I couldn't name.

She pressed her full lips into a hard line, looking at my face with an intensity that made me uncomfortable, that made me think she was carefully cataloging all my flaws, but instead of disgust, or aversion, or fear, she looked at me…with yearning. As if she might have wanted me to come closer, to join her in the room, and—

The moment passed, her face settling into the same kindness she'd always shown me, the heat of the previous moment gone, or maybe just imagined completely. "Thank you, Xollen," she murmured, walking back to join me in the doorway. After a moment of hesitation, she grabbed my hands, threading our fingers together and smiling at me. "For everything. Thank you. I can't even tell you how much I appreciate what you're doing to help me. What you've given up, what you're going to give up. It really does mean a lot to me. I mean—you saved my life. I can't—just…thanks."

I swallowed, my fingers tightening around hers. All of my earlier grumpiness about what I was giving up fled me. Because it was worth it. It would all be worth it, to have her bright and shining light safe and sound and living in my guest room.

After a moment she dropped my hands, biting her soft-looking lip, then she surged forwards and threw her arms around my middle, clinging tight and pressing her face into my chest. I was too surprised to do anything at first, but as the warm clutch of her body seeped into me I brought my arms up and wrapped them around her shoulders, pulling her in closer and leaning my cheek against the top of her head. This was one of her human hugs, I remembered, and was a sign of affection. I think I loved hugs. It was shocking at first, but once the shock settled something melted internally at the contact, thawing out parts of me that I hadn't even realized were frozen.

"Sorry I'm always hugging you," she said as she pulled away, looking bashful. "I'm not usually so touchy-feely, but—um. Sorry, and if it makes you uncomfortable I'll stop."

"No! No, it's alright, It's not uncomfortable at all," I blurted, desperate for her to keep doing that, to keep touching me and holding me. Now that I'd had a taste of it I was starved for it.

"It doesn't gross you out? Because of all those hygiene laws?"

I shook my head. "Not at all." I considered whether I could convince her to let me put her into one of those slings I saw parents carry their small children around in, letting me touch her soft skin and keep her sweet warmth near me always.

"Well, that's good. Seeing them all listed out on those forms was pretty intimidating. You guys really don't mess around with germs. Technically I'm breaking the law by hugging you and holding your hand and stuff."

I nodded. "Yes, but since you come from a different culture you would not be arrested so long as I have consented. And I do!" I rushed to add, lest she start hanging back from me. "And I made sure to register us as roommates, so we do have non-family proximity permits."

Her lips twitched like she wanted to smile. "How thoughtful," she said wryly. "What does that allow us to do, then?"

"Cohabitate lawfully," I began listing, holding up a finger. "Share utensils and dishes, and enter airspace without PPE. Or at least, those are the big ones."

Her dark brows shot up towards her hairline. "You mean before we got that permit living on the shuttle together with the others was illegal?"

I nodded. "Oh yes, that was what several of the fines were about. Luckily the medical exams revealed we were all clean, or else it would have been much steeper fees." Thinking of the fines was starting to sour my mood, so I changed the subject. "Can I show you around to the rest of the apartment?"

She nodded, smiling at me strangely, and I led her through all of the common areas, demonstrating how to use the food synth, the holoscreen, how to adjust the atmosphere of her rooms, where all of the toiletries were kept, and where my room was in case of emergency. I didn't let her in though, not quite ready for her to see my most personal paintings. We ended the tour back at the kitchen, selecting our dinners. We'd agreed that after a quick meal we'd go to bed for the evening.

I'd selected a nice refreshing bowl of *ujenni* soup—a chilled yet spicy delicacy with noodles and various vegetables that Joss tried and liked immensely—while she had the synthesizer whip up a custom dish that she called "space chicken parm". It was alright, but my people were not partial to meat.

"Your ID chip should be ready for implant tomorrow," I reminded her, "so we'll be able to get that taken care of, and then I'll start the process of requesting government assistance. I suppose until you're a full citizen I'll list you as my dependent."

She laughed. "Ew, like I'm your kid?"

I chuckled, taking another spoonful of *ujenni*. "No, it just means that I am responsible for you," I told her. "No one would confuse you for a child."

"Not even when I'm the smallest person in the room?" she teased; aside from Wren, she had been the smallest person on the shuttle, a fact which Uraka had gently teased her for repeatedly. Joss had almost seemed to like the teasing.

"Of course not." *Your body is far too lush to belong to a child.* "You are just a small adult, it's obvious." She grinned, taking another bite of her food.

"I guess once you're all set up with the assistance we should start working on the plan, maybe even start getting you packed up. How long will you have before you'll have to leave this place?"

My appetite fled me. "I just paid rent before I left to go to Quellor," I told her, my tail winding around my lower leg. "So I have another three weeks—that's fifteen daycycles here—before they'll start taking action against me." I set my spoon down, my *ujenni* tasting like ash now.

"Wow, so soon?" She put her utensils down, surveying the wide open space around us. "It'll be a busy few weeks then, but I think we'll be fine. We'll just have to save all the sightseeing for once we're settled into the new place." While we'd been on the shuttle I'd promised her several times to show her around Escheva, to get her acquainted with billieuan culture.

"If you say so," I said, hating the glum and sulky sound of my voice. I crossed my arms over my chest and kept my eyes locked on my half-empty bowl of *ujenni* on the table.

"Hey, it'll be alright, Xoll," she said gently, leaning towards me and trying to make eye contact with me. "I know this is going to be super hard for you, and I hate that you have to do it in the first place, but we'll get through this, and then we can rebuild. Most things can be replaced—"

"Some of these things are priceless. Irreplaceable. One of a kind," I snapped, interrupting her. I knew she meant well, but she wasn't understanding just how much some of these things meant to me. Like my paintings—there wouldn't be enough room to store them at a government dorm, and even if I didn't love every single one, most were precious to me.

"Then we'll hold onto those things," she assured me, her brow wrinkling. "We don't have to get rid of *everything*, I promise—"

"No, we'll probably have to. The dorms are going to be small, and we'll have to squeeze in both of our things—"

"I don't have anything, Xollen. Just the clothes that you gave me." She frowned, pushing her plate aside. "Are you okay? You seem tense."

"Of course I'm tense!" I burst, my arms flinging wide. "My whole life is crashing down around me! And for what, just because I decided to help some strangers? Why is the Goddess *punishing* me for that?" My breaths started coming in angry pants, my hearts thundering in my chest. It felt good to finally give voice to that. Until Joss flinched and leaned away from me.

"I'm sorry, Xollen. I know this is hard and you're right, it's not fair. I wish I could help more but I'm not—Um, I think I'm done with dinner, so I'm going to just go to bed now." She grabbed her unfinished meal and dumped it into the recycler, her back stiff and kept carefully facing me. "I'll see you in the morning!" she called over her shoulder with a cheer that felt false. "Good night!"

Then she was hurrying away, leaving me alone with my fury and my congealing meal.

Chapter Thirteen
Growing Pains

Okay, so that had gone about as shitty as it could go.

I hated the tears that were streaking down my face as I marched back to my room. Thank god I wasn't anywhere near his room—I was in the mood for a good cry now and it was comforting knowing he wouldn't overhear me.

His anger had really upset me. He'd basically said outright that he regretted rescuing me and the others, just because it meant that he wasn't rich anymore. Did that also mean he resented me? Was he going to be that mean all the time now? My stomach sank at the thought. I hoped he was just cranky from what a long day we'd had and had had a moment. If he talked to me like that all the time…

It would be like being with Alex all over again. He'd constantly criticized me, telling me I was lazy, that I ate too much, that he didn't want to spend his money on me when I wasn't "taking care of myself", because in his eyes that made it a waste. Like if I wasn't living my life how he wanted me to, then I didn't deserve his help or his care. It was a wound that still really fucking hurt.

I shoved my frizzy blonde hair back from my tear-streaked face with a huff. *That* was because of Alex, too—my natural hair color was a dark brown with hints of red in the sun, and I'd loved it, but Alex kept telling me how much prettier I'd look with highlights, then after awhile it was that I'd look better fully blonde, and because he didn't want to help me pay for a salon visit I'd done it at home and fried my hair. He'd been happy, but I hated it. I missed my old hair, missed how long and wavy and flowing it had been. Now it was just a frizzy tangled mess, but it was also my security blanket, and I didn't want to cut it all off.

Dread settled like a cold, heavy rock in my gut. Had I made the mistake of a lifetime hitching my wagon to Xollen's horse? It suddenly hit me that I'd decided to shack up with pretty much a literal stranger. I'd just gone with my insane urge to live with a guy I'd just met because he was hot and the idea of it was interesting. But shit—Uraka might have been right about this guy. He could have been faking being nice to make me comfortable with him. Hadn't a whole bunch of famous serial killers done that sort of shit? I could be dealing with the alien equivalent of Ted Bundy for all I knew.

Now safe in the privacy of my room, I gave into the looming freakout. I tore my borrowed clothes off, tossing them to the floor in a rumpled puddle, and slipped on my familiar old pajamas, the only things I truly owned in all the world anymore. They were starting to get ripe, but it was a comfort to have something so familiar touching my skin. It was enough to let me get some decent breaths in, to stop my anxiety attack from spiraling into a full-blown panic attack. I also got up and locked the doors, finding an option that let me set a passcode that would let me keep Xollen out, if it came to it. That also made me feel a little more secure.

Once I'd finished getting ready for bed I'd calmed down a little more, and I realized I was doom-spiraling. Dr. Jackson said it was normal for someone like me who'd had the worst happen so often in my life, but that I couldn't let myself turn the possibility of something bad happening into the conviction that something bad definitely *would* happen. Because it hadn't happened yet it could also be that the *best* outcome would be what went down, and I needed to remember that.

Sure, Xollen could be a narcissistic control freak who was planning on either murdering or taking advantage of me, but he could also still be the really great guy I'd been crushing on so far who had just had a super bitchy moment. There was no point in convincing myself that he was space Bundy. I could be cautious, make sure that if that was what was going on that I was prepared and protected, but I should also keep myself open to things being good.

Feeling calmer, my exhaustion slammed back into me. Between the long boring day full of bureaucratic nonsense and the stressful end to our dinner, I'd used up every single spoon and had had to borrow more from the next day or two. I was beyond excited to finally have a bed I could sleep in, too; sleeping on the floor had gotten really old really fast back on the shuttle, especially with four other people crowded around me every night. I pulled back the fluffy duvet-type blanket and settled into the silky sheets, sighing in contentment as my head sank into the pillow.

I was asleep in minutes.

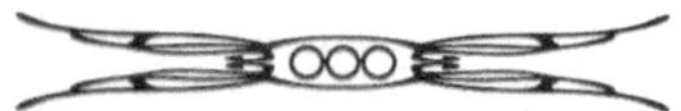

Okay, so Xollen wasn't a serial killer.

But he was proving to be a huge pain in my ass.

"This chain is solid platinum, Joss," he told me. "It was a graduation gift from my parents!"

"And I respect that. I know that that sentimental value is important to you." It was taking every drop of my patience to keep a civil tone with him. My years in retail were letting me give him a pretty solid customer service voice, even though I wanted to punch him square in his handsome face. "I'm not saying you *have* to get rid of it. I'm just asking you if you could see yourself being *okay* with getting rid of it."

"And the answer is no!"

I choked back a sigh. We were getting nowhere with this. "Listen, Xollen, I know that it's hard looking at things that were presents and having to decide if you can let it go, but you still owe 10,000 credits in fines and *while I agree that that is unfair,*" I told him firmly before he could interrupt with yet another protest, "the fact is that you do owe it, and there's no way out of it because they're not bogus charges. So you have to make the money somehow, and this is your best option for getting it by the one-month deadline. Unless you have a job you haven't told me about that pays you that much in a month."

He sat there, glaring at me and pouting. Clearly, he wasn't used to having to make these kinds of tough decisions, to have to pick and choose between different wants and desires to figure out what was really important. "I'm not trying to hurt you, Xoll," I said, trying to be more gentle with him. He was frustrating as all hell, but I knew that change took time, and it was hard to do. "I'm just trying to help you in any way I can. Do you need to take a break, calm down? We don't have to take care of this right now, we can start packing or looking for a storage situation for your paintings."

He kept sitting there, his tail whipping around in irritation like a cat's, for several heartbeats. Then something shifted in him, and he sighed, uncrossing his arms and looking up at me sheepishly. "You're right, I'm sorry," he admitted, his fingers playing over the gleaming silvery metal on its velvet pillow in front of him. "This is so much harder than I thought it would be. I'm being unreasonable about this, I know.

But I just keep thinking about how unfair it is, that I'm having to give everything up just because I wanted to help people."

I wanted to snap at him and tell him to get over himself, but that wasn't going to help anything right now. "I know. When me and my mom lost our place and wound up on the streets I felt something similar. *I* hadn't missed rent payments, *I* hadn't spent all of my money on my mom's nasty new boyfriend, but I was the one who was having to sell off her tablet and jewelry from her abuelita so we could afford to at least keep the car and live out of that. The fact of the matter is sometimes you can do everything right in a situation and still have it break bad. You can't control the actions of other people, all you can control is what you do, you know?"

He blinked at me, his face darkening. "Ah, *vrakaash*, Joss. I'm being an infant about this, aren't I?" He groaned, scrubbing his long fingers over his eyes. When he looked at me again his violet eyes were swirling wildly. "You're right, I wouldn't have chosen things turning out like this but I have some control over what happens next. Feel free to hit me if I start whining again."

I wanted to gasp in shock. He actually *listened* to me? I'd begun worrying he was too spoiled for that, or maybe just too much of a stubborn male, but here he was listening and trying. "Alright, I'll get a spray bottle full of water. Spray you down when you get testy."

He cocked one heavy eyebrow. "Why would you do that?"

I chuckled. "On Earth it's like, a training technique for pets. When they don't listen to spoken commands you deter them from doing certain things by spraying a little water on them. It's harmless but they hate it."

He laughed. "Does that work?"

"Honestly? It never worked with my mom's old cat. Frankie did whatever the fuck he wanted, and he didn't care if he was soaking wet when he did it."

"Well I do hate getting my clothes wet, so it might actually work on me," he admitted, grinning. His eyes drifted down to the chain in front of him again. He sighed, closing the lid of its box and sliding it towards me. "I don't even like my parents," he told me with a bitter sigh. "I don't know why I'm clinging to this one so much. I haven't worn it once since they gave it to me seven solars ago." I'd figured out that on Billieu they used "solars" to refer to years (I guess because it was the length of time it took the planet to orbit around its sun once) while "lunars" were months (one full lunar cycle). It had been confusing as hell at first but I was getting used to it now. At least weeks and days were the same...except when flying through space—but hopefully I wouldn't be doing that again any time soon.

"If it's that long and you haven't touched it then I'd say that's a strong maybe," I told him gently, adding it to the one other piece he'd agreed to part with. "So…you're not close with your parents either, huh?"

He nodded sadly, the two small silver hoops piercing his earlobes twinkling in the bright afternoon sunlight. "I have not been what they envisioned their child would be like," he murmured, opening another box and stroking the jewelry within. "They wanted someone who had their business sense, who was ruthless and cunning like them. And instead, they got…" he swept his hand down, indicating himself.

"Someone who loves art and pretty things?" I offered as a guess.

He smiled wryly. "In part. But also someone overly sensitive and prone to daydreaming. Someone who couldn't win any of the fights that were brought to him. Someone with a birth defect that left him hideously disfigured."

My eyes widened. Okay, that was a lot to unpack. "First of all," I said, getting mad at his parents on his behalf. No wonder the poor guy was so snippy with me; he probably saw all criticism as an attack, with parents like that. "You are *not* hideous, you're gorgeous." My face was burning up but I was determined to make him feel better and embrace boldness in my new life. "By Earth standards, you're pretty enough to be a model. And for two, there's nothing wrong with being sensitive. A…friend of mine told me that when someone complains about you being too sensitive, it's almost always because they want to be mean without getting into trouble for it. Your parents sound like awful bullies, Xollen. I gotta be honest, I don't think I like them either."

He looked stunned. "Bullies? But they're my parents. Can parents even *be* bullies?"

I nodded emphatically. "Oh yeah, big time. My mom was my first-ever bully. They don't see it like that, they see it as 'raising you right', or 'disciplining you', but if that stuff is done with love and care it doesn't make you feel like shit in the process. When they care more about being right and being in control than your feelings, then *that's* when it becomes bullying."

I think I'd just rocked his whole world. "Sweet glory of the Goddess," he murmured, his eyes wide and swirling like crazy. He just sat there staring at me for a long minute, turning it over in his head. "I want to say you're wrong," he rasped, his posture wilting in a way that made me ache with regret. Maybe I should have kept that to myself. "I want to…but I can't. My best friend Derris has had to set me straight many times over the years, but when he does it, he's…gentler. More careful about how he says things, more concerned for me."

I put my hand on his arm, squeezing. "I'm sorry, Xoll," I said, feeling guilty for turning a simple pre-move purge into an existential crisis. "I didn't mean to drag all that up. I just get so mad when I see people getting shit on by their parents. Are you okay? Maybe we should take a break, huh?"

He looked up at me and smiled, his eyes still a little sad. "It's alright, Joss," he said, leaning into my hand on his arm the littlest bit. "It's hard to hear, but I think a part of me needed to hear it." He looked down at the pile of jewelry he'd already said he didn't want to get rid of, before picking up several of the boxes and sliding them over to me. "I don't think I want things from my parents anymore. I think you're right, and I think—I think that these gifts might have been more about them looking like better parents than they really were. Or maybe they were a way for them to feel less guilty about how they treat me. I don't know, but what you just said…*vrakaash*, Joss, it feels true."

I gave him a sad smile. "That's both good to hear and a little sad. Because it sucks to realize. I've been there and I wouldn't wish it on anyone, especially not someone who I consider a friend." The urge to jump up and give him another hug, to maybe slide into his lap and hold him close and breathe in his spicy-sweet scent was so overwhelming that I had to pull my hand away and sit back in my seat.

His full lips fell open in shock, before spreading into a brilliant smile. "I'm your friend?" He flushed, the smile on his face looking a lot less sad. Damn him for being so cute. "You um…you're my friend too, Joss. I'm really glad I met you."

Man, when he wasn't busy throwing fits about jewelry the guy was pretty darn sweet. There was a chance that he was manipulating me, that he was being nice to get what he wanted from me like a lot of people had done my whole life, but his smile seemed genuine. I couldn't believe that all of that softness and vulnerability I'd just seen was some kind of ploy.

"I'm really glad we met, too," I told him with a smile of my own. *Ave María*, the things this male was doing to my insides. Were we having some trouble getting used to each other? Absolutely. But as stressful as it could be, I didn't want to throw in the towel. I didn't regret my decision, and in moments like these I could see us being friends. Or maybe, just maybe, being more.

Chapter Fourteen
Packing Up

<u>XOLLEN</u>

Once me and Joss had gone through all of my jewelry we took a break, and I decided it was time to reach out to Derris like I'd promised. I retreated to my bedroom and opened up my contacts on my wristcom, flicking down the very short list to his name and initiating a secure call.

He picked up after a handful of rings, his handsome face smiling warmly. "Xollen, are you planetside again?"

I nodded. "I am."

"Then I can finally get caught up on whatever insane thing you got up to while you were away. Where did you go, again?"

I sighed. "Quellor Station."

His brow pinched. "Why in the glory of the Goddess did you go to that scrap heap?"

I closed my eyes, bracing myself. "You have to keep an open mind, Derr," I started, leveling a stern look at his bust floating in front of me. "This is…very embarrassing for me to admit."

He nodded, his copper eyes swirling mildly. "Alright, Xoll," he agreed. "Please tell me. I'm getting very nervous."

I loosed another sigh, my tail wringing the life out of my leg, as I carefully related how my last week had gone: my failed attempt at securing a sex worker, meeting the th'rak slavers, deciding to rescue the females, Joss wanting to stay with me—everything. I could tell that

Derris was beyond shocked, but he listened well, nodding and gasping but keeping his thoughts to himself until I'd finished.

"Wow, Xollen…you weren't kidding when you said it was a busy week for you." I forced my tail to loosen its grip on my leg, for air to fill my lungs all the way. This was *Derris*; he wouldn't just cast me aside. He'd at least try to understand first. "Are you going to be okay, my friend? Do you need some credits? I can cover the fine if you'd like. Or you could stay with me and Gesea."

I was touched by his generosity. I was sorely tempted to ask for the credits for the fine, but he was newly mated and might soon have a child, and I had found plenty of valuables already that I could sell off to cover it.

And I was surprised to discover that a part of me wanted to do it the hard way, just to see if I could. "I appreciate your kind offer," I told him, "but I'm fine. Joss is brilliant, and has already gotten me working on my next steps."

"She sounds really special, Xoll. I'm glad all that worked out. But if you need me you know I'm there, just give me the word." I nodded; I knew this well. Derris had been there time and again, no matter what. "Do you think I could meet her? I have to say I'm wildly curious to see such a rare species of alien."

For some reason, that bothered me. Joss wasn't some curiosity to be gawked at. She was an intelligent and kind-hearted being.

"I can ask her," I hedged. I didn't want to share her, but I had no good reason to avoid her meeting my best and oldest friend. I would make it her choice, though. "Let me put you on hold and I'll ask her." I flicked the hold call button, then stood to find Joss.

She was in the living room, flipping through channels on the holoscreen. "Xollen, how the hell do you ever find anything to watch on this thing?" she exclaimed as she turned to look at me over her shoulder. While we'd been out getting her ID chip installed this morning we'd stopped at a clothing shop and gotten her some clothes with the last of my credits, and while I loved seeing her in my clothing I had to admit that she was a vision in garments that were actually designed to fit her. The dress she'd chosen hugged her curves deliciously, showing a tantalizing expanse of skin on her chest and along her lower legs.

"I actually don't watch it all that often," I admitted, sitting beside her on the sofa. "Are you free? I've been talking with my friend Derris and he says he wants to meet you. Would you be amenable to that?"

She looked shocked. "What, now?" I nodded. She bit her lip, her small hand patting at her hair and smoothing her dress down. She shifted, arching her back more and sitting away from the sofa back, which looked uncomfortable. "Sure, I'd love to meet your friend!" she told me, her smile looking just a bit tight. I had told her a little bit about Derris during our talks back on the shuttle, but perhaps she was still nervous to meet him. I toggled the call back on and Derris's bust began floating in front of me once more.

I could tell when he noticed Joss beside me, his eyes widening and his mouth falling slightly open. Beside me the soft sweet-smelling female that had entranced me and boldly inserted herself into my life stiffened, her fingers twisting into the skirt of her dress viciously. I frowned. She must have been *very* nervous. Without thinking, I reached out and clasped her hand that was closest to me, prying her fingers loose from her skirt and rubbing them gently. She didn't react aside from squeezing my hand back.

Derris recovered quickly, blinking and smiling brightly at the little human by my side. "Hello, Joss! I understand you are to whip our dear Xollen into shape in the coming weeks?"

She returned his smile, her posture still too stiff. Her free hand was roving all over herself, combing through her hair, adjusting her dress, touching her face. "I don't know about that, I'm just trying to help," she replied, voice tight. "It's very nice to meet you, um, Derris."

"And I you, little human. I am sorry for what the th'rak have put you through, but I hope that you will find Billieu to be a pleasant place to live. Do you have your ID chip yet?"

She nodded, lifting her right wrist, her free one. "Yeah, I got it in this morning. Still aches like the dickens but there's no mark at all. Alien medicine is amazing," she chuckled, tucking her pale gold hair behind her cute rounded ears.

"I have to say, I'm surprised you would volunteer to live with dear Xollen, Joss."

She stiffened further beside me, her smile looking forced. "Oh? And why is that?"

Derris grinned at her, clearly about to tease me. "Because I think we both know he can be very dramatic. Has he yelled at you about how you hang clothes up yet?"

Joss blinked, looking surprised, before she returned his grin. "No, he hasn't. He must like me more than you."

Derris burst out laughing, throwing his head back. "I like her, Xollen," he managed after several minutes, wiping at his eyes. "My mate Gesea would have loved to meet you as well, but sadly she is at work and won't be back for several hours yet. You two should join us for dinner soon! Perhaps once things have calmed down?"

Joss smiled, her cheeks flushed but her eyes soft. "Yeah, that would be nice. I'm sure you have tons of great stories about Xollen that I would *love* to hear. How long have you known each other, again?"

Seeing Derris and Joss getting along settled something in me. I had been more nervous than I'd realized for those two worlds to collide, and now that they'd interacted and liked each other the relief was making me weak. It had felt vitally important, that when these two people whom I cared so much about met that they like each other.

They chatted for a time, trading jokes about space travel and government agencies, before Derris said he wanted to tell me something in private before he cut the call and got back to preparing the evening meal for his mate. I excused myself and went back to my bedroom.

"She's delightful, Xoll," Derris grinned once I was alone once more. "I like her a lot better for you than Verilla."

Pursing my lips, I considered what he might mean by that. "Better for me how?" I asked, uncertain as to what he meant.

He cocked his eyebrow at me. "As a potential mate, of course."

I sputtered, shocked. "I'm not trying to *mate* her!" I cried, clutching at the front of my black shirt. "I know that was why I went to Quellor, but that's not why I helped. I would never—"

He held up his hands in a placating gesture. "Easy, Xoll," he said. "I didn't mean it like that. I only meant I think she would make a good one. She seems relaxed and easy-going, like she would help you with your anxiety. How have your attacks been since you met her?"

Now that he'd mentioned it, I hadn't had any major attacks since she'd come tumbling out of that crate after Uraka. Derris must have seen as much on my face.

"After Verilla, I should hope it would be obvious you need someone less severe, someone who will be kind and supportive, and I think Joss seems like that type of person. And she is even lovely, despite not being billieuan. But Xollen," he warned, his chin tucking in and his tone going hard with warning, "you need to treat her well. No snapping at her, no jumping down her throat. If you hurt her I'll rip your horns right off your head and shove them up your ass."

Sputtering, I reared back. "Derris! I thought you were supposed to be my friend!"

He shrugged. "Sometimes the best thing a friend can do is beat some sense into you, and I know you, Xoll—you'll push her away rather than risk getting too close and getting hurt. Which I understand, I've met your parents, but you can't do that forever, my friend. Eventually, you'll have pushed everyone away and made yourself lonely and miserable, and I don't want that for you. Do you hear me?"

I nodded, my eyes sliding down to my hands. "You know, she said earlier that my parents are bullies," I blurted, my voice raspy to my own ears. "She said that they don't treat me right."

Derris snorted. "I've been saying this for years, but now you listen to it?" His tone softened. "That makes me even more certain that she would be good for you. I think it's proof that she cares about you, that she understands the kind of person you are. So don't go screwing this up for yourself—I mean it. Give her a chance, Xoll."

I offered him a weak smile, hoping I could do as he said. I'd already snapped at her a few times now, though I didn't want to admit that to my old friend. But she hadn't walked out on me, and had even managed to stay calm and kind to me. I'd known that I found her physically attractive, the allure of her sweet face and delicious curves throbbing through me anytime we were close together, any time our conversations turned deep and emotional or light and fun, but I hadn't yet considered that I might court her, that I might one day join my life to hers in the beauty of matehood. I tried to picture it, picture a lifetime of her smiles and easy laughter, of her silly jokes and gentle teasing, and it made me warm and soft in a way that scared me.

Immediately, all the reasons not to roared through my mind. I might be labeled a deviant, since humans were from a primitive planet people might assume she was a lower lifeform. My parents would completely disown me, publicly shaming me and stripping me of my name. Every one of my friends and business connections outside of Derris would abandon me. I might never have children naturally with a non-billieuan mate. The government might not even sanction such a union, given that the human homeworld was locked away in restricted space. We might be persecuted, hunted. It would be a difficult life, and I couldn't help but imagine that she would grow to resent me for my part in her hardship. How could she not, when being alone would have granted her more peace? Or even if no one challenged our relationship, who was to say that she wouldn't tire of me? That she wouldn't also get tired of dealing with my moods and my anxiety attacks?

Everyone else had.

I told Derris none of this, only promising weakly that I would behave myself, and that I would keep him up to date on our progress with the move. I disconnected the call and sat back against my chair, letting my head fall back to the top of the backrest, desperately swallowing down the bitterness threatening to choke me.

Chapter Fifteen
Temper Tantrums

<u>JOSS</u>

All told, the stuff that Xollen sold brought in a truly staggering 18,000 credits—enough to pay off the fines almost twice over. Most of it had been jewelry and designer clothes, but the furniture he didn't want to have to squeeze into a government dorm also brought in a lot of cash, as did some of his art collection. Not his personal paintings—he didn't want to sell those, and I respected that, not everyone wanted to sell off all their art. But there were several people who offered to buy something on the spot when they picked up the other item they'd paid for, and if nothing else I think that that made Xoll feel a little better about the situation—even if it was like how throwing a glass of water on a bonfire did *technically* help put it out.

Once things started disappearing from the apartment, Xollen's mood got a lot more unpredictable. He'd go from being clinging and sweet one minute to a total brat the next, making me want to scream and walk out. In those moments, I was tempted to figure out where Uraka and Djelani were living—I knew they were somewhere in Escheva, and I had Uraka's comm channel number to call her if I hit my absolute limit. When Xollen got especially pissy I missed Uraka's overbearing affection and giant muscles a *whole* lot.

If felt like he was picking fights with me on purpose, and that just confused the hell out of me. Why did he feel the need to turn on me like that? We were supposed to be a team, working together on Project

"

Xollen, but when I tried to gently coax him towards the more practical course of action he acted like I was trying to burn his whole life to the ground and then take a shit in the ashes.

The only reason I hadn't actually abandoned him was those glimpses of the softer person beneath, the one who reached for my hand and wound his tail around my leg when he started having an anxiety attack. The male who insisted on making all of my meals for me and making sure I never went too long without eating because he wanted to take care of me. The Xollen who smiled at me like I was the sun in his sky, his eyes swirling and sweet. I couldn't leave the grouchy bitch when he spent a good chunk of the extra money he'd earned from selling his stuff on a fancy wristcom and several new shoes for me, just because he'd wanted to thank me for my hard work in helping him.

"I couldn't have done it without you, Joss," he'd told me softly, helping me fit the wristcom onto me. "You deserve only the best." Once he'd latched the accessory to my arm his hand had lingered, his long fingers trailing over the delicate skin at the inside of my wrist and making me shiver. "I don't think I can ever thank you properly for all the ways you've helped me when you didn't have to."

My heart had melted into a mushy pile of goo at that, and I'd been sure that he would try to kiss me then. He'd leaned in closer, his pouty lips parting the littlest bit and the swirling of his purple eyes going wild as his pale blue pupil went wide. I'd leaned in too, my pulse throbbing all through my body and my skin tingling with anticipation as his gaze had locked on my mouth. But he hadn't kissed me, and now he was being a dick.

"Have you seen my plum Heverra?" he called from his wing of the penthouse. I closed my eyes in frustration, trying to keep my annoyance from my voice when I responded, hauling myself up off the couch in the living room and walking towards his room like a sane person instead of continuing to shout from several rooms away.

"The one with the green stripes?" I called back.

"Yes, that one!" He popped his head out of his room, his handsome face pinched with annoyance. "I can't find it anywhere, do you have it?"

I resisted the urge to roll my eyes. "No, we sold that one. Like a week ago, now."

His brows slammed together in anger. "You *sold it*? When did I say that that one was good to sell? I *love* that shirt!"

"You—you said you never wore it and told me to rehome it. You said 'it's not getting the attention it deserves with me so I might as well find it a place where it'll get more love'. You *said* that to me!"

His tail whipped furiously behind him, so fast I could hear it slicing through the air. He crossed his arms over his chest and frowned at me. "I don't remember that conversation," he seethed, making me see red.

"Well, that's not my fault!" I exploded, the pitch of my voice creeping towards a screech. "And quite frankly I'm getting really sick of you blowing up at me like this. If you don't want me around then I'll just go stay with Uraka instead." I hated the tears that were springing to my eyes. It was just so *hard*, going from feeling like Xollen was moments away from kissing me one day to feeling like he wanted to toss me in a dumpster with the rest of the trash the next.

I didn't deserve this kind of treatment.

When I blinked the tears out of my eyes and I could see Xollen better, I was shocked to see how upset he looked. His eyes were big and sad, the swirls slowed to a crawl. His whole body had slumped. His tail had stopped whipping around and had begun to twine around his leg. For a while he just stood there, looking at me with a miserable expression on his face that shouldn't have made me feel guilty…but it did. "I'm sorry," he rasped, before he spun around and retreated into his room, closing the door behind him and leaving me feeling brittle and cold.

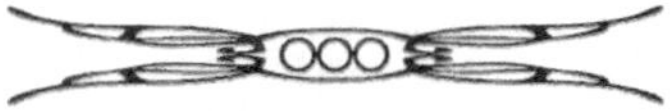

I didn't see Xollen that day, or the day after. In fact, I didn't see his beautiful, infuriating face for two more days, when it was time to move everything out of the swanky penthouse and into the public dorm he'd secured.

When I saw him waiting for me in the kitchen I froze and was tempted to go back into my room and hide, but we had too much to get through today. So I straightened my spine and took a deep breath and walked in like I owned the place and his presence didn't bother me.

To be honest, I wasn't even mad at him. Mostly I was just…hurt. Hurt that he kept believing the worst of me when I'd been trying so hard to show him my best. It left me feeling so uncertain and scared. I was completely at his mercy until my citizenship went through and I could get help from the government. I guessed I could always crash with Uraka and Djelani, especially now that I had my own wristcom and could call them, but I thought Uraka might show up and literally rip Xollen a new one if she found out I needed to get away from him. As mad and frustrated as I was with the big jerk I didn't want him maimed.

"Good morning," I said tightly, heading over to the food synthesizer to grab some "oatmeal". They didn't have oats here but they had this seed stuff that tasted pretty similar.

Sad violet eyes locked onto my face, his throat bobbing with a heavy swallow. "Joss. I'm sorry about the other day," he said. "I didn't mean to blow up at you like that. You didn't deserve it. I-I got you a little something, to say I'm sorry." He slid a small wrapped package across the table towards me.

I sighed, feeling so, so tired all of a sudden. "Xollen, I don't want a present. I don't need one. What I *need* is for you to work on your temper. I can't keep doing this with you, even if I do like you a lot. It's not fair to either of us. Not fair for you to be so triggered all the time and not fair for me to get yelled at for just trying to help."

I felt bad, seeing how much he looked like a kicked puppy, but I stayed strong. Healthy boundaries made for a healthy relationship, Dr. Jackson liked to say. This was a line I was drawing in the sand, and I really did think it was best for both of us. I'd had a lot of time to think about it. "A-alright," he whispered. "I guess that's fair." His voice gained more strength when he asked, "so does that mean you don't accept my apology?"

I considered. "I'll accept this one," I told him, crossing my arms over my chest. "But if there's a next one, for this exact same reason… I don't know that I will. I like to think I'm pretty forgiving and easy-going, but Xollen…this is getting to be too much. I don't want to leave but if you keep pushing me away and picking fights I might have to leave. Do you understand what I'm saying?"

He nodded, looking like he might cry himself. "Yes, I understand. I just wish—I wish I knew what to do to be better for you." He stood up from his seat across from me and crouched beside me, flinging his arms around my waist and pressing his face into my side before I could react. One of his horns was jabbing me in the ribs, but I felt him shivering against me, his breaths quick and unsteady. "What do I *do* Joss?" he repeated into the side of my gut, which was nice and fluffed out since I was still sitting. My impulse was to shove him away and hide it, but he was breaking my heart with this.

I sighed and wrapped my arms around his head and shoulders, making soothing noises while I got up my courage. "Have you ever considered trying therapy? Getting help from someone whose specialty is in helping people with their thoughts and emotions?

He squeezed me tighter. "I already see one of those, an emoreg. Emotional regulator."

Jesus, this was Xollen *with* therapy?! My heart sank, the thought that he might truly be beyond help making my stomach sink.

"What do you do with this—uh, emoreg...person. What sorts of things do you talk about?" I asked him.

He shrugged, nuzzling his face closer to me in a way that made me ache. "I talk to them once a month, they ask me how I've been feeling, and if I've been feeling bad then they adjust my medications. They're very nice, they always listen to me and my problems."

Hope bloomed. Maybe he just had a therapist—or emoreg, I guess—that was a bad a fit. "They don't have you do any thought exercises or give you ways to cope or self-soothe? They don't encourage you to establish corrective experiences? What about tackling behavioral adjustments, do they do that?"

He pulled back to look up at me, his brow furrowed. "No, never. Am I supposed to be doing that?"

"I don't know, probably? It might look different here but those are the sorts of things Dr. Jackson was doing with me back on Earth. Once we're settled into the new place maybe see about trying a different emoreg doctor, see how the experiences compare."

His eyes filled with hope. "You think that would help?"

"It won't hurt, right?" I gently combed his silky deep blue hair back from his face, un-snagging it from around his horns and his jewelry for him. He closed his eyes at my touch, a look of bliss crossing his features as my fingertips skimmed over his scalp and horns. God, he was so fucking beautiful it made my heart hurt. It wasn't even just that he was pretty—though hey, that didn't hurt. It was moments like these, where he was soft and vulnerable with me, showing me that he was just scared and hurting underneath the anger and the freakouts, showing me that he needed me, that he *wanted* me. He wasn't grossed out by gut or my rolls, didn't think my body hair was nasty, didn't mind that I was kind of loud when I got excited. He didn't think I was trashy because I was and from the south side of Chicago. I swallowed hard, trying to get myself under control before I launched myself at him and broke a bunch of their hygiene laws. "I want to see you feel better, Xollen, so promise me you'll at least try it."

His eyes cracked open, his expression dazed and hungry when he looked back up at me. "Of course, Joss. I'll try it."

Smiling, I gave his silky strands one last finger comb and released him. "Good. Thanks. Now we should probably finish breakfast and get ready for the movers, right?"

Chapter Sixteen
The Move

It was heartbreaking, leaving the apartment that had been the first place I'd made my own, away from the controlling presence of my parents, but I had to admit that I was eager to be done with the move itself. I was regretting clinging to so many of my things, knowing that it meant that there was now that much more to cart over to the next place. Did I really need to keep five boxes' worth of designer clothes and shoes? Did I really want my collection of crystal figures, a gift from my late grandparents, at this new place? Where would I even put them in a public dorm? But it was too late now; I was stuck with it all for the foreseeable future.

Every time I passed Joss, directing the movers, it felt like every nerve in my body lit up, remembering the tender moment we'd shared this morning. I had come dangerously close to blurting out my feelings for her, telling her that I ached for her, that I felt like I was starving to death with every day that I wasn't kissing her, holding her, breathing her deep into my lungs so that she sang through my blood. Once Derris had mentioned that she'd make a good mate it had been all I could think of, and I was a male obsessed. Which made it even more difficult for me to deal with the idea of her leaving. How would I survive without her smile, her sweet words, her boisterous laughter that lit up the whole room? How could I go back to my life knowing how much brighter it was with her in it? So if she wanted me to see a different emoreg then

I would—I would do anything, I decided, to keep Joss.

I just had to not mess things up before then.

And avoid kissing her until I'd brought up entering into a courtship agreement and had gotten the correct permits. I'd had quite enough of hygiene fines.

It took the better part of the day to load everything up into the hover vehicle and get it to the new place, and by the end of it I was feeling very wrung out and tired, but the work was only half done. Joss was wearing loose, comfortable clothes, her hair thrown up into a messy knot on the top of her head that drew attention to her delicate little ears and displayed her lovely features to their full effect. The sweat dewing her skin made her glitter in the harsh indoor lights, and I kept finding myself distracted by how stunning she was as she unpacked boxes and put the things within away.

After a few more hours we had about half of the boxes unpacked, and we were both flagging hard and dragging our feet. Joss yawned hard enough to crack her jaw and I called it an evening. "We can finish tomorrow," I told her. "We both need sleep."

She nodded, smiling sleepily and stretching her arms up. "When you're right, you're right," she agreed. "I just hate leaving things unfinished."

"It'll be here tomorrow. You've worked hard today, and you need to rest." I stood from the crouch I'd been in, slotting holo recordings into their low shelf beneath the holoscreen. I strode up to her, putting my hands on her shoulders and squeezing. "You've done very well today, Joss," I told her in a murmur. Her lovely round face turned up to look into mine, her warm brown eyes heavy with fatigue but also alive with something that I felt sparking in answer in my chest. Unconsciously, I took a step closer to her, closing the distance between us and bringing our bodies into the barest of contact. She was so warm, so soft against me, even if it was just the barest of presses, and I didn't think I'd ever felt something so wonderful before in my life.

It had never been like this with Verilla. I had been such a fool to think that I'd actually cared for her. If I would have known that beings like Joss existed out in the wider universe I never would have stayed with Verilla for as long as I had.

Gulping, I swayed closer to her, more of our bodies coming into contact, and my hands slid from the tops of her shoulders down her back, stopping at the small of her back and tightening against her silky heat. Her own hands came up slowly, hesitantly, as if she was afraid of me, afraid of how I'd react, and a pulse of shame soured my stomach; of course she'd be afraid of my reactions when I'd spent so much of the last few weeks being an absolute bastard. But my Joss was brave, far braver than I would be in her position, and after a moment her little hands settled on my heaving chest, her palms right over my thundering hearts.

I couldn't tear my eyes from her, all signs of her fatigue vanished. Her full rosy lips were parted slightly, her face lightly flushed and her eyes bright and shining. Her pink little tongue darted out to lick at those lips, wetting them, and I couldn't quite stifle the groan that ripped from my chest.

"Xollen," she breathed, her fingers curling into the fabric of my shirt as if she wanted to yank me down closer to her. "Xollen, what is this?"

"I don't know," I answered just as quietly, my arms tightening around her, pressing her more firmly against my feverish body, my eyes no doubt swirling wildly. "What do you think it is?"

She licked her lips again, making me ache, and then her gaze settled on my lips, making my wakening cock spring fully to life in my pants. "It feels like you want to kiss me," she responded after a moment, her face tilting further up towards me, as if she was encouraging me to do exactly that.

My head was ducking before I could think, my body screaming at me to finish closing the distance between us, to meet her lips with mine and devour her at last. She raised one of her hands and placed her trembling fingers to my lips, stopping me from getting closer. "What about the hygiene laws?" she whispered, her eyes still locked on my mouth.

I kissed the tips of her fingers, grabbing her hand and turning it so I could place a kiss on her palm, to the inside of her wrist, making her shiver. I'd just been vowing I'd do everything to avoid more fees, but with her pressed closed, looking at me with such heat…"I don't care," I promised her. "I know I should, but I just can't. Joss…can I kiss you?"

She whimpered, biting her bottom lip. She pulled her arm out of my grip and looped her arms around my neck, yanking me down until I was finally, sinfully, kissing her.

There was nothing that could have prepared me for what it was like. I'd never kissed anyone before, not like this, not even Verilla, and it was the most incredible thing I'd ever experienced. I knew I was clumsy, having to pay attention to Joss and what she was doing in order to figure out my own moves, but it was still so…much. This close, her delicate scent was wrapped all around me, her flavor bursting into my mouth as our lips caressed. My arms wrapped around her tighter, hauling her up higher so that I didn't have to hunch so low, her moan of pleasure licking down my spine and settling into my aching cock. She tilted her head, forcing our mouths to line up differently, deepening the kiss, and then her slick little tongue was swiping at the seam of my mouth, asking me to let her in, and I did so gladly, without any hesitation, and then her tongue was in my mouth, licking and sweeping over every inch of me, learning me, and I couldn't take it anymore.

Sliding my hands to the round globes of her ass, I hauled her up even higher against my body, lifting her up off the ground. She squealed, breaking the kiss and wrapping her legs around my hips on instinct. "What are you doing?" she giggled, her mouth deliciously flushed and swollen.

"I'm bringing you to my bed so I don't have to keep leaning over, tiny human," I growled out, pressing another kiss to her hungry mouth. "We don't do anything you're not comfortable with," I added after a moment, as the door of my room slid up at my approach.

"I appreciate that," she told me as I dropped us on the mattress, her curves bouncing from the impact and making me groan and clench, precum seeping out of my achingly hard length. She was just so *perfect*, so sweet and soft and delicious in my arms. I pressed her back into the bed, following her down and doing my best to mimic what she had been doing earlier with my own tongue, trying to learn every inch of her that I could. One of my knees settled between her thighs, the other to the side of her leg, my tail flicking and twitching in the air behind me. Dimly, I realized that the knee between her legs was dangerously close to the juncture of her thighs, the blistering heat pouring off of her from there making my mouth water.

She moaned under me, her hands wrapped tight around my neck while her fingers dug into my scalp, cupping the nape of my neck, sliding forward to cup my face with a tenderness that made me throb with need. Her hands slid up again, cupping the base of my horns, and the sensation that rocketed through me made my hips buck, my pelvis dropping to press into hers. My cock gave a mighty jerk and I worried I'd spill in my pants, it felt so *good*. I ripped my mouth away from hers, biting my lip.

"Sensitive," I ground out, shuddering as I struggled to maintain my control over my body.

"Sorry!" Her hands went back to my shoulders, stroking soothingly. "You alright?"

I nodded, squeezing my eyes shut and concentrating on breathing. I was *not* going to embarrass myself. "Yes, I'm fine. You're just...so incredible. It's um—a lot."

I opened my eyes, gazing down into the warm depths of hers, the black of her pupils nearly swallowing that beautiful brown that made me feel so safe and cared for. She smiled at me, her lip wobbling the littlest bit and her eyes going glassy. "Thank you," she croaked, swallowing and blinking quickly. "That means a lot to me, to hear that."

I huffed, plucking her hair tie from her ruined bun so that her pale gold locks could tumble free. "To hear that I'm untried and close to losing control?" My voice came out sounding harsher than I'd meant it to, my tone bitter, so I pressed kisses to her jaw to show her I wasn't mad at her.

"No, not that, you dork," she chuckled, swatting at me lightly. "Calling me that. Incredible. No one else…well, it's not something I've ever heard before."

I reared back, my ponytail sliding over my shoulder and tickling the side of my face. "How?" I asked incredulously, examining the flawless beauty of the female below me. How could anyone look upon her and see anything less than miraculous perfection?

She bit her lip again, her eyes growing even more hungry, before she pulled me down into another searing kiss. I lost myself in her then, the focus of my whole existence narrowing to Joss, to her taste, her scent, the feel of her against me, the sounds she made as I ran my hands all over her body and tasted her mouth over and over.

I readjusted my position over her, and when I did my knee between her thighs slid higher, pressing into the junction at the apex of her thighs, and she sucked in a breath beneath me, shivering and hips arching into my touch. I moved my leg again, rubbing at the place where she was hottest, and her pleasure noises intensified, a whimper ripping from her throat that I swallowed greedily. Wanting more of those sounds, *needing* them, I kept doing it, surprise and pleasure mingling in my chest as her hips started moving with me, increasing the friction and making her moan and pant against me.

After a moment of this she stopped kissing me, her eyes going dazed and her brows drawing together tightly as she became overwhelmed by what I was doing to her. Was she about to orgasm? Was I about to make her come? The thought sent pleasure spiraling through me, making my cock so hard it almost hurt, but I couldn't have stopped what I was doing even if I wanted to. Her hips began moving faster, her breaths coming in pants that were peppered with little keening noises. I was rock-hard in my pants, but so focused on Joss, on how I was affecting her, that I quickly stopped noticing. Her little fingers were sunk into my hair, her tiny nails digging into my scalp, and her eyes were heavy-lidded and locked on my face.

"Xollen," she gasped, her eyes rolling up into her head as her body began bowing up off the mattress, pressing her curves into me and making me shudder. The rhythm of her hips was faltering now, but I kept working my leg against her, increasing the pressure just a little.

She cried out, arching off the bed, and I felt something throb and flutter against my leg. Her thighs clamped tight against me, my mouth landing on hers to swallow up her faint cries as she rode out her orgasm against my leg. I didn't let up the pressure and the movement until she pushed at me, telling me she was too sensitive.

I had to make sure I had it right. "Was that…did you?…"

She nodded, face flushed and a look of amazed bliss on her face. "Oh yeah. Big time." Then she smiled at me, looking a little embarrassed. "Sorry about that, I didn't mean to steal the show—"

I silenced her with another kiss. "That was amazing," I promised her when I came up for air. "I can't believe I made you come." I looked down at her, tousled and so beautiful. "Can I do it again?"

She laughed, throwing her head back. "Let me catch my breath, you animal!" But her smile was sweet and full of affection. "Do you want me to…take care of you?"

I shook my head. My cock was aching fiercely in my pants, but I didn't think I was ready for her to see me yet, to touch me there. I wanted this to be about her, to be for her pleasure. "Not tonight. I think it will be too much for me. Is that alright?"

"Of course. I don't want to make you uncomfortable."

I smiled down at her, my chest clenching with affection for this beautiful little alien female. I wanted to tell her how much I cared for her, how deeply my feelings for her had taken root in the lunar that I'd known her, but the words stuck in my throat, too scared of what she'd say in return to let it out.

Instead, I kissed her again, trying to pour all of the tenderness and warmth of my feelings into the press of our mouths.

Chapter Seventeen
The Star

JOSS

Okay, so—last night.

I was still freaking out about it. But also tingling about it, hot and bothered about it, and ridiculously happy about it. I mean, what a way to christen a new place, huh? Insane make-out session with my sexy roommate where he makes me come *definitely* tops my list of ways to make a house a home.

But I was a little nervous about how things would look now that we'd had some rest and had calmed down. Like, would Xollen regret it at all? Would he realize how many hygiene laws we'd broken and flip out? Would he want me to move out and get some distance from me because he didn't really want me and had just gotten swept up in the moment?

Dammit, there went my insecurity again. It wasn't like either of us had been drunk or anything; he'd been fully aware of what he was doing. He hadn't had beer goggles on when he was looking at me like I was all kinds of incredible sex goddess. Xollen liked me. He was attracted to me. So that annoying little voice that was saying he'd regret breaking hygiene laws because it had been with me and not someone hotter—gag, right?—could just shut the hell up.

Of course, easier said than done. But as much as I wanted to hide in bed for hours, the urge to pee became too intense so I rolled out of bed and scurried out to the one hygiene room we were now sharing, relieved that it was unoccupied. I waddled in, squeezing my legs together so I didn't wet myself, then locked the door and took care of my business. I also brushed my teeth and combed my hair while I was in there, hopping into the sonic shower when I still didn't hear Xollen up on the other side of the door.

Refreshed, I headed out, unlocking the door and almost walking into a very sexy and sleep-tousled Xollen.

"Oh! Hey," I squeaked, surprised. He was looking at me with knee-weakening intensity, his rumpled appearance making my pussy jump to life with memories of last night.

He didn't say anything, crowding close to me, herding me back until I bumped into the wall next to the hygiene room door. My pulse throbbed through me, my breaths starting to get tight. He leaned in, his hands sliding along my sides, caging me in with his much taller frame. His head dipped further, his flat nose just skimming along my jaw, making me shiver. My hands cupped his face, holding him there and basking in the way his touch was lighting me up. His lips started trailing down my throat, the little nibbling kisses setting my blood on fire. I was panting now, holding his face tighter. I might have been moaning his name, but it was so hard to concentrate outside of the feel of him against me, his mouth lighting me up like a Christmas tree.

One minute I was struggling to stay on my feet, my legs going shivery and weak from his attention on my neck, and the next he was hauling me up, holding me aloft and pressed against the wall like I didn't weigh almost 250 pounds. I made a very un-sexy squeaking noise as my feet left the floor.

"Oh my god, Xollen!" I said breathlessly, squirming as he grinned at me, his fangs glinting. "I'm too heavy, put me down. You'll hurt yourself!"

He just growled—honest to god *growled*—and pressed his hips into the cradle of my own. "You're not heavy. You're right where you need to be, my star."

Oh, fuck.

Before I could form another protest he was swooping in, slanting his mouth over mine and kissing me like he would die if he didn't. I melted into him, my arms wrapping tight around his neck, my hips trying to grind against the hard bar I felt throbbing against me through our sleep clothes.

He groaned, sucking on my tongue, as I managed to get a little rhythm going. "Joss..." he rumbled in my ear, his hands going tight on my ass. "You are the sweetest gift I have ever gotten, but if you don't stop that I'm going to..." He hung his head, burying his face where my neck met my shoulder, making the edge of one horn bump my face. I laughed, the sound more throaty than I'd ever heard from myself.

"That's kind of the idea, babe," I told him, trying to grab a handful of his ass and failing. Stupid short arms.

He pulled back, his heavy-lidded eyes boring into mine, the color swirling frantically and his cheeks flushed with color. He studied me for a moment, his lips parted slightly. I leaned forward and kissed him gently, softly, caressing his lips with all the tenderness I could muster. "You did it to me last night," I reminded him. "Now I want to do it to you. And besides," I rolled my hips again, my own breath hitching, "it feels good for me, too."

I started up a rhythm again, and this time he didn't try to stop me, his eyes rolling up as he leaned further into me, kissing me and increasing the pressure, the friction, between our pelvises.

I felt the slow lick of an orgasm beginning to build low in my belly, the sensation of his hard heat pressing against my aching clit sending lazy swirls of pleasure spiraling through me.

"Sweet Goddess, Joss," he groaned into the side of my neck, his breaths coming in sharp pants now, his hands clutching at my ass hard enough that it almost hurt. "You feel amazing. Even like this, you feel… so good. So damn *good*." He lifted his head, his hair even wilder from my playing with it, gripping it, and grinned down at me, the pace that he was grinding against me picking up. "You're so beautiful. All the time, but especially like this. Are you close, my star?"

I nodded, the words too hard to get out past the fog of lust. *He thinks I'm beautiful.* Just woken up, barely cleaned up, and he thought I was beautiful. He *wanted* me like this. I bit my lip, feeling myself beginning to crest, the delicious tension in my body all pulling taut at once. I gasped, grabbing the base of his horns and running my thumbs along the skin just below where they started, using my grip to guide his face back to mine so I could kiss him as I came, heat and release thundering through me. I cried out, his mouth catching the sound and swallowing it, then I felt him twitch and surge against me. He cried out with his own release, clutching me tight against him, every muscle in his body going tense. After a moment he sagged against me, panting, before gently setting me on my feet. Once he was sure that I was stable he sank backwards, flopping onto the floor.

"Oh my god, are you okay?" I crouched down next to him, my hands fluttering around him, unsure of what to do to help. "Do you need…something?"

He shook his head, his horns scraping into the floor, before one arm came around my middle and pulled me down on top of him. I went eagerly, giggling at the blissed-out, mind-blown expression on his gorgeous face.

"I think I just need a moment," he rasped, pressing a kiss into the top of my head. "Holy heavens, I was not expecting that." He squeezed me against him, his other arm wrapping around my hips, his thumb rubbing against me in small, soothing strokes. "Is it always like that?"

I giggled again. "Dry humping? It's never been that amazing for me before. But from what I hear actual, you know, *sex* is even better. But I've never, um…gone all the way with a guy before." I pursed my lips, then blurted out the question that was boiling in my gut: "Have you?"

He stiffened a little underneath me, blowing out a breath that ruffled my hair. "Had…sex?" He hesitated, then held me closer. "No, I haven't. Does that bother you?"

I shook my head. "No. Does it bother you that I haven't?"

"Of course not. I uh—I may have already known that."

I started, pulling back to look down at him. "What the fuck? How?"

He looked uncomfortable. "The uh…the th'rakkans said so. That all five of you were…untouched."

"Oh." Well, that was weird. But I guess it made sense if they were selling us as pleasure slaves. "Well that's good though, no more secrets there. Are you…happy with this? I know your people have a long list of hygiene laws and we're breaking them left and right doing this. Does it bother you?"

"Goddess, no. But that does remind me, I wanted to ask you something." His face flushed again, his tail winding around my ankle tightly, like he was nervous I'd run. "I was wondering, Joss, if you might want to—to enter into an official courtship with me. We can get proximity permits that would allow for this, we just need physicals and some blood tests."

A smile broke wide over my face. "Oh my god, are you asking me to go steady?"

His brow furrowed in confusion. Which—fair. That was an old and unused phrase even back on Earth that I'd picked up from watching too many old movies. "I don't…"

I waved a hand dismissively, sliding up his body to plant a kiss on his lips. "Don't worry, it's just a goofy Earth saying. Yes, I think I'd like that a lot. My answer's yes."

He beamed at me, pulling me in tight for a bone-crushing hug that made me squeak.

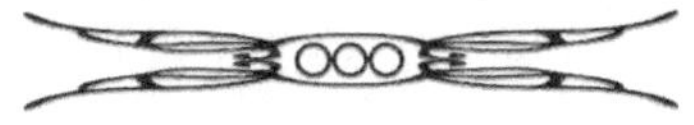

* * *

I wasn't sure what I'd been expecting in terms of a timeline once Xollen had asked me to be his…girlfriend, I guess? But I wasn't expecting same-day. But I should have figured he'd want to get it taken care of as soon as possible. He was a bit of a control freak, my Xollen.

The security guards at the front of the records building grinned at us, recognizing us from our many trips to this exact building, getting me my chip and citizenship (which was still not all the way through, since I still had a couple of tests to take).

"How you two doing?" A rather scary-looking but sweet yvrenii male named Hellem greeted us with a warm smile and a wave. "Good to see you back again so soon."

I smiled back, leaning a little closer to Hellem. "We're getting courtship permits!" I fake-whispered theatrically.

Hellem's three eyes widened, then a broad grin split his face, stretching his lips taut over his jutting tusks. He laughed, a loud booming belly laugh, then clapped Xollen on the shoulder hard enough to make him stagger. "This is excellent news, my friends! I wish you all the happiness in the world!" Xollen smiled back weakly while I giggled. "You know where the office is?" he asked us.

Xollen nodded, "yes, we've been there before. Thank you, Hellem."

"Of course! I expect an invitation to the mating ceremony," he called after us as we headed to the second floor, where the office we needed was.

I looked at Xollen out of the corner of my eye, surprised to see him blushing. Was a mating ceremony not like a wedding? Had Hellem just asked to see us like, bone or something? "You okay, Xoll?" I asked, taking his hand and squeezing it.

He nodded, smiling down at me before tugging me closer against his side with our joined hands. "Yes, I just never know what to make of Hellem. How is he so…friendly all the time? It boggles my mind." I laughed; Xollen *was* very shy.

"I don't know but I wish I could steal it. I have *such* a hard time talking to people," I admitted.

Xollen turned to me, surprised. "Really? But you seem so comfortable with it. I see you talking to other people like they're your friends all the time."

I shrugged, stepping through the office door. "I'm just good at faking it. Inside I'm screaming and throwing up."

He chuckled, squeezing my hand one last time before peeling away to talk to the front desk person. "Well, you had me fooled."

We took our seats in the waiting room. There were only two other couples there and they were getting through people really quickly, so even with the physicals and the bloodwork we were in and out in just a couple of hours. *An Earth office could never.*

Once we were on our way home, officially courting in the eyes of the billieuan government, I noticed Xollen was a little quiet and withdrawn.

I immediately assumed the worst.

My thoughts started spiraling the longer he was silent. Was he regretting this? Was he no longer interested in me now that he had me? Did he regret making this commitment to me? By the time we were walking through the doors, my heart was more than halfway to being broken.

But now that we were alone, I decided to do something about it. What was it helping, keeping it all to myself and locked away? Dr. Jackson would be telling me I needed to communicate, to stop torturing myself and get clarity. Worst case scenario was that I was right, but knowing that meant I could do something about it and start healing.

"Do you regret it?" I blurted as he unzipped his boots. He froze, stopping what he was doing to look at me.

"Why would you say that?" he asked, and my heart cracked a little more. That wasn't a no.

"I don't know, you just seemed really quiet and like something was bothering you the whole way back. So is something wrong? Do you... do you regret doing that with me?"

He blinked at me, silent for a heartbeat, and I couldn't stop the tears that sprang to my eyes and started falling. He finished taking his boots off and kicked them to the side, then walked over to me and pulled me into his chest.

"I don't regret anything, I'm sorry I made you think that, my sweet, sweet Joss." He kissed the top of my head as I buried my face into him, clutching at his shirt. "It's nothing, I promise."

I sniffled, pulling back to look up into his face. "W-what's nothing?"

"Nothing's nothing."

I pulled back further, my eyebrows pulling together as I frowned. "So it's something. What is it? If you don't tell me what it is how can I fix it?"

He pursed his lips, his tail lashing through the air behind him. His eyes slid from mine, the purple swirl slow and hesitant. "Promise you won't get mad?"

Oh boy, he was really going to lay something big on me. "Alright," I agreed slowly, bracing myself.

"I-it was what you said. At the office. About how you fake being nice to people. It got me wondering if maybe…I don't know, if you do it to me. If you don't really want to be with me, if it's just convenient for you so you pretend you like me."

Okay, wow. Fucking harsh, but at the same time I could see where he was coming from. Hadn't I just been worried about the same thing, in my own way? I pressed back into his embrace, holding him tight. "That's not what's happening at all, I promise." I took a deep breath, gathering my thoughts. "I was talking about me pretending I'm comfortable talking to strangers so it's not awkward. But I still like talking to them, and I like making friends and stuff. It just doesn't come naturally to me because of some stuff from when I was a kid." I nuzzled my face into his chest, listening to the strange thrum of his two hearts. "I don't think I could fake how much I like you even if I wanted to. You mean a lot to me, Xollen."

His arms tightened around me, pressing more kisses into my hair.

"I think I understand," he murmured. "I feel like such a piece of *vrakaash*. Once you say it it makes so much sense. This is why I should just keep my thoughts to myself."

I pulled back again, frowning at him exaggeratedly. "What? If anything this is why you *shouldn't*. If we wouldn't have talked about it then we'd both be sitting here thinking we hated each other. Now we understand each other better, and that's *because* we talked."

"Yes, but I've made things awkward. Ruined what should have been a beautiful moment, a beautiful day."

I grabbed his face and forced him to look at me. "You've ruined nothing. Baby, this is just what it's like being in a relationship when you're kind of broken." I stroked my thumbs over his cheekbones, staring deep into those swirling violet eyes of his, so different from mine but still so beautiful. "It doesn't feel good at first, fixing the broken bits. But I've been working on it for a little while now and I can tell you it does get better. It gets easier. And you get happier. That's why I want to see you get better help. And why once I can I'm going to get someone to help me, too."

Xollen squeezed his eyes shut, grabbing my hands on his face and squeezing them. He bent down, touching his forehead to mine and taking a shuddering breath. "I'm so scared of losing you," he admitted in a whisper, breaking my whole heart.

"Sweetheart…" I choked out, wrapping my arms around his neck and pulling him in close. "You want me? You've got me. Just keep talking to me, okay? Keep trying, and I won't go anywhere." He held me tight, pressing his face into my neck and taking deep shuddering breaths.

After a little while he released me, looking uncomfortable. "I uh…I like those things you were calling me. Are they Earth terms?"

I smiled. "Yeah, they're like, terms of endearment. Cute little nicknames you give to people to show how close you are to them. If they don't bother you then prepare to hear it a lot."

"You don't like calling me by my name?"

"No, it's not that. It's more like…I don't know, I call everyone by their name no matter how I feel about them. But if we're a couple, if we're romantic, it feels like it should be different names. More…tender ones, I guess." I paused, considering. "Isn't that why you called me your star?"

He flushed, grinning bashfully. "You caught that, huh? Yes, I suppose that is why. But Earth ones are strange. You call me an infant, and tell me my heart is a delicacy."

I burst out laughing hard enough that I snorted. *"Xollen!"* I gasped, bent double. "It's not that literal! I admit the baby one is kind of weird though. Especially because of all the people calling their partners mommy and daddy. But sweetheart is like…your emotional heart is sweet. As in…kind and gentle and good."

Now he just looked concerned. "You would call your partner the same name you would call your parents? That is…shocking."

My face flamed hot. "Okay yeah, it's kind of strange. It's complicated and I'm probably doing a bad job of explaining it." At least I knew not to try calling him Daddy if we took things to the next level.

He didn't have that kind of energy anyway. If anything it'd be hot for him to call me Mommy—

Okay, no, nope, not going there. Not discovering a new kink today.

"So what nicknames do you like to be called?" I asked him, trying to distract myself from my dirty thoughts.

"Hmm." He grabbed my hands and twined his fingers with mine. "I have never thought about it. No one has called me anything except Xollen. Or Xoll. At least, that's all anyone has called me out of kindness. When I was young the other children were cruel to me about my facial deformity."

Oh god, I bet they had been. My poor, sweet Xollen. "I don't like that you call it that," I told him, freeing one of my hands so I could cup his face. "Your face isn't deformed, it's just different. There are other species of aliens right here on Billieu that don't have the cleft. You have a different face shape, that's all. And it's beautiful."

He gave me a shy lopsided smile, nuzzling into my hand and kissing my palm. "You're the beautiful one, sweet Joss. But I will accept that you think I am pleasing to look at."

I huffed and pursed my lips at him, but at least it was a start. "Alright, then I guess if I call you something you don't like just tell me. Like, if I call you pookums…"

He laughed. "Is that a real Earth name?"

I giggled. "Not really. I called my dog that growing up. What about sugar? Or sweetie pie?"

"I think I am concerned about how many of these names imply you wish to eat me. Should I be worried?"

I couldn't help laughing. "I guess that depends. Most guys want their partners to eat them." I bit my lip, cocking an eyebrow at him suggestively. Just to make sure he really understood what I was implying, I made sure to take a long look at his crotch. When I looked back up into his face he was blushing furiously.

"You would…oh my."

"Oh yeah." I went on my tippy-toes and kissed him. It was hard being confident and sexy, I was finding. Half the time I was worried that I came off as a weirdo, or that I looked ridiculous. But Xollen never made me feel like that—it was all me, getting too much in my own head. And maybe it made me a bad person, but in a weird way it helped that even though he was objectively gorgeous by my standards, by his own he wasn't. It meant he'd lived his whole life thinking he was ugly, just like me, when in fact he wasn't in the slightest, and it helped me to believe that maybe something like that was happening to me, too.

Sometimes Xollen was a bit of a dumbass, but I couldn't deny that I was falling for the guy. He was broken in a lot of the same ways that I was, and so he understood what I was going through when I had a moment of insecurity, and I really thought that so long as we kept the channels of communication open that we'd be alright.

"Where will you sleep tonight?" he blurted, pulling me from my thoughts. What an interesting question.

I considered it for a second. "I guess…that depends on where you want me to sleep."

"With me," he replied without taking a single second to think about it. "It doesn't have to be anything besides sleeping, I won't push you. But after you left last night it…it was so lonely. And my bed is plenty big for both of us."

See, this was why I couldn't stay mad at the guy when he got bratty. I felt myself melting, my body swaying forward into his so I could hug him tight. "I think I'd really like that," I mumbled into his chest. "I'm kind of a wild sleeper though. You might get hit."

His chest rumbled with his laughter against my cheek. "Is that a threat, my star?"

"No," I chuckled. "Just a heads-up. I thrash a lot in my sleep. Toss and turn and fling my arms and legs around. When I went to sleepovers as a kid they made me sleep off in a corner by myself because they got tired of getting hit."

"So violent, even in sleep," he chided me. "You'll just be tenderizing me for when you eat my sweet meat pie."

I laughed, pressing my face into his warmth. "Stop teasing! I'm not going to eat you…like that." I tilted my head back to look up at him. "I promise if I hit you it's not on purpose. And if it's too much then I'll just sleep in my room. I get it, I can be a lot."

He combed his fingers through my hair, gently working out the inevitable snarl. "I will wear my battle wounds with pride, my m—my star. Maybe you just need a big strong male in your bed to help you fight your sleep demons, and with me you will finally know peace."

I laughed again, the mental image of sleepy Xollen helping me fight off invisible monsters utterly hilarious. "Maybe. I guess we'll see."

Chapter Eighteen
Sleep Fighting

I thought when my Joss had told me she was a "wild" sleeper that she was exaggerating for comedic effect like she does for many things.

My bruised nose said otherwise. Sleeping with her in my bed would be an adjustment, but one that I was excited to make. I had never shared that kind of intimacy with another person, having no siblings and almost no courtships in my life, and despite being elbowed and kneed and smacked in the face, there was something so soothing about having another warm body in the bed beside me.

For one, I was fairly certain that having Joss with me helped with my sleep paralysis and nightmares. Both were things that had resisted medical treatment, plaguing me from my grade school days, but there was no sleep paralysis that night, and when I awoke from a nightmare, panting and hearts thundering in my chest, I pulled Joss in close to me, wrapping my bigger body around her, and having her scent in my nose, her adorable sleep noises drowning out the echoes of my bad dream, helped lull me back to sleep, and I wasn't bothered by any other bad dreams. If it wasn't for her hand smacking me square in the face when she flopped onto her stomach it would have been the best sleep of my adult life.

But I wasn't mad. Perhaps I should have been, but it hadn't been on purpose, and I would have forgiven anything of her when we woke up later that morning, her body so warm and plush against mine. I felt so…cared for, so safe, with her leg thrown over mine, her arm draped across my chest, her face pressed into my upper arm. I was fairly certain that the dampness soaking into my skin there was her saliva, which should have horrified me, but instead I only found it…cute. She slept like she did so much else: with her full focus, a bit recklessly, but ultimately with a lot of charm and character.

I pulled her closer to me once I was awake, coaxing her head onto my chest and wrapping my arm around her shoulders so I could stroke the soft skin of her arm. She snorted and twitched but stayed asleep, giving me a long stretch of time to simply hold her and lie there peacefully.

It was still unbelievable to me, that she should want me as much as I wanted her. No one ever had before, except for Derris—but it was different with friends, anyway. It scared me as much as it thrilled me. It felt so likely, so inevitable, that she would get tired of me and want to separate. What did I really bring to this relationship? She found me attractive, said she thought me sweet, but as much as I wanted to believe her I also wanted to grab her by the shoulders and demand she tell me *how*, that she tell me *why*. It couldn't be that easy, to find someone who saw me and just…*liked* what they saw. After a lifetime of the opposite, why should it suddenly work out now? Was Joss really that different from every other person I'd ever met? She wasn't the first alien I'd tried courting—there'd been a disastrous attempt to woo a felican female in an economics class in university—so it couldn't just be that she wasn't billieuan that explained it.

But maybe I was thinking too much about it. Perhaps I should merely accept this as the gift from the Goddess that it was. Maybe all I really had to do was open myself up to it, accept her affection as fact, and do everything in my power to keep her, to keep her happy.

It should have been an easy decision to make. I shouldn't have had to think about it all, because the feel of her in my arms was such perfection. But that perfection was exactly the point: I'd never been allowed to feel that before, in my twenty-six solars, and a part of me that I just couldn't seem to silence insisted that now would be no different. Suddenly, I was uneasy, my skin crawling as I lay there with Joss in my arms.

What if she struck me on purpose in her sleep? What guarantee was there that she was truly unconscious and unaware of what she was doing? Or maybe she was just pretending to like me and her real feelings were coming out when she wasn't awake to control them.

It was an ugly thought, and I hated it as soon as it slithered through my mind though I dismissed it almost immediately.

But I couldn't quite forget it. Checking to see that she was still definitely asleep, I pulled up the text comm app on my wrtistcom and composed a frantic text to Derris.

How do you know a female's feelings are genuine? I asked him, shame prickling at me. But Derris was so happy with Gesea, and I trusted that he would answer my question honestly.

I was surprised by the gentle vibration of a response at my wrist just a few moments later; it was early, and I hadn't expected him to be up yet. *I take it things are going well with Joss, then?*

I grinned. *Yes. We are courting and have applied for our permits. She sleeps with me even now.* My heart clenched with affection, taking another greedy breath of her intoxicating scent before I continued my message. *But I can't help but worry that I am imagining things that are not there. What if she only thinks she likes me? Or what if she only pretends because she wants me to help her and protect her? I do not know what to do, Derr.*

Derris's response was once again quick. *Xoll, you're overthinking. I know you have a hard time with this stuff, and you know I love you like a brother, but if you keep on thinking like this you're going to lose your cool and do something foolish. It was obvious when I saw you two together during our comm that she is just as fond of you as you are of her. She sleeps beside you, shows you affection, yes? These are not the actions of a female who speaks false feelings. Please, find some way to calm yourself down, Xollen.*

I huffed, relief and embarrassment warring in my chest. He was right, of course. Verilla hadn't been able to hide her disgust of me, not completely. She'd tried valiantly for the sake of my wealth and connections, but in little quiet moments, she'd shown her true self: flinching from my embrace, refusing to sleep in the same bed as me, not wanting to move in even after several months of courting, not introducing me to her friends or family. Looking back the signs were so obvious, but at the time I'd only thought of making her comfortable.

Thank you for putting my mind at ease, Derr, I sent back to him. *You're right, I'm overthinking and need to put my mind to something else. Perhaps I'll get up and draw.* I hadn't done much drawing since getting back from my trip to Quellor, being too busy with the move and preoccupied with my blooming feelings for Joss, but now that the idea was planted in my mind my fingers were itching for my drawing tablet.

I like the sound of this, my friend. He responded. *Show me what you come up with!* After another moment a second message came through. *Gesea wants to know when you two are free this week, so we can have that dinner and finally meet this hoonin mate-to-be of yours*. My hearts swooped and throbbed at those words: mate-to-be. That was the implication of an official permitted courtship, but it was thrilling nonetheless to see it spelled out like that.

Human, I corrected him, *They are from a primitive planet in restricted space called Earth*. I'd insisted Joss teach me the proper way to say and spell these words, and I wanted to make sure others knew it too. *We should be free all week. Today we will be finishing unpacking and getting the new place set up. It is not too bad, for a public dorm,* I added. Maybe it only seemed that way because of Joss, but it really was not as bad as I had thought it would be. It was small and didn't have nearly the number of windows as my last apartment, but it was still a nice space, with good light and solid construction. Joss had declared it superior to her apartment back on Earth, which she had said was much smaller, much dingier, in an unsafe neighborhood, and had still cost over 1000 "dollars" a month for her to rent.

It warms my heart to know you are settling in well. I was expecting several frantic comms by now, asking to live in our guest room or begging me to save you from the squalor. Joss is very good for you. I could practically hear the teasing smile in his text comm. I rolled my eyes and grinned. *How about we plan for dinner tomorrow night?*

I will make sure this works with Joss when she wakes, but I don't think there will be any issue. I silenced my wristcom, beginning to carefully extract myself from Joss's grasping hands. She'd practically climbed onto me by this point, she'd wrapped herself so tightly around me as I'd been texting Derris. As much as I loved the feel of her against me, my bladder was beginning to ache from the need to relieve myself, and I thought drawing for a little while before Joss woke up would be nice.

It took some careful maneuvering, but I was able to slide out of bed without waking my beautiful human. I took care of my business, washing up in the hygiene room and quickly changing into clean clothes. I grabbed some tea and curled up on the little dorm couch in the living room, which fit neatly against the large windows there. I placed my tea on the window ledge, since the coffee table was buried under boxes still, and powered up the drawing app I preferred on my tablet.

I didn't even have to think about what I wanted to draw, the lines flowing from my pen without thought, constructing the beloved contours of Joss's face. I had studied her so often, so thoroughly, that I could bring her to life from memory alone. Before I knew it I was lost in the process, my mind drifting among sweet memories of my mate, her face held firm in my mind as I sketched her over and over. I drew her smiling, I drew her sleeping, I drew her with her teasing grin and her expressive eyebrows lifted in surprise. I drew her in the ratty clothes she was wearing when I rescued her and the others, in the clothes she had borrowed from me and worn during the trip here, the simple garments taking on new sensual life when draped over her lush curves.

When something brushed against my ear I swatted at it absently, utterly focused on my tablet and irritated at the intrusion. My hand connected with warm flesh, and I froze, my head whipping around to see Joss giggling and rubbing at her cheek.

"Alright, no sneaking up on you when you're in the zone. Consider the lesson learned." She leaned in and pressed a smacking kiss to my cheek. "What are you up to, babe?"

I blushed, my instinct to hide what I'd done. Verilla hadn't liked it the two or three times I'd tried drawing her, saying it was creepy and obsessive. But Joss was not Verilla, and I didn't think her reaction would be disgust. I pulled her into my lap, running the back of one of my fingers over the slightly reddened patch of skin I'd smacked. Luckily it hadn't been hard at all, but I still felt awful about it.

"I'm sorry I struck you, my star." I nuzzled her jaw with my nose. "I thought an insect was crawling on me."

She leaned into me, resting her head on my shoulder. "It's okay, I know it was an accident. What happened to your nose, though? It looks like you hurt it." I prodded at the tender spot, remembering that I had seen a mild bruise there when I'd been cleaning up.

"You happened," I teased, wrapping my arms around her and holding her tight. It was such bliss, to be able to pull the female I craved in close and give in freely to my urge to cuddle her, to caress her and tell her the tender things that crawled into my throat and begged to be spoken. "It's fine though, it will heal quickly."

She made a noise of distress and pulled back, trailing her little finger over the injury in a featherlight touch that tickled. "*I* did this? Oh god, I beat you up in my sleep, didn't I?" When I nodded she groaned. "You should have woken me up and sent me packing! I hate that I hurt you." Her pout was adorable.

"And miss out on the spectacle of your sleep acrobatics?" I grinned at her, catching her chin and tilting her face up to meet my gaze. "I regret nothing, sweet one. I will do it again tonight if you let me. Besides, if you turn me into one big bruise right away and just get it over with—"

"*Xollen!*" she groaned, rolling her eyes.

I kissed her gently, pouring all of my affection into the soft sweep of my lips on hers. She melted against me, her arms slipping around my neck and pulling herself closer to me. Derris was right; the chances of her faking such ready affection were slim.

I released her, nuzzling my nose against hers before pulling back and smiling down at her. "Are you hungry? I can get the food synth set up and make us some breakfast."

She nodded, her eyes still heavy-lidded from our kiss. I stood, setting her down on the spot I was vacating. After a moment of hesitation I turned my tablet back on and handed it to her to look at. "Do not refer to the fact that you have seen this. *Ever*. I don't think I could handle it."

She laughed, taking the tablet and hugging it to her chest. "I promise nothing, you goof."

I turned and headed into the kitchen to grab us our food, nervous about how she would react to the digital canvas covered in drawings of her beauty. Would she be flattered, or would it repulse her like it had Verilla? I was glad for the distraction of setting up the machine and preparing our food, my hearts in my throat as I wondered what she would think.

Chapter Nineteen
Joss is Beautiful

<u>JOSS</u>

It's...it's me. Xollen had filled up the entire digital canvas with drawing after drawing of me. He was such a talented artist that there was no mistaking my face, but somehow, it didn't feel like I was looking at myself, either.

I mean, there wasn't anything about my face that was worthy of this much care and attention, was there? But seeing all of those sketches, one after the other, rendered with so much care and emotion, I could see what Xollen saw when he looked at me...and it was lovely. *I* was lovely. Even though this wasn't an idealized version of me—I snorted and winced at the drawing he did of my smooshed-up sleep face—I could still see nothing but my own beauty in the dozen drawings he'd done of me.

Immediately, I was tearing up. There had been a part of me that had thought Xollen was into me for my personality, and that he just didn't mind how I looked because he didn't know any better. But this... you couldn't fake this kind of care and affection. The way he'd drawn me made me look like I was every inch the star he kept calling me. It made me feel like I was swelling up with emotion, ready to burst apart at the seams with it.

It was so different from when I was with Alex. I'd had to change just about everything about myself to keep that asshole with me, and even then he'd barely hung around for a couple of months. He was the reason my beautiful hair was fried, the reason I sucked my stomach in all the time when I was around new people, why I didn't believe that anyone would ever think I was attractive as-is. I'd thought Xollen's attraction had been in spite of my weight, but from these pictures, he was just *into* me, rolls and all.

He strolled back in a few minutes later, a smile bright on his handsome mint-colored face, proudly holding two bowls of cereal aloft. But when he saw my expression, saw me crying, he set the bowls down on the first flat surface he could find—a box that got a healthy amount of our breakfast sloshed onto it—and rushed to my side, taking the tablet from my hands so he could grab them tightly.

"Joss, my hearts, what's wrong? What happened?" He combed my hair back from my face, his violet eyes swirling sadly. "Did my drawings upset you? I'm sorry they're not very good, I shouldn't have shown you them..." When that only made me sob harder he made a distressed sound in the back of his throat, almost like a dog whining, and flinched away from me.

Sucking in a breath, I slipped off the couch to join him kneeling on the floor, flinging myself into his arms. He was stiff against me for a second, then wrapped me up tight, running his hands soothingly up and down my back as I sobbed into his chest.

Once I could get enough air to speak, I pulled back, surprised to see we were back on the couch, me cradled in his lap. Jeez, I'd been super out of it. And I was amazed he could lift me that easily, considering how slim he was. "I'm sorry for all the tears," I croaked, swiping at his soaked shirt with my fingers like it would do anything. "They're good tears though, believe it or not."

"I will be honest with you and admit I do not entirely believe those tears were happy, but I trust you would not lie to me." He was combing my hair back from my face while he rocked me gently. I nuzzled into the warmth of his chest, letting the strange rhythm of his heartbeats soothe me. "Was it something I did?" He sounded so tense, so scared, that I couldn't help pulling him down into a kiss.

"It was good, I promise babe," I told him in between kisses. "The drawings you did of me were just so beautiful, it overwhelmed me."

He nodded, looking like he understood. "Yes, I am also overwhelmed by your beauty. I am just shocked that my silly sketches were able to capture you well enough to elicit that reaction." I started crying again at that, making him squeak in panic and swipe his thumbs over my cheeks to try and capture my tears.

"I don't think I'm beautiful," I admitted in a whisper, my voice sounding so small and scared in the quiet of the living room. "Because

I'm fat, and kind of plain, and—and no one's thought I was beautiful before. So that's—that's what I find so overwhelming. The girl in those pictures…that's not who I see, and it's amazing to me that that's what you see when you look at me. I-I wish I could see myself like that," I confessed in a rush, my voice cracking on the last bit as fresh tears stole his sweet face from my vision.

He pulled me in close against him again, rocking me harder and trying his best to comfort me even though he still seemed very confused about what, exactly, I was so upset about. "Joss, Joss, my sweet heart, the star in my skies…I don't understand how you can't see how gorgeous and perfect you are in all ways, but I can understand the feeling. Because of my own struggles with my face, and how it is so different from others billieuans." Okay, so maybe he was less confused than I'd thought. It was so easy to forget that he saw himself as ugly when all I saw when I looked at him was miles of drop-dead gorgeous alien hunk.

Oh shit. That was it, wasn't it? He saw me with the same kind of attraction that I saw him with…and we each saw ourselves as hideously ugly. What a fucking pair we were.

"How do you know exactly what to say?" I murmured into his chest, clinging to him tightly.

"I have helped?"

I nodded, swiping the moisture from under my eyes. "You helped a lot. Thank you, baby." I got to my feet, grabbing the congealing cereal and handing him the bowl that had lost less to his panic. But he just held it, not making any move to start eating.

"You're sure you're alright, my star?" He set the bowl on top of another box so that he could cup my face in both of his big warm hands, his thumbs tracing along my cheeks and wiping away the leftover moisture. "I didn't hurt your feelings with my drawings?"

I shook my head, chuckling and smiling up at him. "Not at all. It made me very happy. You're an amazing artist, Xoll. We really have to figure out a way to show the world what amazing talent you have." I took a bite of the soggy cereal, grimacing at the texture but choking it down anyway. But then my eyes landed on the tablet again, and suddenly I remembered the conversation we'd had back on the shuttle, when he'd told me that aliens didn't have comics. "Oh my god!" I shouted, putting my food down, too. I wasn't really all that hungry anyway, and with their recycling system, the waste would be minimal. "We have to get you drawing a comic!"

His brow furrowed in confusion. "The story drawings you were telling me about? The idea is wonderful, but I don't know what story I would even tell."

"I can help!" I'd always wanted to try writing a comic. I even had some ideas tucked away, though my ideas notebook was lost to me now, back on Earth somewhere. "Do you ever daydream stories or characters? We can always start with something really vague like that and build it up into a full story."

He flushed, looking embarrassed, and I wanted to pounce on him, he was so fucking *cute*. His tail flicked with embarrassment down by our feet, the tufted tip gently swatting at my shins. "Well, when I imagine stories for comfort, they are usually…fantasies. Romantic fantasies," he admitted, his whole face flushed bright green now. I bit my lip, resisting the urge to tackle him.

"Romantic stories are great! People love romance, right? Can I ask what sorts of stories you'd make up for these fantasies, or will you set yourself on fire with embarrassment?"

He snorted a laugh, pulling me against his side and burying his face against my neck, hiding. "I like to imagine…that I do something brave, or charming, and it causes a female to see past my ugliness and fall for me anyway." Oh god, Xollen…jesus this guy was so fucking sweet that he made me want to start screaming and flipping furniture.

I cradled his head against my neck, combing my fingers through his silky hair and scraping my nails against his scalp like he loved. "You are breaking my heart, babe," I muttered, pressing a kiss to the side of his head. "But I think it's a great idea for a story. We have a fairy tale back on Earth that kind of goes like that. A prince does something that gets him trapped in an enchanted castle, cursed to be a hideous beast until he can win someone's love. We call it Beauty and the Beast."

He pulled away, smiling tentatively down at me. "You think it could be a good story? I've always thought it was silly nonsense, just my loneliness getting the better of me."

I shook my head. "No, it's great! I'll start making some notes, and you make some sketches, and then we'll start hashing it out!" Excitement was thrumming through me now. I had no fucking clue how to make a comic but since no one else had done it yet it wasn't like I could actually screw it up, right? And the idea of being able to work closely with Xollen, doing something big and creative alongside him, had me feeling warm and fizzy. In fact, that might have been the best part.

He was surprised, one side of his mouth quirked up in a little grin. "You want to start now? With the very first idea we come up with?"

I stood, picking up our abandoned breakfasts. "Hell yeah, babe. It's a great idea! And it's not like we have all that much else to do, right? We can keep brainstorming while we unpack, even."

He trailed after me, helping me clean the bowls and prepare fresh portions in the food synth. "I have to admit, that does sound exciting. I've never had someone encourage me to do nothing but art with my life. Even Derris would suggest I do art in my spare time, but still work with my parents. For the stability, and to give me the best chance of attracting a mate, I think." He wrapped his arms around me from behind, nuzzling into my neck again, while we waited for the food synth to finish up. "But who could have foreseen that someone as beautiful and sweet as you would fall into my arms without any care for wealth or reputation?" He pressed light, fluttering kisses along my throat, making my nipples tighten and heat throb between my thighs. I squeezed them together tight, my hands clutching at his forearms. He nipped at the top of my shoulder, licking the small hurt, and I couldn't take it anymore; I turned in his arms and threw my arms around his neck, kissing him deeply.

We were never going to eat that cereal.

Chapter Twenty
Settling In

Eventually, we came up for air and got ourselves together enough to sit down and eat. Apparently, magic and fairy tales were another Earth special, and it took me a while to get him to wrap his head around the fantasy genre.

"It's like, if you didn't know how hover vehicles worked, you might believe that there was a powerful force outside of your knowledge making them fly, right?" I tried.

"But it is a powerful force, it's an antigrav field. Is this magic a blanket term for ignorance?"

I huffed, trying to figure out a way to explain something like that to a guy who'd grown up in a hyper-advanced alien civilization. "No, it's like, a force that you can't study. Sometimes it's a part of people, sometimes it's like a force of nature, but it's made up. Magic isn't real, and we all kind of know that, but it's fun to pretend that you can be all-powerful and do whatever you want, like fly or make things appear from nothing."

He still looked deeply confused. "It isn't real, and yet you have so much of your culture dedicated to it? Why is this?"

"Because it's *fun* Xoll!" I laughed. "People on Billieu don't ever use their imaginations, huh?"

Snorting, Xollen leaned towards me and leveled an annoyed look at me. "We still use our imagination! But we use it for good, to imagine what could be instead of inventing nonsense."

I laughed again, swatting at his arm. "Excuse you, that sounds totally boring, I prefer the magic!"

For all that he kept insisting it was silly and didn't make sense, I think the idea intrigued him. Once breakfast was done and cleaned up we went back to unpacking, starting with the kitchen since we were already in it. We settled into an easy rhythm, me opening the boxes and handing what was inside to him, and Xollen putting everything away where he thought it should go, since he cared more about that kind of stuff than I did. While we worked we started spit-balling ideas for our comic.

"I like the idea of freeing a person from a curse, from the fairies tale you were telling me about," Xollen mused, taking a pair of drinking glasses from me. "What sorts of curses are there?"

"*Fairy* tale," I corrected him. "Usually curses are punishments for something bad the person who gets cursed did. They're meant to teach a lesson. So a vain person may be cursed to be ugly, a greedy person to have nothing, stuff like that. Sometimes it's on more than one person though. In 'Sleeping Beauty' an entire castle is punished by a curse because an evil fairy didn't like something the king and queen did."

He thought for a second, playing with the fall of silky navy blue hair coming from his high ponytail. "And you said that sometimes people get cursed to be animals, like the frog and the swan?"

I nodded. "Two different stories, but yeah. You got an idea?"

"Perhaps. What about one person who is cursed to only ever say the opposite of what they mean to say, meets someone who is cursed to take any form but their true form, and in order to break the curse they are tasked with getting someone to fall in love with them. Maybe…they team up to try and figure out a way to do it, and accidentally fall in love instead?"

I stood there blinking at him in amazement. I almost dropped the glasses I was holding, I was so stunned. "Oh my god, babe, that sounds so fucking cool!" My mind was already whirling with ideas, symbolism, and metaphors that we could work in, what they could have done to earn their fates…I ran out of the kitchen and snatched my tablet from its charging dock. When I brought it back into the kitchen and immediately started hammering out notes Xollen came over to look at what I was doing. He was quiet, apparently content to just watch me for the long minutes I sat typing at the screen.

Once I stopped he stood there looking at me with a stunned expression. "All of that came from my silly idea?" he asked, pointing at the paragraphs I'd churned out.

"No, it came from your *good* idea," I corrected. "Sorry to derail the unpacking, I just wanted to get the ideas out before I could forget them."

"It was fascinating watching you work. You made a lot of interesting faces."

I chuckled, going back to handing him dishes to put away. "Yeah, people have told me I get really into it and make crazy expressions." I shrugged. "I don't notice it when I do it so I can't tell you why it's happening."

When he turned to me again the look on his face was soft and full of adoration. "You are truly a marvel, my star."

I felt myself flush with pleasure. "Careful, I'll start believing you when you say stuff like that."

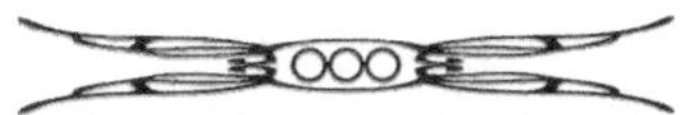

Once the kitchen was put away we couldn't help ourselves any longer: I parked myself in front of my tablet and started working on an outline, and Xollen grabbed his drawing tablet and started sketching out character ideas.

It was amazing how we just fell into a flow, like we'd been working together for years. I'd ask Xollen for his opinion on a story beat and he'd show me his sketches for my input, and it was just easy and seamless switching our focuses like that. And more importantly, it was *fun*. I'd never worked with someone on a creative project before, and a part of me had definitely been nervous about that. What if he got really bossy again? What if I didn't want to take his criticisms? What if once we got going our artistic visions were just too different? But I hadn't let those nagging doubts stop me, and now I was having some of the most fun I'd ever had in my life with my boyfriend. Mate. Whatever word I was supposed to be using.

Dr. Jackson would be proud of me for pursuing such a strong corrective experience.

By lunchtime, we were sketching out pages and finalizing the first chunk of the story. By dinner we had the first three pages roughed out, and we were completely exhausted. But even so, we were both humming with excitement. It wasn't just a far-off dream, all of a sudden. We were already in it and making strides. It was scary and amazing all at once.

I crawled into my bed—my actual bed, since I was sure Xollen wouldn't want a repeat of last night's beatdown no matter what he'd said—and got settled in. It felt weird to be in a room without him when we'd spent pretty much every moment together for the last couple of days though. It was…lonely. But it was my own fault for sleeping like a crazy person.

I was almost asleep despite how lonely I felt when a heavy weight settled against my back, followed by limbs draping over my shoulders and hips.

"What are you doing?" Xollen murmured in my ear, his nose nuzzling the sensitive flesh just under it.

"Going to sleep. What are you doing?" I croaked back.

Instead of responding he pulled the blankets up and slithered under, wrapping himself around me once again. "I didn't realize we were sleeping in your bed tonight. I was waiting in mine, or I would have been here sooner."

Guilt flooded me. "I didn't think you'd want to sleep with my again, given how I hurt you last night," I admitted.

He snorted, holding me tight. "You thought wrong, my star. I want nothing more than to sleep wrapped around you every night for the rest of my life." My heart soared in my chest, lodging in my throat and making my eyes prickle. "You can try and fight me off all you want but until I hear a 'no' I want this. Do…do you want this?" he asked haltingly, his voice going soft and uncertain.

I flopped onto my other side, burrowing into his chest. "Of course I do. I'm sorry, I should have said something." Man, this open communication shit was *hard*.

He kissed the top of my head, pulling me closer against him. "All is forgiven, my mate," he promised. "We both have much to work on, as you've said. I'm just relieved you haven't gotten sick of me always hanging around you."

My heart jolted in my chest, slamming into my ribs. He'd called me his mate. In my favorite alien romances that was more intense than a declaration of love, it was a borderline marriage proposal. But maybe on Billieu that wasn't the case. Maybe it was just that they didn't use terms like boyfriend, girlfriend, or partner. He was saying it casually, without any hint of his usual anxiety, so it must not be a big deal.

But fuck, I kind of wanted it to be a big deal.

I decided to play it just as cool as him, glad that he couldn't see my face. "Not at all," I murmured into his chest, placing a kiss between his pectorals, right in the middle of his two hearts. I was starting to think I'd never get sick of him. It was entirely possible it was just because it was so new—I knew the honeymoon phase was no joke—but this was different from how I'd experienced it before. It wasn't just that I was having trouble noticing bad things about him and feeling obsessed with him. It was more about discovering a person who complimented my quirks, who challenged and excited me, who needed me in a way that no one else had before.

If I wasn't mistaken, was actually *falling* for this guy. I was living my best life out here, falling in love with a hot-ass cinnamon roll alien, just like I'd fantasized about back on Earth hundreds of times.

Xollen was quiet and still for so long that I was sure he'd fallen asleep, but suddenly he spoke, startling me from my thoughts. "I care about you so much, Joss," he admitted in a whisper. "So much that it scares me. Is this what love is?"

I swallowed around the lump in my throat. Fuck, maybe "mate" *was* a big deal kind of word. "You think you love me?" I asked in a whisper just as quiet as his.

"Yes. I'm fairly certain, actually. I've never felt this before, and it's so wonderful and intense that I'm terrified by it. Of doing something to ruin it. Of hurting you."

"Oh, Xollen…" I was at a crossroads. I could either lay it all out, give him my heart on a silver platter and hope like hell he didn't chuck it in a blender, or I could play it more cautiously, play it safe. But was that how I should be thinking? Wouldn't it make more sense for me to think about what I *wanted*? To do what would make me *happy*? Maybe it would be worth it to be stupid and to just get it out there, to take the leap. Xollen had found the courage to do it, after all. Maybe he'd drop me and let me fall on my face if I took this leap of faith, but wasn't it also possible that he'd catch me and make something beautiful with me?

I ripped the words free from my throat before I could think about it too much and stop myself. "I-I think I love you too. Just so you know. And I think that the only way you'll ruin it is if you go back to pushing me away and not talking to me. We can't fix what we don't talk about, right?" It sounded so reasonable and logical, but I knew it was all too easy to fall back into that kind of behavior, to retreat and stick with what was comfortable and familiar instead of what needed to be done. But I didn't want to think about that right now, not when he was pulling back and looking at me like I'd hung the moon, like I was the most beautiful and amazing thing he'd ever seen. Not when he was sliding down to kiss me, his lips on mine so hot and soft and sweet.

I'd been exhausted when I lay down, but with his mouth slanting over mine the fatigue burned away almost immediately. I moaned into his mouth as he deepened the kiss, his tongue slicking over mine and plunging deep into my mouth to taste me hungrily. His tongue was a slightly different texture than mine, almost ribbed, and I just knew that that was going to feel amazing on my clit once we got to that point. It made me breathless and trembly, imagining that tongue all over my body, laving at my neck, suckling at my aching nipples, licking at all of the sensitive places on my body.

My hands came up and tangled in his hair, locking him against me and making him rumble deep in his chest. His own hands trailed along my sides, his fingers brushing ever so lightly against my oversensitive skin. I arched into his touch, trying to coax him into palming my breasts. They felt so heavy and sensitive that if *someone* didn't touch them soon I'd lose my mind.

He seemed to understand what I needed at last, one big warm hand cupping the heavy weight of my breast and the thumb dragging over the beaded nipple so deliciously I had to break the kiss to gasp and pant. "You like when I touch you like this?" he asked huskily, grinning at me in the dim light of the room. I nodded, pressing myself more firmly into his grip.

"You should use your mouth," I blurted, my voice breathless and needy. My face heated at how brazen that was, but I was too far gone to care much.

"You're sure?" he asked, pinching my nipple gently through my clothes and making me cry out. "Can I use my mouth…everywhere?" His hand left my breast, making me ache with its loss, and started trailing lower and lower, until he was cupping my mound through my old shorts. "Even here?"

I bit my lip, nodding. "Especially there," I panted. No one had ever gone down on me before and I was *dying* to try it. Xollen grinned at me, his expression going hungry. If I could see his eyes better I was sure they'd be swirling wildly. I'd never seen him this bold and confident before, and it was *doing* things to me.

He took my mouth again in a searing kiss that made my pussy throb with need, so full of promise and heat that I whimpered.

"I love the sounds you make, my sweet Joss," he growled, easing the fabric of my pajama shirt up so that my breasts were exposed to the cool air. His warm breath fanned over my sensitive skin, making me shiver, before his mouth descended, his tongue swirling over the tight peaks. I cried out, my hands going to his head to hold him because I had to hold onto *something*. I was careful not to get too close to the sensitive base of his horns, not wanting to overwhelm him when we'd just gotten started.

I wanted to draw this out as long as possible.

I could tell he'd never done some of this stuff before, but he was a fast learner; he paid attention to my responses and went harder at the things that made me cry out the loudest. I was already panting and squirming under him, thrusting my hips up into his tight, warm body as a not-so-subtle reminder of what I wanted from him. I wasn't about to get bossy in bed—I hadn't managed *that* much healing—but I was starting to get a little impatient. Playing with my breasts was nice, but I wanted to *come.*

Xollen released my nipple with a wet pop, grinning up at me as one of his hands slid down my body to capture my gyrating hip. "Are you eager for my mouth on you, my star?" he purred, his fingers slipping under the band of my sleep shorts. "Should I take these off and take care of you?"

I nodded, biting my lip and grabbing at the waistband to pull them down, but he swatted my hands away, growling low in his throat. I had to admit that Bossy Xollen, in this context, was fucking *hot.* I whimpered as he tugged my shorts and panties off, exposing my hot, wet sex to the cool air, making me shiver.

He slithered down the bed so that his head was between my eagerly spread thighs, his hand stroking the delicate skin of my inner thighs and gazing down at my pussy like it was the most magical thing he'd ever seen.

Bossy Xollen slipped away a little, and I saw my sweet and slightly uncertain male instead. "I-I don't know what to do, exactly," he admitted, looking embarrassed as he continued to stroke my skin in gentle sweeps. "I think I need you to show me."

"Of course," I told him, sliding my hands down my body so I could show him what I liked. I was so wet that I didn't need to spread my moisture around, so I just spread my lips with my fingers and started pointing things out and rubbing. I started with the most important bit, the star of the show. "This is my clit," I told him, rubbing it in firm, slow circles that made me catch my breath. "This is the most important part for human females to get a release." I felt a little silly, giving a lecture like this, but if I didn't show him he wouldn't know—it's not there was any information on human sexuality way out here, where there weren't even really any humans. "This is how we orgasm. Penetration feels nice, but it's the clit that gets the job done. There's more of it under the skin, and the rest of it is just inside the actual vagina. We call it the g-spot but I don't know what that stands for." I plunged two of my fingers inside myself and curled them up, just barely managing to hit the edge of it. I sucked in a breath, giving myself a few more strokes before slipping my fingers out and going back to my clit. "Rubbing along the sides also feels good, if you're using your fingers. And when you use your mouth, it feels good if you use your tongue on it, a-and if you suck it." That last part I was just guessing on, but it seemed popular in romances so I figured there had to be something to it.

He nodded, watching my fingers like they were spelling out the path to his own personal salvation. "Can I try?" he asked in a dry rasp, making me clench. I nodded, moving my hand away, but he caught my wrist and guided my hand to his mouth so he could lick my fingers clean. He closed his eyes and shuddered as my taste hit his tongue, his hips bucking into the mattress. I whimpered, my pussy clenching on nothing. Jesus Christ, that was so *hot.*

"Sweet Goddess, you taste so good, Joss," he murmured, releasing my wrist so he could wrap his arms around my thighs and position my hips how he wanted them. He pressed kisses to my inner thighs, making his way slowly to my wet and aching folds. "You are so beautiful, so eager for me. I can't believe you don't know how beautiful you are." He pressed a kiss to my mons, nuzzling the damp curls there. I grabbed a couple of pillows and wedged them under myself so that I could watch him better, my boobs and tummy getting in the way otherwise.

It was one of the most erotic things I'd ever seen, watching Xollen's full lips part, letting his soft ribbed tongue slide out to lick a stripe down the seam of me, the tip swirling deliciously around the hard bud of my clit once he got there. His eyes burned up into mine in the dark, the look on his face predatory and hungry and making me shudder. It made me the littlest bit uncomfortable, having that much intense attention on me, but he was so into it, so…*worshipping* of this body that I'd hated most of my life, that the self-consciousness didn't last.

If he started off uncertain and a little clumsy, Xollen was soon tonguing me within an inch of my life. Unlike in the romance novels I loved so much, I didn't ever seem to come all at once. It was more like I had a lot of little ones, each one more intense than the last, until I had one big one that was almost painful—and sometimes I couldn't quite get there. But I honestly wasn't mad about it, especially when I had a devoted male between my thighs, bringing me to peak after peak like it was his job. I was a mindless puddle underneath him, lost in the sensations of his tongue working me over.

He grew a little more bold, releasing one of my legs and bringing his hand over to the entrance of my channel. He stroked along the entrance of my pussy, then dipped his finger in experimentally, groaning when he sank into me. "You're so hot and wet, it's the most incredible thing I've ever felt," he rumbled, watching my face as he tried to mimic what I'd done earlier. "You said the spot is the other side of the clit, right?" I nodded as he probed deeper, gently prodding at my walls, trying to figure out my anatomy.

His persistence paid off, his finger sliding against that sensitive spot inside of me and making me cry out and throw my head back. I was so worked up already that just that brief touch had me heading towards another orgasm. When I looked back down at Xollen he was grinning wickedly and looking very proud of himself. "Was that it? Did I find it?"

I chuckled, biting my lip as he stroked me again, then added another finger. "Oh yeah, you found it, baby," I managed to gasp as he started stroking into me more firmly. His mouth descended back onto my clit, the ridged flat of his tongue feeling so incredible that I was coming again in no time, this one intense enough that I could feel moisture flooding my folds.

As I was coming down from that peak and heading for another, my pussy clenching hard around his fingers, Xollen's lips closed around my clit, and then he was sucking me, and I was losing my goddamn mind.

I was actually, literally screaming, the orgasm that barreled through me from the dual stimulation was so intense. I'd never come that hard in my life, and getting my clit sucked was every bit as wonderful as the books had made it out to be. I lost track of myself in the storm of sensation, fireworks of light sizzling behind my eyelids. Distantly, one of my feet was cramping from how hard my toes were curled, but I couldn't muster up the strength or awareness to care. All there was room for in my mind was the waves of pleasure carrying me out to sea. My damn ears were ringing, he'd made me come so hard.

When I finally came back to the mortal plane Xollen was staring at me with deep concern. "Are you alright?" he asked me, his brows drawn together in concern. "I—I'm sorry. Did I hurt you, my star?"

I laughed weakly, unable to do much more in my newly weakened state. "No, you did *not* hurt me. I've never come so hard in my life. It was out of this world." I giggled at my joke. When I next managed to pry my eyes open and look at him, he looked like he couldn't decide if he was more concerned or proud of himself.

"Come here," I told him, holding my arms open for him. He came eagerly, scooping up my limp body and cradling me against his chest. "Once I recover it's your turn."

He stiffened against me. "Oh, you don't need to do that," he assured me, nuzzling his face into my tangled hair. "I didn't do it because I was expecting you to touch me, too." He was such a sweetheart.

"And that's wonderful, really it is. But I am *dying* to see what your dick looks like." I trailed my fingers down his body until I was palming the hard length of him. He sucked in a breath, his pelvis pressing harder against my hand. There were definitely some interesting textures going on down there, making my mouth water in anticipation. I couldn't wait to see what sorts of goodies Xollen was packing. Unveiling the alien peen was always one of the most fun parts of the books, after all.

Chapter Twenty-One
What That Dick Do?

XOLLEN

Bringing Joss pleasure might have been the single greatest accomplishment of my entire life. Even though she was the one who had experienced it, the sense of satisfaction I'd gotten was surprisingly intense all on its own. There had been a part of me that had believed that there was no way that I could bring her that kind of pleasure, that I'd fail at that just like I had so much else and leave her wanting.

But now that I was thinking about it, most of the other things in my life that I hadn't been successful with and had abandoned were things that I hadn't really wanted to do in the first place. I'd gone to business school to appease my parents. I'd dated Verilla to keep them happy and because it was expected of me. I'd remained sensitive and prone to moodiness because I didn't actually want to be tough, to lose the side of myself that Joss was so drawn to *because* of its tenderness, rather than despite it.

Great Goddess's boon, had I ever pursued *anything* in my life just because *I* wanted it? All I could come up with was that I'd kept drawing, kept painting, despite everyone except Derris telling me to stop. And I was with Joss knowing my parents and their entire social strata would be horrified and likely shun me. And look at how much happier I was even with just those two changes.

"You're right, Joss," I told her as I nuzzled her, careful of my horns on her delicate skin. "I need a new emoreg."

She snorted. "What on earth were you thinking about instead of me sucking your dick to get to that conclusion?"

I blushed, grinning. She wasn't wrong to be surprised. "I just realized that the reason I've been miserable and thinking I've been bad at everything my whole life is because I've only ever tried to do things that other people wanted for me, instead of what I wanted that would have made *me* happy. I feel like Dr. Gish'ren should have caught that."

She chuckled as she pulled me closer. "Yeah, I should fucking say so," she said, her tone incredulous and a little angry—for me, I realized. "Kind of weird that you're the one having post-nut clarity even though when I was the one who came." She wriggled out from under me and pushed me back into the mattress with a firm hand on my shoulder. "Let's fix that," she purred, rubbing her palms up and down my torso, squeezing at my pectorals when she passed over them. I shivered, suddenly so nervous that the powerful throbbing ache of my cock was starting to ebb.

Joss had taken everything else about me in stride, but I couldn't help worrying about this one last piece of me that she hadn't yet seen. Verilla had never seen me naked, but there were several times she hadn't quite been able to disguise the look of disgust and resignation in her eyes at the sight of me. Obviously, the female in front of me was about as far away from Verilla as could be, but I still couldn't tamp down the anxiety.

"Y-You don't have to. Really, I'm fine. Touching you was more than enough." I pressed my fingers into the sides of my legs to hide their trembling, praying Joss wouldn't notice that my tail was squeezing my leg tight.

She clicked her tongue, her face softening. "If you really don't want me to, I won't," she told me softly, her hand caressing my side. "But is this an 'I don't think Joss will like it so I'm going to say I don't want it' thing, or something you're actually wanting to wait on?"

I didn't want to answer her, ashamed of my answer, but her hand on my side was so warm, so gentle, that I sighed and fixed my gaze on the ceiling and admitted the truth. I had promised her I would, hadn't I? "The first one," I muttered.

Joss made a sound of distress and my eyes shifted down to see her face filled with feeling. "Why don't you think I'll like it? I've done it before with people I was much less into than you and I still enjoyed it. If that helps."

Jealousy flared hot and bitter in my gut, but I tamped it down. She'd already told me she'd had other relationships, and she'd just said that she liked me better than all of them. I shouldn't be jealous. And it was some sort of comfort, to know that the act itself was something she was confident she wouldn't object to. But what if once she saw me she found me lacking compared to those previous lovers? What if the fact that she liked me wasn't enough?

I swallowed, the words not cooperating. I wanted to tell her, to tell her everything, but it was so *hard*.

Joss seemed to realize my struggle, because she grabbed her tablet from its dock and opened it to its note-taking app, and handed it to me. "Here, write it out. Sometimes it's too hard to say it out loud, right?"

I took the tablet, my hands trembling, but it did seem less awful than trying to figure out how to turn the mess in my head into something another person could understand.

I worry the way that part of me looks will alarm you. That it will be too different. That you won't like it, or find it lacking. It feels too much like a fluke that you've found even this much of me to be attractive. I hesitated before handing the tablet back to her. She took it and read over what I'd written, her smooth brow wrinkling as she read.

"It doesn't matter how different you are, Xollen," she said quietly, taking my hand and squeezing it tight. "It doesn't matter because it's still *you*, and that's all that matters to me. I want to make Xollen feel good by touching him because I care about him and I want him. The rest is just…technicalities. You might have to show me what you like like I showed you, but so what? It's all still you, and I want to put my mouth on it."

I didn't know if I wanted to laugh or sob more, so I compromised with a strangled sound in the back of my throat and pulled her down onto my chest for a kiss. I tried to pour everything I was feeling into it, using my lips and tongue and teeth to tell her in this way, since they so stubbornly refused to shape the words. She moaned and melted against me, her pelvis grinding into mine and stirring my cock back to life. Soon she had control of the kiss, conquering my mouth, her hands exploring my body with heady boldness that had me straining against her, my entire groin throbbing with need for her, for her touch.

She broke the kiss, smiling at me wickedly as she slid down my body until she was kneeling between my spread legs. "If you don't have any more objections?" she mused, her fingers trailing over the fastener of my pants to punctuate her question. My tail slid off my leg to wrap around hers, the comfort from that contact immediate. I nodded, helping her undo the fastener and get the tight pants off of my legs, leaving me in my underwear. She hooked the band with her fingers and then that, too, was gone, and I was totally naked. I returned my legs to either side of her, feeling exposed and vulnerable. I lay there, tense and awaiting her judgment, my eyes firmly locked on the far corner of the room.

"Oh, baby," she breathed, trailing her hands up and down my thighs. "You're absolutely beautiful." I couldn't help shooting a look at her face, awed by the reverence and delight I saw there. She leaned down, keeping my eye contact and her tongue darting out of her plush mouth. She grabbed me at the root and squeezed, knocking the air from my lungs, as she used that slick little tongue of hers to lick a stripe up the center of me, the tip of her tongue laving each of the raised rings that trailed up and down my length. When she got to the oblong, egg-shaped head of me she swirled her tongue all around it, then pulled me into the wet heat of her mouth.

I'd never felt anything like it—it was an almost overwhelming sensation as her tongue continued to swirl against the underside of my cock even as she took me deeper into her mouth. She made a sound of pleasure low in her throat, and I could *feel* the vibrations of it straight down to my tightening balls, making me arch off the bed and cry out. Her one hand was stroking the length of me not seated in her silky mouth, and her other hand was stroking along my thigh, inching closer to the thatch of thin hair-like tentacles that sat just above my cock, on my pubic bone. They were a sensory organ used during mating to ensure both partners were ready and releasing the correct hormones to ensure a successful coupling, but I'd noticed that Joss didn't have them, that she just had thick dark curls of hair decorating her sex.

Her fingers found my thatch, and the tiny tentacles grabbed onto her eagerly, the flavor of her skin sinking into my blood and making me relax. I saw her eyes widen, her lips tightening around my cock in a wicked grin, and then she was petting the tentacles, tickling them and stroking them, making my hips buck up into her mouth. Joss groaned in approval, the pace of her hand and mouth quickening, and all too soon I felt my balls pulling almost painfully tight against my shaft, my release boiling up my cock and setting my spine on fire.

"I'm—Joss—wait—" I tried to warn her, my hands going to the sides of her face to lift her off of me, but she held on tight, meeting my eyes with a challenge, and I could hold back no longer. My eyes rolled up into my head as everything in my body tightened, my seed erupting from my cock into Joss's hot sweet mouth. She made a sound of pleased surprise, doing her best to swallow me down, and I thought I might cry at the sight of her.

It felt like my orgasm ripped through me for hours, Joss's grip on me the only thing keeping me from floating away, but at last I was wrung out and spent, my vision still clearing from the stars that had filled it with the force of my orgasm.

Joss gave a happy little hum and finished delicately licking me clean, making me jump when her tongue trailed over my now too-sensitive cockhead.

She finally released me and lay beside me on the bed. "Sooo…how was it?"

I couldn't think of anything to say. "Guh," was the embarrassing sound that slipped out when I tried.

Joss laughed, looking immensely pleased with herself. "A five-star review if I've ever heard one." She snuggled up against my side, her head on my chest and her leg draped over one of my thighs. "I wasn't expecting it to taste good. Earth men taste kind of bleachy most of the time, but you taste good, like honeydew melon." I had no idea what that was, but I was glad she found it pleasant. "And it was the same purple color as your eyes. Is that normal?"

I grunted. "Of course. The mating fluids are always the same color as the eyes. Is it not this way for humans?"

She laughed. "Not at all! It's always the same color, white."

"For everyone?"

"Yes!" She snorted. "It can't be that unusual out here."

I shrugged. "Perhaps not for other species, but for all billieuans it is so."

Her fingers played along my stomach, tracing the faint outline of my abdominal muscles. "I like your little tentacle things too. They're very sexy. What are they for?"

"Sensing. During mating, they taste to make sure the partner's hormones are aligned for a successful coupling."

"Can you…control them? Move them around and stuff?"

An interesting question. "Somewhat. I can't control each one but I have some control over the thatch as a whole. Why?"

"Just wondering!" she squeaked, wriggling against me. "I just, uh… those would probably feel amazing on my clit. When we, you know, have sex."

My eyes widened, realizing what she was saying. I could use my tentacle thatch to stimulate her clit even as I pumped into her slick well.

I could not wait until we got to try that.

Chapter Twenty-Two
Dinner with Derris

<u>JOSS</u>

Xollen had said it slipped his mind, when he failed to tell me until this morning that we'd be going over to his friend Derris's house for dinner with him and his mate, Gesea. He was shocked that I was so mad about it.

"But you've already spoken to Derris. His mate Gesea is very kind, and very sweet. Derris is the bold one, so if you found him palatable then you will have no issues with her."

I sighed loudly and rolled my eyes. "That is not the *point,* Xollen! I need time to psych myself up for shit like this."

"It is this—this *shit* to have dinner with my best friend?" He was getting that pissy look on his face that I hated, that meant he was getting himself wound up.

"No, that wasn't what I meant. It's hard for me to go out and meet new people, I need a lot of time to prepare myself!" Goddammit, I still had to shave, curl my hair, figure out the alien makeup Djelani had given me a couple of weeks back, find an outfit, figure out if we were supposed to bring something and then get it...

"What is there to prepare for?" Xollen scoffed. "It's just Derris and Gesea. We're not even going to a fancy restaurant!"

I was getting so frustrated. It felt like he wasn't really listening to me. But maybe I just wasn't explaining myself well enough? For all that it felt like he understood me better than anyone, we were still from two completely different cultures—in a lot of ways. I took a couple of deep breaths to calm myself.

"Look, Xollen, I know all that. I know it in the logical part of my brain, but that's not the part of me that's freaking out. That part sees any interaction with someone I don't know really, really well as...I don't know, like...a battle. Or a trial. I always feel like I have to prove myself, because of how I look, because I'm not where I want to be in life compared to other people my age, because all my life I—" A*h shit, here come the waterworks*, I thought bitterly, my next words catching so hard in my throat I had to swallow several times to force them out. "All my life people have seen me like trash. Even people who were supposed to care about me, so I can't help it. It's going to take a lot of time for me to be able to walk into something like this on the spur of the moment, without all of the extra stuff I feel like I have to do to be... safe."

I'd stopped looking at Xollen a while ago, the force of my emotions too much to also have to look him in the eyes while I said it. So I was surprised when he was there, practically out of nowhere, wrapping me up and squeezing me tight in his strong arms. I melted into him, the plush warmth of his chest and the scent of his skin already so familiar and comforting to me. A few more tears leaked out, but Xollen was quickly pulling me beyond them, thawing my fear with the solid warmth of his presence.

"I'm sorry, Joss. I didn't know. I feel like I should have, but I am realizing I am not the smartest male, especially when it comes to females. Next time I will tell you right away, I promise."

I clung to him tighter, my fingers digging into his back. "Thank you," I said softly. He was rubbing my back with one hand and using the other to cup the back of my head in a gesture so tender it ached. "Maybe I overreacted. You're right, it's not that bad. It's just the two of them and it's at their house. But they mean a lot to you, and I want to make a really good impression."

He pulled away and kissed me gently. "And you will. Derris is already ready to adopt you into the family, and Gesea likes everyone. Except for my parents. And Verilla."

That was a name I hadn't heard before. "Who's Verilla?"

He flushed, looking uncomfortable. "Oh. She was...we had a relationship. Before I met you. It...wasn't good, but at the time I thought she was amazing. Further proof my head is full of space dust, because now that I have met you it's obvious she was cruel and trying to use me for my parent's influence."

I knew I shouldn't be jealous of an ex—it wasn't like I didn't have any, after all—but that name, Verilla, brought to mind skinny, glamorous socialites without a single hair out of place, always dressed in something new and ridiculously expensive, flitting about parties like glowing butterflies and catching the attention of everyone in the room. In comparison, I was so…dumpy.

Xollen pulled me close again, burying his face in the crook of my neck and breathing deep. "You are nothing like her," he rumbled. "You are beautiful, you are kind, you are funny, and so compassionate. You will amaze my friends and charm them even if you show up covered in *vrakaash* and wearing clothes made of garbage." He lifted his head to look into my eyes again, his expression going somber. "And if they do not love you then they are not friends that I want anymore."

I gasped, my eyes widening. Derris was like his brother—he couldn't mean that. Could he?

He kissed me once more, then released me, smiling softly. "We still have a few hours before they are expecting us. What can I do to help you get ready in that time?"

I was feeling a lot less panicky after talking to him. Was this why Dr. Jackson was always telling me I needed to communicate more? Because this was pretty damn great. I was even feeling a little saucy now. There was just something about a guy being willing to burn everything to the ground for you that really soaked the 'ole panties.

"You can keep kissing me," I purred at him, fluttering my lashes and thrusting my chest forward. "Maybe even on the mouth."

His brow furrowed, the look of confusion on his face quickly replaced by heat and lust once he got it. "My Joss," he groaned, grabbing me and hauling me up so that our faces were at the same level. I squeaked, clinging to him with my arms around his neck and my legs around his waist. His mouth slanted over mine, claiming me hungrily, making me pant and whine with the rush of need flooding me.

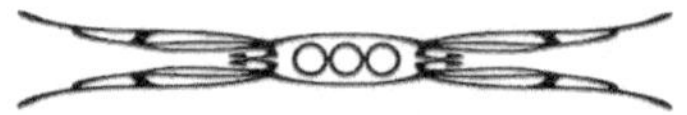

Derris and Gesea were lovely, of course. I'd known there wasn't *really* any reason to worry—but anxiety had a way of getting to me like a greased-up freight train with busted breaks.

When they'd met us at the front door I was feeling uncomfortable about how slippery I still felt between the thighs from Xollen's pre-dinner attentions back at the apartment. Luckily the billieuans didn't have the hyper-sensitive sense of smell that so many aliens in the romances I loved had. *That* would have been more embarrassing than I could stand. As it was, they were both smiling warmly, Derris's arm casually wrapped around Gesea's waist.

Derris looked pretty much the same as how I remembered him from the video call a couple of weeks back, copper eyes swirling warmly, and his skin a deeper and greener shade than Xollen's, kind of like oxidized copper. I didn't think I'd ever get over that cleft they had running down the center of their faces, but at least I no longer felt tempted to start giggling when I saw it. Gesea was a delicate-looking female, her slight willowy build reminding me a lot of Ghena. Her complexion was closer to Xollen's pleasant mint, her eyes a bright and hypnotic gold that her cobalt hair complemented well. Her cleft was also less deep than Derris's, reminding me more of a peach than a full-on butt.

"Warmest of welcomes to you, Xollen and Joss. We're so glad you could make it," Gesea greeted us, her voice soft and sweet. I immediately felt like a bull in a china shop. I took Xollen's hand, squeezing tight, and he looked down at me, his eyes so full of affection that it took the worst of the edge off. Dr. Jackson used to tell me all the time that I was probably the only one in a room judging me as harshly as I did, and I had to admit, looking around at the group, that that did seem to be the case. Gesea and Derris were being genuinely warm and welcoming, and no one was staring at my big tummy or my double chin. I relaxed the tiniest fraction.

Our hosts led us on a quick tour of their home, since not even Xollen had been there yet, then we settled into the dining room to eat and drink. They'd prepared a wide selection of dishes, making me uneasy. Were more people going to be coming by after all? Had Derris mentioned how big I was and they'd prepared extra food because they thought I'd eat it all?

Gesea waved a hand at all of the dishes, looking sheepish. "I went a bit overboard with the cooking, I'm afraid. I didn't know what humans liked to eat so I made a wide variety to make sure you'd have something you like, Joss." She shot Xollen a brief frown. "*Someone* was absolutely no help when we asked him what you liked."

I laughed, feeling a little guilty for my minor freakout. *Corrective experience, Joss. They're not messing with you!* "Yeah, I'm not too picky so I'm sure it'll all be delicious! When they did my medical scans at the port they didn't identify any food allergies so nothing should kill me."

"See, I told you! She likes everything!" Xollen cried, throwing his hands up. "I know my Joss," he pouted at a laughing Derris.

"So you did, Xoll. You have our apologies."

I squeezed Xollen's thigh under the table, giving him a little smile.

He put his hand on top of mine and squeezed me back. So far it wasn't too bad. I was still tense and nervous, but it wasn't nearly as bad as it usually was when I found myself in these sorts of situations. I wasn't ready to just jump into the conversation yet, but it was still nice to sit there and listen to the three of them talk.

Over the course of the meal—which was delicious, the dishes full of fresh vegetables and soft grains—I learned that Gesea had gone to the same school as them for most of their childhood, and had been one of the few people outside of Derris who hadn't bullied Xollen and had actually tried to be his friend. She'd been born with only one heart instead of two, and could identify with Xollen and his struggles since most of her young life had been spent with a kind of pacemaker device hooked up to her chest. She'd had to move away and switch schools when she was a young teen, and they'd fallen out of contact.

"But the Goddess had a plan," Derris interjected smoothly, tucking a strand of his mate's wavy blue hair behind her pointed ear. "I'd had a crush on her for many years, but hadn't wanted to make things awkward if we started a contract and then had to nullify it. But then once I got to university, guess who was in my very first class on my very first day?"

Gesea tilted her head back to meet Derris's adoring gaze, the smile on her lips blooming bright and beautiful. "From there it was a bit of a whirlwind," Gesea continued, her voice dropping an octave and getting a bit husky. "He had a relationship contract drawn up by the end of that first week, and because *I* had always harbored a secret crush on *him*, of course I signed it. Within a month we'd moved in together, and after a year we were talking about getting engaged."

I couldn't stop myself from sighing and leaning my head on Xollen's bicep. "Oh my god, that's so romantic! I can't believe it worked out like that," I told them. Xoll kissed the top of my head, careful not to muss my meticulously curled hair, and Derris and Gesea looked surprised at the gesture, but both of them smiled brightly at us.

"You two have quite the story, too, do you not?" Derris asked, putting his arm around his mate's shoulder and holding her close against his side. "How was it that you met again, Xollen?"

My alien man flushed, ducking his head and making the decorative chain he'd draped over his horns tinkle. "You know how, Derr," he grumbled. I frowned at him, wondering if he was ashamed of how we'd met.

"You rescued me and four other females from some slavers you ran into on Quellor Station. You even cleared out your savings to do it!" I swatted at his arm gently. "I don't know why you're being so shy, Xoll."

He stiffened beside me, his hand leaving mine under the table. *What the hell?* Had I embarrassed him? Xollen cleared his throat and shifted in his seat, pulling his leg out of my grasp.

Cold dread filled my stomach, making it sink like a heavy stone. My meal was going sour on me. I *had* upset him by telling them that—but how? Why would he be embarrassed about the fact that he'd rescued all of us? Maybe he thought that just that bit made it sound like he was taking advantage of me.

"He was a perfect gentleman the whole time," I plowed on, my hands tangling together in my lap. I was starting to get sweaty now. I had to fix this. I had to make sure I explained it all so everyone understood. "I offered to stick around instead of moving in with one of the girls or trying my luck with the shelter because even then I was drawn to Xollen. And the rest is history!" I smiled up at my quiet alien boyfriend, hoping I'd fixed things.

He was looking straight ahead, his jaw muscles tense and ticking, his purple eye swirling wildly.

I had not fixed things.

I shoved back from the table, keeping a bright smile plastered on my face. "Where is your hygiene room?" I asked. I needed to get away, needed to calm myself down and regroup.

Gesea stood, smiling gently. "I'll show you. There's a lot of turns to get there from the dining room and it'll be easier if I just take you."

I nodded, feeling grateful. With how upset I was getting I probably wouldn't have been able to remember directions anyway.

Once we'd made our way there, Gesea put a delicate hand on my arm, startling me. "It'll be alright, Joss," she said softly. "Xollen gets in these moods sometimes, I'm sure you know. But it's obvious that he cares for you, and Derris will get his head out of his ass. He's very good at it."

The smile I shot at her felt too wobbly, and before I could stop them tears were gathering in my eyes. Gesea clucked and pulled me into a hug. I didn't usually like it when strangers touched me but this was nice.

"I just don't know what I did," I whimpered when she released me, feeling both too big and too small all at once. "I don't know why he got upset. He promised me he'd work on this shit." It reminded me that for all of his promises about getting better help, he hadn't done it yet, hadn't even started, as far as I knew. He'd been pouring all of his energy into our comic, and into spending time with me.

Oh god, what if this had all been a mistake after all? What if I'd hitched my wagon to Xollen and he wasn't ever going to actually do what he needed to do to be a good partner? *He grew up lonely and not used to having to take the feelings of others into account. He comes from a whole shitload of privilege.* I smiled at Gesea, muttering something about how I was sure Derris had it, before making my escape into the bathroom.

How had things gotten so terrible so fast?

Chapter Twenty-Three
Trouble in Paradise

<u>XOLLEN</u>

It was an exercise in restraint to stop myself from grabbing Joss and carrying her out of the house before she could say anything else to embarrass me.

I'd told Derris why I'd gone out to Quellor Station, but Gesea hadn't known, and to have Joss spell it out so plainly was utterly mortifying. Just about every billieuan of a certain age knew that Quellor was the safest place to hire a sex worker, and the fact that I'd rescued people that had obviously been meant to be bed slaves…well, I didn't know if we'd get invited over to dinner again anytime soon.

Worse yet was how Derris was scowling at me. He probably didn't like that I'd gotten so irritated at her, but why should I apologize for getting upset that she wanted to spill our secrets to everyone?

Derris sighed, leaning back in his seat and crossing his arms over his chest. "You are such a *vrakaashaad*, Xoll."

I bristled, crossing my own arms. "Shut up, Derr. How was I a *vrakaashaad*?"

He snorted, looking incredulous. "Are you serious? She has no idea what the significance of Quellor is. She's not from Billieu, you stubborn fool. And if she doesn't know, whose fault is that, hmm? So stop acting like a child and go apologize to that lovely female."

"She's in the hygiene room," I grumbled, making no move to get up. "And I didn't even do anything."

Derris slammed his hand down on the table, rattling the dishes and making me jump. "Xollen, I love you like a brother, you know that. But right now I want to strangle you. Joss is such a sweet, kind person. She's *good* for you. And if you screw this up for yourself by pushing her away I might just have to murder you."

Was I pushing her away? Maybe a little bit, but only because I felt like I was being attacked. She should have followed my lead and kept it vague. And when I first showed that I was upset, she should have *definitely* stopped then. She was always talking about clarity and communication, and how much clearer could I get than that? Would she have preferred that I cut her off and tell her to stop talking?

But I didn't want to go through this with Derr right now, so I sighed and stood up. I passed Gesea on the way to their hygiene room, and she shot me an angry look. It was strange, seeing her angry. I couldn't think of many times in my life when she'd been mad, and knowing that she was mad at *me* only upset me more. Why were my friends suddenly turning against me? Why couldn't they sympathize with me in this?

Joss was still in the hygiene room when I got there, so I leaned against the opposite wall to wait for her to get out. I'd apologize for upsetting her, we'd finish dinner, and then hopefully just get back to it.

It was several moments before she emerged, and I felt a pang of guilt when I saw that she had obviously been crying. Her eyes and nose were pinkened, and her makeup looked more smudged than it had before she'd excused herself. Her brown eyes widened in surprise when she saw me, but she refused to look at me for more than a second.

"I'm sorry, Joss," I managed, uncomfortable. "Please don't cry."

She frowned, crossing her arms over her chest in a mimic of my own pose. "What's bothering you?" she asked, her voice tight and edged with anger. I tensed, taking issue with her tone. *She* was mad at *me?*

"Nothing's wrong," I snapped. I wasn't going to start this with her while we were here.

Anger warred with hurt on her face and her lips flattened into a hard line. "You told me you weren't going to do this anymore. That you were going to talk to me when something was bothering you so we could talk it out. You fucking *promised*, Xollen!"

"Fine!" I snapped, my tail squeezing my leg in a death grip. "Something is bothering me, but I don't want to go into it right now, okay? I'd rather do this at home."

Her jaw jutted as she worked her mouth angrily. "Fine." She

uncrossed her arms and put her hands on her hips. "But you have to actually talk to me when we get back. Promise me right now."

"Fine. I promise. Happy?"

She sucked in a breath, her eyes looking glossy again. "No, not really," she rasped, spinning on her heel and returning to the dining room.

I felt really guilty, then. She'd looked so sad, so disappointed, and knowing that it was partly that she was disappointed in me, in my lack of communication, hurt something fierce. But we were out in public, at a friend's house for a dinner party, and surely she hadn't really expected me to hash it all out here? Having those sorts of conversations where anyone could hear them wasn't a good idea, right?

I shook my head to clear it, prying my tail from its death grip on my thigh and trailing after Joss back to the table.

When I walked back in Derris and Gesea were telling Joss a funny story from when we were children.

"…Ser'Yannic was so upset that Xollen had called his bluff about the fitness test that he had to go home early!" Derris was saying, making both of the females laugh.

"I had forgotten how much he used to hate exercise," Gesea chuckled, leaning into Derris at her side. "He was very quick, and fairly strong, so I don't know why he did."

"It was the sweat," I grumbled, taking my seat. "I hated how long it took for me to stop sweating once I started and how it would just sit there on my face." It just made my facial deformity more obvious, the sweat sitting on my face and highlighting how flat it was.

The gloss was gone from Joss's eyes, and the smile she flashed my friends seemed genuine, but I didn't miss that she was leaning away from me in her chair and that she wasn't looking at me.

It didn't feel right, that I should be the one who was hurt by what had happened but that Joss's feelings were the ones that had to be coddled.

I retook my seat and stabbed at my food with my utensil, but I didn't eat anything else. My appetite was long gone.

Chapter Twenty-Four
Xollen Shits the Bed

<u>JOSS</u>

I felt so bad for Derris and Gesea; they tried so hard to keep the dinner running smoothly after Xollen's tantrum and my obvious discomfort. I tried my best to relax for their sake, because they didn't deserve this, not when they'd been so goddamn nice to me, but pissiness and fury were rolling off of Xollen. He didn't say anything else until it was time to leave, and even that was just the bare minimum of good manners. He refused to touch me or look at me the whole tram ride back to our apartment and by the time we walked in the door I was a raw nerve.

"Living room," I barked at him, wanting to have our talk in neutral territory.

He grunted, tossing his jacket on the back of a chair on his way to sit down on the couch. I followed a moment later after I'd taken my shoes off and hung up my own jacket. When I joined him on the couch I made sure to keep a careful distance between us, even though it was breaking my heart.

When Xollen stayed quiet, glaring at the empty slice of couch between us, I took a breath and forced myself to look at him. "So what happened back there?" I asked, wishing my voice didn't sound quite so small and fearful.

"You really don't know?" he growled, still not looking at me. His tail was hitting the side of the couch with loud *fwaps*.

"No, I really don't. What did I say?"

He gritted his teeth, hard enough that I could hear it. "I didn't want you telling them about that."

I wanted to scream at him. "What was so bad about it?"

"I don't want to say," he huffed.

"If you don't tell me then how am I going to know what *not* to say in the future?" I searched his face, desperate for any hint that he was softening. His attitude was starting to make me nervous. "Are you... ashamed of how we met?"

"I don't want to say, Joss!" he spat at me. I hated the way it made my eyes burn. "I shouldn't *have* to say," he grumbled, his expression dark and stormy.

That hurt. "Well what did you think would happen when you started dating someone from another culture?" I hated the tears prickling at my eyes and making my vision foggy. "I'm sorry but I don't know what I said that's so upsetting to you. But do you not trust me? I just want to understan—"

"*Just fucking drop it!*" he cried, standing up and flinging his arms out wide. "By the Goddess, I said I don't want to talk about it! If you won't listen to me over something as simple as that, and you're asking me to to trust you?"

It wouldn't have hurt that much if he'd actually slapped me. I was too stunned by the pain to move, to speak, my brain screeching to a halt as those words sank in. Tears fell down my face, stinging and hot, and I mused that in the space of a week he'd managed to make me cry on this couch twice, for two very different reasons.

Jesus, it's only been a week.

Without saying anything I got to my feet and stepped around him, needing to leave, needing the quiet and the safety of my room.

He tried to stop me as I passed him, his hand grabbing my arm. I ripped myself free and ran, slamming my door shut and engaging the 'do not disturb' mode so that he couldn't get in or comm me through the door. Once I was certain it was locked and I wouldn't have to deal with him for the foreseeable future I flung myself onto my bed, giving into the urge to sob.

My sheets still smelled like him, twisting the knife in deep.

Chapter Twenty-Five
A True Dumbass

XOLLEN

As soon as the words were out of my mouth I wanted to take them back, wanted to tell Joss how untrue they were.

Of course I trust you. I know that you listen to me, that I'm being an ass and doing exactly the opposite of what I promised I'd do. I'm just scared, Joss. Please don't leave, Joss.

When I'd seen how badly what I'd said shattered her, it had made something shatter in me. I knew I'd gone too far, knew I needed to apologize, to grovel and beg for her forgiveness, but I locked up. It was like I'd lost control of my body, and all I could do was scream silently from inside my own skull.

I watched her face crumple, watched helplessly as her lip wobbled and her eyes grew glossy with tears, my heart shredding itself to pieces in my hollow chest knowing I'd done that, I'd caused that pain to pinch at her beautiful face. And then she was standing, and she was walking out, and then she was gone. And I was immediately seized with the conviction that she was gone *forever.* That I'd really, truly pushed her away now, and I'd never be able to convince her to come back.

"Wait, Joss!" but of course she didn't hear me. The door was already closed with her on the other side. And I was stuck here, alone and frozen.

Why am I like this?

I stood there for several minutes—it might have been just two, or enough to make an hour, I wasn't sure—breathing and replaying the night back in my mind.

I didn't want Joss to think I was stupid or weak, ruled by my baser urges. I didn't want her to think that maybe I had bought them all to be pleasure slaves, only to change my mind. I wanted her to think I was a fine male specimen, despite my looks. I wanted her to see me as a viable partner, a mate. And that meant never letting her see my weakness, keeping her in the dark about the things I lacked. It didn't matter that she'd already seen so many of my ugly parts and called them wonderful; something inside of me was panicking at the thought of her seeing any more, because I was certain that her mind would change about me.

Joss had seen more of me than anyone else, and she hadn't run away. And maybe a part of me was so convinced that she would, that she *should*, that I was pushing her until she did. Because...

Because I was developing some very scary feelings for her. Feelings that had gotten so intense so fast that it frightened me. I'd told her that I loved her...but it was more than that. She was more than beloved; she was *essential*.

But I had to face the fact that in my desire to avoid my own hurt, I'd caused hers. The look on Joss's face as she'd left me here in the living room made pain spike through my chest every time it ran through my mind.

Suddenly I was moving, my long legs eating up the distance between us. I needed to apologize, needed to explain myself, needed to beg her to give me another chance. It might already be too late, I realized, my hearts pounding in my chest and the air too thin in my lungs. She might be lost to me already, and for what? I'd been trying to protect myself from pain, from humiliation, but it hadn't even worked. I'd just shot myself in the foot.

I knocked on her door, the force of my fist hitting the metal sending bolts of pain all the way up my arm. "Joss, please let me in," I called, hoping. "Please, Joss. I'm so sorry. I was an idiot. Can we talk?"

Nothing. I tapped at the keypad to open a comm channel and my heart sank into my stomach: *Do not disturb active.* She didn't want to talk to me. I should have expected that, of course. But it still hurt. And more than that it made me *panic*. Perhaps a part of me had thought that I couldn't push too hard. An arrogant part of myself had pushed at her to prove that even my worst wasn't enough to push her away.

But that wasn't what you did to someone you cared about. It wasn't something that I wanted to do to Joss, not really. I'd been so, so selfish.

Why did I never see this *vrakaash* in time to do something about it? Where was this clarity an hour ago?

My mind started racing, trying to figure out a way to get to Joss to try and fix this. I had to believe that this still *could* be fixed, that I could make it right. But the more time that slipped past me the surer I was that she wouldn't give me that chance.

I could override the lock on her door, obviously, but I knew that that was a terrible idea, no matter how tempting.

What if she decides to just leave? To climb out the window and down the fire escape and out of my life forever?

Well, I could always go outside and go *up* the fire escape. Cut her off and hope she let me make it up to her.

It was an insane idea, of course. My unit was twenty floors up, and I was too unfit to do that much climbing. My bedroom was around the corner of the building and wouldn't let me get at the escape that passed in front of Joss's window, I knew, so if I wanted to go that route I'd be forced to start from the ground. But that was insane, wasn't it? I was starting to feel unhinged, but I was still pretty certain it wouldn't make my case to do something like that right now. I was better off camping outside her door and waiting to catch her when she emerged, like a sane person.

I sat down on the floor and settled in to wait. I pulled out my tablet and loaded up my favorite puzzle game, hoping Joss wouldn't stay in there for too much longer. I mean, she had to come out to use the hygiene room, right?

After an hour I was starting to fall asleep sitting up. Clearly, she meant to really make me squirm. Fair enough; I couldn't deny that I deserved that. I hauled myself to my feet and shuffled over to my room. I dragged a pillow and my blanket off my bed and carried them back to where I'd been keeping my vigil. I'd camp out in front of her door all night if I had to. I had to get to her, had to tell her how sorry I was, how the truth was that my life wasn't *right* without her in it. Just these few short weeks had taught me that. For all that I kept getting annoyed at her for commenting on my shortcomings, it was so satisfying when I managed to fix it and earn one of her dazzling, sweet smiles. She was *proud* of me in those moments. No one else had ever done that—been proud of me.

I settled in and fell asleep quickly, but staying asleep proved far more difficult. Every sound, every shift in the air currents, every scrape of my horns against the floor when I tossed and turned, made me twitch awake, hearts racing.

It was both the longest and shortest night of my life, and I never got so much as a whiff of Joss.

As dawn broke I decided it was time to panic.

After the sun had slipped far enough over the horizon to bleed the sky from steel to olive I abandoned my bedding and charged into my room to change my clothes, also stopping in the hygiene room to freshen up. Then I was out the door, my hearts racing and my head feeling curiously light and fuzzy. What if Joss had already had the idea to leave via the fire escape? What if something had happened to her and she needed help?

What if I never saw her again? What if the last thing I ever said to her were those ugly words?

I had to stop in my tracks and crouch, letting my head hang down between my knees against the wave of lightheadedness and nausea. What had possessed me to say that? What idiotic impulse had that come from? If she'd left me I couldn't blame her. But I was a selfish bastard: I wanted her anyway.

I managed a deep, shuddering breath and continued to the elevator to get down to the ground floor.

I'd never been in the alley next to my building before, and while I was horrified by the smells and mystery puddles it was distant compared to the urgency thundering through me: *must climb.*

Must get to Joss.

Must…Joss…

Joss…

The ladder descended with an anguished squeal when I tugged on it, stopping with a groan a few inches above my head. I frowned, grabbing the rusted steel and yanking on it, causing it to fall another inch or two. I leaned all my weight back, and it stayed firm at that height. I sighed, hoping my upper body strength would be enough to get me up the ladder to the staircase that was the fire escape proper.

It involved a lot of jumping and grunting, and some flopping I was *very* glad no one was around to witness, but I managed to get myself up onto the ladder and begin climbing.

And if I screamed when, halfway up, the ladder suddenly dropped several more feet and almost dislodged me, that was between me and my Goddess.

Limbs unsteady from my harrowing climb, I began my trek up the twenty flights of stairs that would take me outside Joss's window. For the first four floors I was feeling good, surprising myself. I thought, *hey, maybe this'll be easier than I thought. Maybe I'll manage it in no time at all.*

By the seventh flight, I knew I was wrong. Possibly *dead* wrong.

Sweat began pouring off of me, soaking my clothes, and my breaths were getting ragged and painful. In an attempt to alleviate the burning in my legs from the endless climb, I started pulling myself up with my arms.

At the halfway point, floor ten, my arms and legs started cramping painfully. I looked up at the height I still had to climb and wanted to cry. I allowed some stoic whimpering, then forced a deep breath. Joss was worth it. I couldn't let things end between us like this. I wiped at the moisture on my cheeks that was definitely just sweat and not also tears, and hauled my screaming body back into motion, Joss's name like a prayer looping in my head.

Chapter Twenty-Six
Rapunzel

<u>JOSS</u>

I'd slept like shit. Not surprising, but after the day I'd had yesterday I could have used a good sleep. I was ravenously hungry and I had to pee like a bitch, but my desire to avoid Xollen was outweighing those needs.

It hurt to think about him. I was just so fucking *conflicted*, and I hated that I still cared about the bastard. I wanted to hate him, to be able to cast him aside like he had cast me aside. But all the sweet moments we'd shared kept creeping in, making me doubt that he'd actually done that. He acted all tough and aloof but I'd caught so many glimpses of a scared, deeply insecure person that responded strongly to my kindness, like it was the first time someone had been gentle with him. Like he was unused to someone encouraging him, supporting him, so that he treated it like it was the greatest gift he'd ever been given. I knew what that was like, and how much it changed your life to suddenly get that. To feel supported and—and *enough*.

Once I'd given up on sleep I'd gotten back to my searching on the nexus, though my heart was less in it than it had been yesterday at the height of my rage. One moment I wanted to leave this apartment and never come back, the other I wanted to fling open the door and find Xollen and scream at him and hug him and then force him to make me those noodles that I liked so much as penance. But it felt like I was forgiving him too easily, that I was letting him walk all over me and calling it love like I had done so often back on Earth. This was supposed to be my fresh start where I unleashed a bolder, more assertive Joss who didn't let people make her feel guilty about her existence.

I had a page open about how immigrants could qualify for government housing, but my eyes were blind to the words. My thoughts were swirling too ruthlessly around Xollen, around what my feelings for him were doing to my sense of self.

A loud crash against the window behind me had me jumping and nearly falling out of my chair. I whipped around so fast my neck twinged, my heart in my throat.

Pressed up against the glass of my one window, so tired and sweaty it looked like it hurt, was Xollen. He mouthed something I couldn't hear, sagging against the glass and pawing at it, his eyes darting around like he was trying to see through the privacy film.

I was up and rushing to the window before I could think it through, sliding the lock aside and yanking hard on the sash to get the window up. Xollen oozed through the gap, sliding to the floor in a moist mint-colored heap. I took several big steps back, putting more space between us again. Between panting, wheezing, and sweating, I got three words from him: "Don't…leave…me…"

I was torn.

I was still mad at him, still so hurt, but I'd always been a sucker for someone pathetic and in need. Putting others before myself had always been my favorite form of self-harm.

So I stood there, halfway across the room, staring down into his swirling violet eyes, so bleak yet hopeful, and I thought about this.

Did I want to forgive him? Absolutely. But was it the right thing to do? *That* I didn't know.

I sighed, walking over to Xollen's wet noodle of a body sprawled out on the floor. He was still breathing heavily and looking kind of out of it, and I finally put two-and-two together and realized he'd climbed up the fire escape to get to me. To talk to me. I sank to the floor near his head, sitting cross-legged and pursing my lips into a line.

"You hurt me," I said softly, my voice barely above a whisper. "I've only ever wanted to help you and you just…snap at me. All the time. I don't deserve that, and you promised to do better, to get help." My voice sounded meek, and it was one of the hardest things I'd ever done, getting those words out, but I was proud of myself anyway. This was what I'd been working so hard on with Dr. Jackson all those years: asserting myself, stating my boundaries, and loving myself enough to stand up for myself.

"I know," Xollen rasped, closing his eyes briefly and grimacing. "I'm sorry, Joss. Please…another chance?"

I crossed my arms over my chest, thinking. Did I want to give him another chance? In my experience, an abuser only used second chances to keep abusing you. But there was a chance—and maybe I was blind to think it was there—that he wasn't being malicious. That he was being dumb, and emotionally stunted, but that he really was serious about not wanting to hurt me.

"I've been hurt by people promising to change before, Xollen. I gave them second chances, and third chances, sometimes even more, and they just kept hurting me. So if you want me to stay, you have to actually change. Not just *try*. You have to actually do it."

Xollen started thrashing and wiggling on the floor, and after a second I realized he was trying to sit up. I put my arm under his shoulders and heaved, getting him upright. He was panting less now, but he still looked wrung-out and just a smidge delirious. Once he was sitting I backed away from him again, my hands twisting in the fabric of my shirt. It was suddenly too hard to look at him, too hard to be close to him like this, and I wanted to get up and run screaming from this, from the discomfort of these feelings, but we were in my bedroom already; I had nowhere else to hide.

"I'm so sorry Joss," he said again, his voice soft and sad. "I don't want to be like those other people, I-I want to change but…I don't know how. Where do I start?"

I couldn't stop the snort that burst from me. "Now I've got to tell you how to grow up, to be a better person? Jesus, Xoll…" I sighed deeply. "You need to get your ass into therapy. I *told* you this already."

His brows lowered, his violet eyes swirling like a cyclone and boring into me. "Yes, I should have done this already." He swallowed, looking miserable in a way that made me both happy and sad. "I really do not deserve you. I am the world's most pathetic *vrakaashaad…*" He squeezed his eyes shut.

"No one is going to fix it but you, Xollen. I can't fix it for you, and I'm not going to sit here and let you shit all over me in the meantime. What happened last night should never have gotten that bad. You know that, right? You didn't talk to me, you shut me out, you yelled at me and I don't even know *why*."

He nodded, squeezing his knees. He was silent for a time, his eyes sliding to the floor and losing focus. I wanted to scream; he still wasn't talking to me.

Right when I started to wonder if he'd slipped into a trance, or fallen asleep with his eyes open, he spoke, his voice such a small whisper: "I'm sorry. It's just...I went to Quellor to...hire a sex worker. It's shameful and illegal to boot, and Quellor has a reputation for being able to cater to billieuan tastes. So you were basically broadcasting to Derris and Gesea that I'd been...well. I know that you couldn't have possibly known that," he cut in before I could interrupt, "But I just...I panicked. Do you hate me?"

Fuck. A part of me *wanted* to hate him, wanted to be able to tear myself away from him. But that sounded even more awful than him snapping at me after giving me the cold shoulder all night. What the fuck was *wrong* with me, that I couldn't be strong? That I was so willing to let him back in after an apology and some promises?

But the facts were this: I was crazy for this immature idiot, because in the moments when he was good, he was so good it took my breath away. When he didn't let his pride or his ego get in the way he was kind, and thoughtful, and funny. He clearly cared about me deeply underneath his bullshit, and I couldn't deny just how badly I wanted more of that. If I was being honest with myself, that was something that set him apart from the other abusers in my life: he was good to me more than he was mean, and he told me how much he cared about me all the time, not just when he was trying to bring me back in close after pushing me away. It wasn't a whole lot, but was it enough for me to trust him with another chance?

I was crawling across the floor and flinging myself at him in a tight hug before I could even think about it. He was stiff in my arms at first, but after a heartbeat or two he unfolded himself and threw his arms around me too, clinging desperately to me. "No, I don't hate you," I murmured into his cute little elfish ear. "I want to be mad at you but I can't even manage that."

Xollen buried his face into the side of my neck, almost clipping me with one of his sleek horns. "I'm so sorry, Joss," he said again, his voice heavily muffled because he still had his face pressed tight against me. "I love you so much and I don't know why I'm doing this." Now he did move his head a little, resting what felt like his chin against my shoulder. "You make me feel scary things," he admitted softly.

My heart jumped into my throat. I pulled away gently so I could look him in the face. Feeling the boldness of New Joss, I took his hands in mine and squeezed. "What sorts of scary things?"

He swallowed, his eyes swirling like cyclones. "It's hard to say, but —things like...like that I love you. Like...I might want to be with you forever because you are the most perfect and wonderful person I have ever met. You're so beautiful it literally stuns me, and I...I don't know what to do. It scares me." His voice was low and husky, his face tense as he forced the words out. "I want you. I want to talk to you, and laugh with you, and make things with you. I want it all, and the fact that I don't deserve you makes me so crazy."

Well mark me down as scared and *horny,* I thought as Xollen pressed gentle kisses to first one wrist, then the other. He dropped our hands into his lap, his gaze searching my face expectantly. *Alright, big girl pants time.*

"I feel the same way, Xollen," I admitted, pressing my lips together against my nerves. "That's why it hurts so much when you push me away. That's why I want you to get better. Because I want you, too. I've wanted you since I first saw your pretty face back on your ship. But I'm not going to let you hurt me like that anymore."

He closed his eyes, throat bobbing. Then he broke out in the most beautiful, shining smile I'd ever seen. "Then I have to get better," he said, his voice thick with emotion. "So that I can finally say that I've done something to deserve you."

It was all instinct: I lunged at him, my hands letting go of his hands so I could wrap my arms tight around his neck instead. Our mouths crashed together, Xollen's stiff with surprise for a moment, before it caught up to him what I was doing. Then he softened, melting against me like he'd been made for me, my perfect fit, and his arms were wrapping around me, pulling me in close against his long body. One of us moaned—or maybe both of us—and then I was spiraling, my entire world reduced to Xollen: his taste, his scent, his feel. When I gently nipped his bottom lip—so full, like a ripe piece of fruit—and licked away the hurt he surged against me, his mouth slanting and his tongue darting out to demand access to my mouth.

And I gave it, gladly, sighing at the slick heat of his invasion. The taste of him sharpened, deepening now that I was drinking from the source. Xollen was clutching me to him, holding me so tight it was almost uncomfortable, but I found that I wanted *more,* wanted to be even closer, more wrapped up in him, more drunk on his kisses. Kissing Xollen made me think that maybe I'd never actually been kissed before in my life, because no one else had ever felt so right in my arms, their taste so sweet and warm and perfect. He groaned into my mouth, his tongue slicking against mine, his hands clutching tight.

He finally ripped his mouth off of mine, both of us panting and flushed. "I am so sorry, Joss," he whispered in between kisses that had become tender and slow. "I was so scared I lost you. That you'd left and I'd never see you again."

I nipped at his full lip, tracing his piercing with my tongue and making him shiver. "I should have. You're lucky I'm such an idiot."

He growled, pulling me closer. "Not an idiot," he rumbled, pressing kisses along my jaw. "Kind. Generous. Perfect." Each word was punctuated with a wet kiss down my throat, heat flooding my body and pooling between my thighs. He was saying such sweet things, and he was already entirely too good at awakening my body, learning what I liked and memorizing it, trying to perfect his technique every time he touched me.

But I still had to pee, and if I waited much longer I was going to have an accident. "I have to use the hygiene room," I told him as I peeled myself away from him. "And I think you owe me a nice breakfast." I patted his cheek as I walked away, waddling with how hard I was squeezing my thighs together.

"I will make you the best breakfast you've ever had," he called after me. "It's going to blow your mind!"

Chapter Twenty-Seven
No More Chances

XOLLEN

I threw every trick I knew at the food synth to get it to make Joss the perfect breakfast. I knew she liked sweet things for breakfast, but not *too* sweet, so I made her thin *jithla* cakes with *hrasaza* berry compote on top, and some of the fizzy flavored water she liked for some reason.

She swanned into the kitchen just as I was finishing up, looking freshly scrubbed and radiant. She squealed in happiness when she saw what I'd made her, clapping her hands and grinning up at me. "Yay, pancakes!" she went on tip-toes to place a smacking kiss on my cheek. "Thank you." My chest may have puffed out a little at her praise.

I sat down and pulled her into my lap, pulling her legs over so she was sitting sideways. She tensed up against me.

"What are you doing, I'm way too heavy for this!" she protested, trying to wriggle free, but I refused to let her down.

"Nonsense," I informed her, pressing a kiss to her cheek and nuzzling at her jaw. "Would I do anything that would make me uncomfortable? Am I that type of male?"

She froze, then tilted her head back and laughed, her arms going around my neck to keep her balance. "Alright, you got me there," she wheezed when she'd caught her breath. "My man is a bit of a princess."

I knew that calling me a princess was an Earth thing that was her way of teasing me for being too particular and spoiled, but the fact that she had called me hers settled something inside of me that was still raw and frazzled from the last twelve hours. She didn't hate me. She might have even already forgiven me.

Truly, she was a gift.

I reached around her and started cutting into the *jithla* cakes, spearing a bite with plenty of berries on it with the utensil and guiding it to her lips.

She shot me an exasperated look. "You are *not* feeding me," she protested, trying to snatch the utensil from my grasp. But with my longer arms I kept it away from her easily.

"Silence, female. You will let your male serve you as an apology for his terrible behavior." Something shifted in her eyes, something like sadness creeping in.

"Alright," she agreed softly, her arms tightening around my neck. "Maybe after breakfast, we sit down and look for another doctor for you to see."

I wanted to bristle at that, but I had to admit I was terrified of slipping up again and losing her for good. "Alright," I echoed, feeding her another bite. "I wish to take care of this as soon as possible." I dipped my head so that our foreheads met. "I can't lose you," I admitted in a whisper, the confession ripping my chest wide open, leaving my beating hearts so, so vulnerable.

Joss made a sound of distress, then pressed her soft lips to mine. She tasted like *hrasaza* berries and home, the warmth of her body in my arms better than any medicine I'd ever been given to help with my anxiety. She was *potent*, my Joss. I was tempted to let breakfast go ignored and get my fill of her instead, but I didn't want her to go hungry. My drive to take care of her was especially strong this morning.

I ripped my lips from hers and resumed feeding her, making her huff again that she was capable of feeding herself. But if I couldn't have *her* for my meal then the possessive male in me wouldn't let me release her or let her take care of herself. Besides, I think a part of her liked it.

Once I'd fed her everything I let her up so that I could dump the dishes in the sanitizer and hit the terminal to find a new emoreg. I used the terminal in the living room so that Joss could join me if she wanted, and I was relieved when she did, settling into the couch with her knees bent and her tablet balanced on her raised lap.

"I was thinking while you do that that I'd start getting a website set up for our comic," she drawled, flicking at her screen.

"What is a website?" I asked.

"Sorry, Earth term. Um, a nexus page. On Earth, there'd already be platforms for hosting a comic but since we're pioneering that technology I'm going to have to throw it together myself."

I turned to face her fully. "You know how to do that?"

Her brow furrowed. "Huh. Maybe not. I can't imagine you guys use HTML here. Maybe there's a site that does the backend stuff for you though…" she trailed off as her attention slid back to her tablet, her nimble little fingers typing furiously.

It didn't take long to scroll through the available GovCare emoregs and find someone who looked promising. A Dr. Vakkas had a background in family and couples counseling and had very high ratings from her patients. I made the appointment for the next day and filled out the required forms, feeling guilty. Poor Dr. Gish'ren, my usual emoreg, hadn't done anything wrong and it felt like I was being unfaithful to them by seeing this other doctor. But if there was even a chance it would help me keep Joss and, more importantly, keep her *happy*, then I had to try it.

Once it was done I went to my room to grab my own tablet to keep working on the art for our comic. I joined my mate on the couch, shoving my cold toes under her warm bottom and making her yelp.

"Jesus, why are your feet so cold?" she cried as I forced more of my feet under her sumptuous ass.

I shrugged. "They usually run cold. Should I move them?"

She snorted, shaking her head. "Nah. Now I'm worried they'll freeze right off if I don't warm them up." She shifted, pressing her warm flesh harder into my feet and making my cock twitch to life in my pants.

I'd never been so thankful for my poor circulation before in my life.

The next few hours were spent in companionable silence, each of us working on our parts of the comic. Every now and again I'd ask her if she needed something to drink, or she would ask if I wanted a snack, but most of the time we were quietly absorbed in our work.

Reality fell away as I sank deeper into the page I was working on. It was an emotional page, with the person cursed to always be in a different form—Jhalia—upset about how she was never in the form that she needed to be to fit in with her peers or loved ones, and how lonely she felt. I was absorbed in the character, agonizing over her expressions, her posing, to convey her hopelessness, her desperation. This was what I had been yearning to do with my art since I was young —telling a story, crafting drawings that supported a narrative while also telling their own. It was a heady rush, and I didn't notice the day slipping away into night, the living room growing dim around us, until Joss shook me and snapped me out of my trance.

"Babe, what do you want for dinner?"

I blinked, trying to come back into myself and focus on Joss's lovely face. "Something simple. Perhaps noodles? Or a salad?"

She nodded, cocking out a hip. "How about both?"

"Perfect." She leaned down to peck a kiss on my lips before strutting into the kitchen. I saved my work and joined her, setting the table and grabbing drinks from the dispenser. Once the synth had spat out our meal I helped her carry it to the table and settled down to eat. She gave me a wary look as she took her seat, clearly expecting me to snatch her again. I wanted to, but I contented myself with pulling my chair right up against hers so I could wind my tail around her leg and breathe in her sweet smell while we ate.

"I can't wait to show you what I've gotten for the web—for the nexus page. It looks surprisingly professional for how little I know what I'm doing."

"You have something done already?" I raised my eyebrows and tilted my head. "I could never have gotten something together so quickly. You truly are a marvel, my Joss."

She swatted at my arm. "Oh my god, stop. I found a tool that did most of the work for me." She paused, biting her lip. "But…it does still look really good. And I worked hard on it."

I beamed at her, kissing her flushed cheek. "I have no doubt."

She cleared her throat and speared another bite to eat. "What have you managed to get done so far today?" she asked me.

"I've been working on the comic. I think this page is just about done. I'll show you after you show me yours."

"Wow, that's awesome! We're up to what, almost five pages now, right?"

"This will be six." I paused in my eating. "When can we start posting the comic? Do we have to finish the whole thing first?"

Joss shook her head, making her pale gold hair sway. I noticed that her hair was changing color near the root, turning a deep brown that was almost black. "I don't know how it works exactly, but all the artists I followed posted a page at a time, on whatever schedule they could manage, so you had to keep coming back to read it all." Her brow furrowed as she thought. "I'm pretty sure they worked with a few pages already done and waiting to be posted so that if something came up they could keep to the schedule. So if we have six pages done we can probably start posting soon. We just have to figure out what speed you're comfortable working at. Plus I gotta finish the nexpage. Is that how you shorten nexus page?"

I chuckled, shrugging. "It is now. I like it, it's snappy."

She bumped her shoulder into my arm. "Goof."

"It is remarkable that you have managed to make this a reality so quickly," I added, wanting to praise her hard work. A part of me was trying to make up for how I had treated her last night, still. "Only a week and we're already about to begin putting our story out there for others to enjoy."

She smiled softly at me. "Yeah, we really did pull it together fast. We make a pretty good team."

"When I am not being an insufferable *vrakaashaad*, many things are possible," I groused, stuffing the last bite of my food into my mouth.

Joss took my arm, wrapping both of hers around it and pulling it close against her body while she leaned into me. She rested her chin on the shoulder of the arm she was holding, looking at me closely. It felt too intense, the way she was looking at me. "That's why I want you to try a new doctor, though. When we don't work as a team we hurt each other and ourselves, you know?" She got to her feet, releasing my arm so she could pull me into a half-hug. "You're not insufferable," she murmured into my hair, making my throat feel tight. "You just have to work on some things that are super fucking frustrating to have to deal with." I could hear the sly grin in her voice, that minx.

I squawked in fake indignation and stood up from my chair. I swept her up into my arms and carried her to my bedroom, her shrieking laughter filling my ears and making me tingle with delight.

"What are you doing?" she cried, clinging to me.

"Teaching you a lesson," I growled, tossing her onto my bed. "You have been very sassy with me today and I cannot have that."

Her eyes went wide, color flushing her neck. Her lips parted and I heard her breath speed up. "O-oh yeah?" she breathed, flustered and squeezing her legs together tight. I dropped down on my knees beside her and crawled over her, forcing her down onto her back beneath me. "What are you going to do to me?"

I lowered my head, licking a slow stripe up the side of her throat and making her whimper. "Whatever I have to to make you scream, my mate," I promised her, nipping at the delicate golden skin of her throat. She shuddered, her legs falling open between mine.

"I-I'm your mate?" she asked breathlessly as I started to run my hands over her plush body. "Does that mean what I think it means?"

I eased her shirt up, exposing her soft belly. I slid down so I could kiss the skin I was exposing. "What do you think it means?" I asked her between kisses.

Her breathing was picking up speed now that I was close to her sensitive breasts. "In the books I've read, back on Earth, it...oh god, Xoll!" Her back arched as I licked up the valley between the soft mounds. "It means...together forever. Per-perfect for each other."

I hummed, easing her shirt off of her body with her help. "I'd say that's accurate," I agreed as I eased the cups of her bra down so I could lap at the rosy brown peaks. She preferred having the entire breast squeezed and played with, rather than just the nipple, but I could never keep my mouth off the pebbled tips. While I licked and nibbled at one I kneaded the other gently, making her pant and squirm under me.

"You want me...forever?" she asked, the vulnerability in her voice making me pause. I lifted my head to look at her, alarmed to see the sheen of tears in her wide brown eyes. I released her and shot back up the bed to pull her close and cuddle her against my chest.

"Sweet Joss, what's wrong?" I asked, panic gripping me by the throat. "My hearts, why are you crying?"

She laughed tearfully, burrowing into me and clinging. "It's happy tears, Xoll," she promised. "I've never been that important to someone before. Not even to my mom."

My hearts clenched painfully in my chest. "And they are all fools for not knowing what a gift they had in you," I told her fiercely, combing my fingers through her fluffy pale gold hair. "I have been a fool for not appreciating you more. But you have been brave enough to give me another chance, so I will be brave enough to change."

She pulled back, looking at me with wonder and a hope so bright it burned, her eyes boring into mine. She surged up against me, our mouths crashing together, desperately trying to kiss with enough passion to encompass everything we were feeling. It was a rough, messy kiss, but it was exactly what I needed in that moment, my hands running all over her body, desperate to get closer to her, to consume her somehow so that we could melt together, become so deeply intertwined that I never had to be scared and alone ever again.

She pushed me onto my back and clambered on top of me, yanking her bra the rest of the way off and making quick work of the loose shorts she'd been wearing. That quickly, she was naked, her golden skin flushed and looking like an avatar of the Goddess Herself. She dove in to kiss me again, her smooth tongue lapping at my mouth and stealing my breath at the feel of her. Her small hands tore at the buttons of my own clothes, close to ripping the fine material, and for once in my life, I found that I couldn't care less if she shredded every stitch of clothing I owned, if it meant she did it with this hunger.

Our hands were trembling and feverish as we both worked to get me naked. I couldn't help but feel like something big was happening, something that would change things between us. Joss's mouth on mine was insistent, demanding, telling me I would give up control to her and I would love it, and I thought I would. I didn't *want* to be in control anymore, not when I so often made the wrong choices and felt the weight of it wearing me down. I wanted her to guide me, to let me shut off the loudness of my mind and just *feel*.

Joss broke our kiss, peppering the rest of my face with delicate little pecks that felt almost reverent. She traced the outside edge of my ear, pulling the pointed tip into her mouth to suck at it. I cried out at the overwhelming pleasure, my hips bucking off the mattress of their own will. "I want you to be my mate, Xollen," she murmured into my ear, her tongue flicking at my pierced earlobe. "I want to be that in all ways. I want you inside me." I stopped breathing. She couldn't mean that. Not when I'd been so awful to her just last night.

She pulled back to meet my eyes, waiting for my response. I swallowed. "But—but last night. And w-what if we don't get cleared for s-sexual relations?"

She cocked an eyebrow. "Shit, they regulate that, too?" Her mouth twisted as she thought. "I don't think I care. If you don't, then I still want to. I want to feel close to you."

I blinked up at her, thinking. Of course I wanted that—I'd been desperate enough to venture over to Quellor Station to hire a sex worker. But it was more than that—when I was clear-headed and calm I wanted everything that she had to offer. The part of me that wasn't too proud could admit that I liked the person she was encouraging me to be, that I wanted to keep figuring out who I was, under all of the anger and loneliness and bitterness that had been my constant companions my whole life.

I wanted her. All of her.

I nodded, looking up at her and hoping she could see it all in my eyes. I reached up and ran the backs of my fingers over her cheek. I cupped her face in both of my hands, stroking my thumbs over into the hollows of her cheeks, before tugging her back down into another kiss.

"Yes," I whispered when we broke the kiss. Then I was grabbing her around the waist and flipping her over so that she was back on her back. Her legs clamped shut in a reflex, and I growled, using my hands to pry them apart so that I could wedge myself in to get my watering mouth on her gorgeous cunt.

She gasped as I licked a bold stroke along the damp seam of her, squeaking in surprise when I buried my nose in the curls of her mound and breathed deep, taking the musky-sweet scent of her into my lungs.

I wanted to be able to bottle her up, so I could get my fill whenever I needed. She was utterly delicious, so ripe and juicy for me.

I curled one arm around her thigh, using the fingers of that hand to spread her lips wide, baring the flushed and swollen flesh beneath for me. I licked her hard from core to clit, making her gasp, before settling on her clit and laving it with firm circles and flicks. Soon the entire lower half of my face was wet with her essence, driving me wild with need for her. I needed to make her come more than I needed my next breath. I brought up my free hand now, using a finger to carefully circle her entrance, teasing her even as I began sucking at the firm bud at her apex. She shivered, her hips rocking up into my face. I stopped circling and sank a finger into her, groaning at how wet and hot and soft she was.

I pumped in and out of her slowly with my finger, relishing how she tightened and fluttered around me. If she was going to take my cock though she'd need to stretch more than just one finger's worth, so the next time I pushed in I added another. She arched up off the bed, but she didn't tell me to stop, so I picked up the relentless rhythm again, sucking her clit with every push in.

Joss was shuddering and whimpering with pleasure, her hands grabbing at my arms, my shoulders, my head, as if she needed something to grab onto or she'd fly away up into the stars. Her hands settled on the base of my horns, squeezing tight and sending a pulse of hot need straight to my cock, pressed tight into the bed and weeping precum. I didn't relent though, my rhythm picking up speed, picking up intensity, my fingers curling up into her g-spot, and soon she was coming prettily into my mouth, her hips grinding against me desperately, her cries filling the room like the most perfect music.

I didn't let up once she started peaking, carrying her through her orgasm, prolonging it, until she sagged back into the bed, her hands on my horns pushing my face away from her over-sensitive flesh. "Down, boy," she rasped. "Give me a minute."

I chuckled, kissing up and down her soft thighs, relishing how she jiggled and shivered against my lips. "Whatever you need, my mate," I told her, pressing a kiss to her furred mound.

"What if I need you inside of me?" she asked quietly, making my head snap up.

"I thought you needed a minute?"

She shook her head. "Not for that. For…penetration. My clit's too sensitive but I can take you. If you still want to."

Of course I did, but I was worried about hurting her. She was unmated, according to the th'rakkans and her own admission. And we would get in a lot of trouble if someone discovered we'd had sex like this before getting the results of our medical clearance. But my cock was aching and weeping, trapped between my hips and the mattress, and my mate was flushed and wanting in my arms.

I used a corner of the sheets to wipe my face of her juices, licking them from wherever I could reach with my tongue first, then surged up and covered her body with mine. She brought her knees up to open herself for me more, and I stroked my cock once, roughly, before notching the head at her slick and sucking opening.

I started sinking into her with a groan that she echoed, her hands wrapping around my back, just under my shoulder blades, and it took all of my self-control to avoid thrusting into her all at once. I didn't want to hurt her though, no matter that her blunt nails were scoring my flesh, her heels pressing into my buttocks as if urging me in further. My tail wrapped around one of her ankles, holding it in place.

"You can go faster," she panted, looking up at me with heavy-lidded eyes. "It doesn't hurt." I sank into her to the hilt with a groan that came from deep in my belly. She felt…incredible. Slippery and hot, her inner walls clenched tight around my aching length. I sank down onto my elbows, pressing our chests and bellies together, and it was the comfort of holding her with the added edge of our mutual pleasure. I lowered my face to hers to steal a kiss, needing to stay still before the sensations overwhelmed me and made me come before I'd made her come again, this time on my cock.

Once I'd gotten control of myself I rocked my hips, pulling back and then sinking back into her. This time, I felt my thatch tentacles latching onto her, the thin tendrils kissing and stroking over her clit. She gasped, her eyes rolling up into her head. "Fuck, I forgot about those guys."

I froze, despite everything in me urging me to keep pumping into her, bringing her to orgasm so I could follow her. "Is it bad? Too much?"

She shook her head, grinning wide. "Not. At. All." She punctuated her words with rolls of her hips, working herself on me and making me shudder. Goddess be blessed, but she was incredible.

I resumed moving, using Joss's movements to find my rhythm, encouraging my thatch to massage her clit, relishing the taste of her that contact was giving me. I claimed her mouth in another kiss, swallowing her cries of pleasure, drinking them down as greedily as I was drinking her slick with my thatch. Her breaths began to grow shallow and panting again, and I felt her begin to quiver on my cock, the rest of her tightening up beneath me in what I knew was the onset of her orgasm. I tried to hold onto my control, to finish pleasing her before

I took my own pleasure, but the clamp of her beautiful cunt on my cock was too much; I was tumbling over the edge, my movements going erratic, as I began emptying into her sweet body.

But then a curious thing happened: soon after first spurt of my seed, Joss's eyes snapped open wide, then rolled up, her entire body bowing off the bed. She grabbed a pillow and pressed it to her face, screaming so loudly I was concerned. I felt her clench even harder around me, the moisture from our mingled releases soaking our thighs and the bed. Each spurt had her screaming again, shuddering and twisting as if she was coming apart, and I started to get really worried. Was she allergic to me? Was I hurting her? I cursed myself a thousand different ways for not waiting, for not grabbing protection to use, for not being able to hold on.

"Joss, what's wrong? Where does it hurt?" I asked, panicking, slipping from her sheath and patting her down with my trembling hands.

"H…hurt?" she asked, shoving the pillow away from her face and looking up at me dreamily. "Nothing hurts, babe. I feel…" her head rolled back, arching her throat prettily. "I feel *amazing*."

This was good? How could her feeling good look so scary? "You're not dying?"

"I better not be," she breathed. "I think you have magic cum," she added with a giggle. "I feel like I just dropped a bunch of really good molly." After a pause, she added, "Wonder why it didn't happen when I sucked you off."

None of that made sense to me, and I told her so. "What is that? What are you saying right now? Can you understand me, Joss?"

She grinned at me, stretching languidly. "Yes, I told you I'm fine, you goof." She sighed, running her hands all over her body, petting herself. "Your cum is making me feel high in all the best ways. Like… wow. Like really good drugs."

I blinked down at her, relief starting to make me limp. "I don't need to take you to the hospital?"

She shook her head. "I don't think so. Does this happen when two billieuans have sex?"

"No. At least, not like this. There is a compound in our spend that relaxes our partner, opening her up so that the seed can travel up into her womb to hopefully take root—which it won't, I am on birth control like every other unmated male, don't worry my star."

She relaxed again, smiling and writhing on the bed. "Good. I don't think I'm ready for babies just yet." She bit her lip, gasping as another wave of pleasure rolled through her. "How soon can we do that again?" she asked dreamily.

My sated cock twitched to life against my leg, eager for her body. "I don't know. But hopefully soon."

Chapter Twenty-Eight
Better Work, Bitch

<u>XOLLEN</u>

I sat in front of my terminal and accepted Dr. Vakkas's vid comm request. Soon, my screen was filled by a black-and-white furred felican female smiling kindly.

"Xollen Me'Tirri Be'Faan?"

"Yes, that's me." I rattled off my ID number to confirm.

"Excellent! It's so good to meet you. My name is Dr. Vakkas, but you can call me Shiya if you'd like." I was a little shocked that she'd offered her first name to me. In all the years I'd been seeing Dr. Gish'ren they'd never done that. I didn't think I *could* call her by her first name, but it was nice that she had offered.

The next fifteen minutes were spent going over policies and legal protocols I'd already heard from Dr. Gish'ren but wasn't allowed to skip, leaving me with just a little more than half an hour to try and encapsulate the absolute mess that was…me.

"So, Xollen—now that that's out of the way, how about you tell me more about yourself and why it is you're seeing me today?"

My tail started thrashing behind me as my anxiety mounted. "Um. Well, I guess I'm here because my—Goddess, what do I even call her —my friend? Lover? Partner? Mate?—thinks it would be helpful."

Dr. Vakkas nodded, smiling. "I say you call her whatever feels most honest to you. Can I ask if this is a new relationship?"

I nodded. "We have known each other for almost two months but the romantic side of things is only about two weeks old."

"Oh wow, so it's *really* new!" The doctor smiled warmly, nodding her head. "Well congratulations, Xollen. I assume congratulations are in order?"

I couldn't stop the beaming smile that stretched across my face. "Yes, I'd say so. Joss is…she's just amazing. The smartest, funniest, and kindest person I've ever met." My heart soared, thinking of how I'd woken this morning to Joss making us a breakfast that she called "space chilaquiles" and how she'd melted in my arms when I'd come up behind her at the cooking slate.

"I'm so happy for you Xollen, she sounds absolutely wonderful. Can you tell me more about why Joss feels you'd benefit from additional emotional regulation?"

I pursed my lips, my tail winding around my lower leg. "It's because I keep pushing her away. And I pick fights with her. And she deserves better than that."

"Can I ask what these fights are about?" Dr. Vakkas asked gently.

"Well, she came into my life because I rescued her and four other females from slavery by buying them, which wiped out my entire savings. So she offered to stay with me to help me figure things out and get back on my feet. But then once she started doing what I had agreed to, what I was asking for, I don't know…I guess it just freaked me out. Reminded me of my parents and my former prospective mate Verilla."

Dr. Vakkas blinked, shocked. "Wow, that was a lot all at once. Could you walk me through that again more slowly? How exactly did you meet Joss?"

"It's kind of a funny story," I chuckled. "See, I'd gone to Quellor Station…for business, and while I was there I stumbled on th'rakk slavers selling Joss and four other females. I couldn't just leave them there so I bought all five of them and freed them. Joss decided she wanted to stay with me since she's human and her planet is in forbidden space—so, you know, she can't get back there legally—and she's been my roommate ever since."

I'd clearly only further shocked the poor female, but she shook it off and nodded, her expression going still and calm. "There's a lot to unpack there, so I think if it's alright with you we'll save that for another time and focus on your relationship with Joss. Unless you'd rather spend the rest of your time discussing something else?"

I shook my head. "No, that's what I need the most help with, so that works."

"Excellent!" her warm smile made another appearance. It was

very different from how me and Dr. Gish'ren talked, but I had to say I liked it. "So you were saying that you fight when she directs you on how to do things and live your life—can you say more about that? What do you think triggers you about it?"

I thought for a moment, frowning. "I think it's because I have a hard time with criticism. I was born with this defect," I said, waving a hand to indicate my face, "and I was never the kind of child my parents wanted. I was too…unfocused. Dreamy. Head among the satellites and all that. And then Verilla was even worse. We were together for almost a year before she called it off. And I really like Joss, so it messes me up inside when she tells me the things that she doesn't like about me."

"That sounds awful, Xollen. I'm so sorry you had to go through all that. I'd say it's only natural that you'd struggle with criticism. Can I ask you a question, though? When Joss criticizes you, does she *say* she doesn't like things about you?"

I thought about it, my tail twisting the fabric of my pants. Now that she mentioned it, *was* that what Joss had been saying? "I guess I don't know," I admitted. "It feels like that, but when I think back to what she actually says to me…" I thought back to our most recent argument. "Last time it happened because she was telling a story to my friends at a dinner party that I hadn't wanted her to tell, and she didn't pick up on the fact that I was upset. But when we talked about it later it was obvious that she just hadn't realized it was a story that I wanted private."

Dr. Vakkas nodded, smiling gently. "Can you remember what was going through your mind when you got upset?"

"It felt like she was trying to humiliate me. That if she cared about me it should have been obvious I was upset about what she was doing. But she made the excellent point that I hadn't said anything, and that she's from a whole other alien culture and wouldn't just *know* things like that."

The female felican nodded again. "That certainly makes sense. It's always tough figuring out how individuals fit together when they enter into a relationship, and you two have the added hurdle of culture shock." Dr. Vakkas looked thoughtful, smoothing her whiskers against her cheek. "Is better communication part of what you're trying to achieve here, Xollen?"

Nodding, I looked down at my lap. "Yes. Joss says that this is very important for us moving forward, and I agree."

"But?" the emoreg prodded gently.

I hesitated, swallowing. "But I can't shake the feeling that if she was truly my mate, then she would know me well enough to be able to avoid hurting me like that. And it doesn't feel right that I have to set aside my feelings just to keep her happy." The ugly words left me in a rush, and my face immediately flamed with embarrassment. I sounded so childish.

"I understand where you're coming from," she reassured me. "Your feelings are always valid, Xollen. Always. Can you speak more about how you're setting your feelings aside during these disagreements with Joss?

I squirmed. "It's like…I have to set aside the fact that I'm upset so that I don't make her upset."

"Does she not do the same for you?"

My mouth fell open and I gaped at the screen, stunned. I thought of all the times that Joss would look annoyed, or hurt, or mad, only to take a few breaths and look at me with kindness, instead. She would tell me what she was feeling, and then we would talk it through and move on.

Dr. Vakkas chuckled. "Did you just realize something?"

I nodded slowly. "She does. She said she was seeing an emoreg back on Earth, and when I think back on our arguments she *does* get upset, but she stops herself from shouting at me or saying harsh words. Like…like I do."

I was shocked to find tears prickling at the backs of my eyes. The lump in my throat was too big for me to speak around. Merciful goddess, how had Dr. Vakkas *done* that? "She wants me to see you so I can learn how to do those same things," I rasped, pressing my lips together to stop their wobbling.

"Unfortunately Xollen, we're almost out of time," Dr. Vakkas interjected softly. "So what I'd like you to do, the next time this happens with Joss, is to slow down and give yourself time to process. When you feel yourself getting upset and overwhelmed, take a second to pay attention to your breathing and make sure that it's nice and slow and even. And then I want you to ask yourself what Joss is saying, and why she might be saying it. And if you feel like she's out of line, try and let her know that, but stay calm as you can. How does that sound? Doable?"

All I could do was nod.

Dr. Vakkas wished me well for the upcoming week and signed off, leaving me gaping at my blank comm screen.

After several moments I leaned back in my chair and rubbed at the nape of my neck. Then I stood and opened my bedroom door. "Joss?" I called, searching for her.

"Yes, sweetness?" she called from the hygiene room.

"You were right."

"Duh!" the door slid open and Joss emerged, grinning and patting her damp hands dry on her hips. "What about this time?"

I strode towards her, getting on my knees once I'd reached her and pressing my face into her soft stomach, just under her breasts. I wrapped my arms around her tight enough that her breath left her lungs with a surprised huff. "Everything," I said into the fabric of her shirt. "Dr. Gish'ren isn't good for me. I've been so unfair to you." I pulled back enough to be able to look up into her adorably shocked face. "I'm so sorry for how I've been treating you. I think I've just been getting some wires crossed and—and you didn't deserve any of it."

"So it was a good session, then," she murmured, her arms coming up to wrap around my shoulders. "Thank you for apologizing, I appreciate it. Do you…want to talk about it?"

I shook my head, returning my face to Joss's soft warmth. "I think I'd rather hold you," I told her.

Her arms tightened around me, making me feel warm and fluttery. "How can I say no to that? Why don't we go to your bed then? So you can get up off the floor."

"Not letting go," I informed her, tightening my grip around her middle. "You'll have to drag me."

Joss laughed, squeezing me again, as I pulled away and got to my feet. I took her hands and then leaned down to kiss her, pouring all of the softness, the tenderness, the *joy* I felt for her into it. I brought my hands up to cup her face, holding her right where I needed her.

She was flushed and dazed when I pulled away, a slow smile tugging at her reddened mouth. I took her hand and led her back to my bedroom so I could cuddle her in comfort.

Chapter Twenty-Nine
The Truth Never Lies

<u>JOSS</u>

To my utter relief, Xollen took to therapy with his new doctor like a man possessed. Over the next several weeks he got so much better at talking things out with me, with taking time for himself when he was feeling overwhelmed so we could discuss things calmly. It wasn't easy for either of us—his willingness to be so open was making me aware of how much work I still needed to do on myself—but once we were past the uncomfortable moments of having to talk to each other about the things we were too used to keeping all to ourselves, we agreed that we both felt better.

Which was very fortunate, because our revolutionary "new" form of storytelling was taking off like you wouldn't believe.

The first week was pretty slow. Me and Xoll had decided to try doing two updates a week and see how that felt. We got maybe a dozen views on the first page, then a couple dozen on the second, but by the third update we were seeing over a hundred, and then someone big must have talked it up because by the end of the second week we had over a thousand people visiting our nexpage and reading our little comic even though our brainchild was only four pages long.

Now, a month and a half in, we were getting *millions* of visits to our nexpage a day, news outlets had started reaching out asking for interviews, media companies were looking to secure rights and bankroll exclusive projects, and we were making a *lot* of money.

I'd set up some revenue streams along with designing the nexpage. There was ad revenue, just like back on Earth, but the more lucrative avenue had wound up being the commissions and digital tip jar. Even though we were barely out of the prologue, something about our little story was really resonating with people, and it was making them unexpectedly generous. And people loved Xollen's art (which made a lot of sense, my male was seriously talented) and went crazy for the quick sketches we were letting people request as commissions. We got messages from people all the time showing us how they'd printed their commission out and framed it on their wall, or turned it into their terminal's background image, and a couple of people even turned it into a shirt (a weirdly Earth-like phenomenon, I told Xollen).

It was a crazy, beautiful time, and I should have known that the other shoe was going to drop. The universe just couldn't let me have it that good: I was going to get too powerful if it let me have fame, fortune, a sensitive guy with magic drug cum and a package that made me see stars every time we fucked, *and* peace and quiet—something had to give.

It was going to be another chill day, Xollen lounging on one end of the couch with his tablet, drawing for our comic—which we'd named "The Truth Never Lies"—while I tapped away at my novel on the other end. I'd always wanted to write the monster romances I'd loved so much back on Earth, and now that I was living one and didn't have to work thirty-nine hours a week to stay afloat on top of going to school, there was no better time to take the plunge. Which was probably another reason why the universe felt the need to start throwing wrenches.

Xollen's comm beeped with an incoming call, and since the only person who bothered to call him was Derris, he flicked accept without even glancing at the interface. "What do you want?" he drawled, his eyes still locked onto his tablet with an adorable intensity that made me real quivery in the pussy.

"Is that any way to address your father?" a stern, slightly nasally male droned, and Xollen yelped, dropping his tablet and sitting up like he'd been shocked.

"Father?" he asked, jumping to his feet and pacing across *la sala*, his tail wound so tight around his thigh he was limping a little. "I'm just —um, I'm surprised to hear from you, is all. I thought you and mother —well. The last I'd heard you didn't want to see me."

"We said we didn't want to watch you throw your life away, but that if you ever managed to get yourself sorted we'd be happy to have you back, dearest," a female with a husky voice said, sounding just like every WASP-ish mom on TV I'd ever seen. I'd let my tablet slip from my fingers, my mouth hanging open in shock at the blatant manipulation they were throwing at my poor sweet Xollen.

"Oh. I must have misinterpreted what you meant, then," he mumbled, and I widened my eyes at him, trying to convey that he was falling for their gaslighting. He cleared his throat, grinning sheepishly at me. "Um—so what's going on? Why are you calling me now? I still haven't gone back into the business program at Sett U." I noticed his hands starting to tremble, so I got up off the couch and put my arms around his waist from behind, trying to give him all the courage and support I could.

"We've heard about the success of your little art project, son," his father said. "We've heard Se'Gittrak and Se'Ushaar have made offers and we said to ourselves, 'well now, I wonder if everything's alright with our Xollen, that he wouldn't come to his own parents for distribution and adaptations'." My arms tightened around his waist. How fucking *dare they*?!

Xollen sucked in a shaky breath, his free hand clamped tight on my forearm. "I didn't think you wanted to hear from me for this, my *art project*." I was proud of how much venom he'd managed to stuff into those words. Most of Billieu was going crazy for "The Truth Never Lies" and his asshole parents were calling it a *little art project*. I wanted to laugh, and then find them and choke them out. I patted Xollen's chest, letting him know I liked that. He grinned at me over his shoulder, so beautiful my heart clenched.

"Of course we want to see you, sweetie!" his mother crooned, sounding fake as hell. "We'd treat you well, of course. It's only right that our own son get the best service that we can offer. Sixty percent of merchandising, creative control, forty percent of revenue from adaptation streams…" she trailed off, sounding coy, like she was just so fucking confident she had him right where she wanted him.

Xollen twisted and yanked me around to his front, pulling me against his long shivering body and holding me tight. I could see the panic swirling in his violet eyes, and I knew where it was coming from, too. That was the best deal we'd heard so far, by a lot, and would make us absolutely filthy stinking rich. We'd be able to live like kings, and while I knew Xollen didn't mind our modest new life in the public dorms, he wasn't entirely satisfied either. I was constantly catching him looking at fashion blogs and designer nexpages like other men looked at porn. And a lot of the time when we were lying in bed, talking about how we were doing, he'd bring up some of the pieces he'd had to sell that he missed, how he wished we had enough room to invite Derr and Gesea over. He missed some of the creature comforts he'd gone his whole life being able to indulge in, and income like that would let him get it back.

"Tell you what, how about you come over for dinner tonight and we can talk it out some more? It's not good business to do these sorts of things over the phone."

Xollen was definitely panicking now, so I reached up and cupped his face in my hands, tilting his head down to look at me so I could encourage him to do his breathing.

"A-alright," he said, and I kept my face carefully neutral. I wasn't crazy about having dinner with them, but if Xollen wanted to do this then I'd be right by his side, supporting him as best I could.

"Perfect!" his mother cried, raising my hackles. "We'll see you eighteen hundred, then?"

"Sure."

"See you then, son," his father added blandly, and then the connection was cut.

"I regret all of that," Xollen moaned, collapsing against me dramatically. I chuckled, holding him and running my hand up and down his back.

"You did great, baby. It's a process." I bit my lip. "Do you think you'll take their offer?"

He sighed, straightening up. "I don't know. It's such a good offer, but knowing my parents it's going to come with a lot of strings attached. It might even be a trap. It's definitely not coming from a place of love. They didn't care at all about me, it was all about them and how they could weasel their way into this to make money."

I squeezed him. "Yeah, that's how it sounded to me, too. I'm so proud of you for seeing that and for standing up for yourself."

He snorted, flushing. "I didn't stand up for dick, as you would say." I laughed. I'd been teaching him some of my weird English slang. "I practically rolled right over."

I swatted his ass, making him jump and grin at me with more than a little heat. "Nonsense, you told them you'd give them a chance to say their piece, but you're making them work for it just like anyone else. The old Xollen would have just agreed outright. And you're paying attention to what they're doing, seeing through their games, so you can approach this with a clearer head. Dr. Vakkas is going to agree with me, you just see."

He smiled down at me softly, one of his hands sliding up to cup the back of my head. "What a strong and fiery mate I have," he murmured before dipping to capture my lips in a sweet but searing kiss. I was tempted to take him back to his room and ride him like my life depended on it, but there wasn't enough time before we'd have to start getting ready for dinner. "I love you with all my hearts," he added when he broke the kiss.

"I love you too, Xollen," I told him, pressing my face into his warm chest. "Just say the word and I'll fight both of your parents. I'm a Chicago girl, they'll never know what hit 'em."

He laughed, holding me close, but he didn't say no.

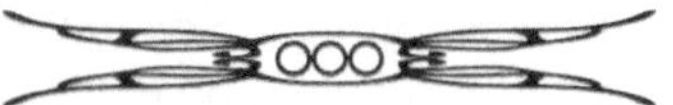

It was one thing to know that Xollen came from money, and another thing entirely to see it. I'd thought his old place was bougie and ridiculous, but now that I was seeing his parents' place it looked positively squalid in comparison.

His parents were the kind of rich that wanted everyone to know about it and feel bad for their lack. There was no reason for two people to have a mansion as big as an Earth city block, with an attached garage as big as a large house unto itself stuffed full of hovers that looked like they'd never seen a drop of the outdoors. Most of the rooms had to be empty and unused; there was no way so few people were able to fill all of them with something meaningful.

Xollen was clutching my hand tight, his large palm clammy and his fingers almost too tight on my hand, but I wasn't going to let go of him. I could deal with a little bit of cold sweat if it meant I could help him keep his cool. We'd spent a lot of the time in between when we'd gotten the call and now talking things out, coming up with a loose plan and working out our anxieties, and now we just had to see it all through.

The idea was to hear them out and then shut them down no matter what. The whole thing felt manipulative and shallow, and I could practically hear the alien fish man yelling that it was a trap. If it were me in charge of this I'd've just sent them a comm telling them no, but these were Xollen's parents, so I was letting him take point, and he wanted to see them and give them a chance. I understood where he was coming from, and when I'd been in this position with my mom, or with friends, lord knows I'd done the same thing. When you love someone and want them to love you back, you'll let them do some pretty shitty things to you just in case *this* was the chance that they took and didn't take for granted.

But that didn't mean I'd let Xollen just welcome them back with open arms. I wanted to protect him, to keep his beautiful, delicate hearts safe, and I *knew*, on no uncertain terms, that his parents weren't going to take care of him like he needed.

When we pulled up to the front entrance, a valet met us to take our rented hover and park it for us. Then we were met by an honest-to-god butler, who announced us, just like in the regency shows I liked back on Earth, and then led us into the formal dining room—implying there was more than one dining room, I realized—to meet his parents and begin the meal.

Xollen looked more like his mother than his father. He had her eyes, her full lips, her complexion, but all of Xollen's sweetness and humor were missing from her features. She oozed cool, calm, collected, and powerful, and I knew she'd be a powerful enemy if she decided I was worth her time to take down. Her facial cleft wasn't as deep as her husband's, and she was lithe and almost as tall as her husband and son. His father was surprisingly dad-like, wearing khaki slacks, a white button-up that made his dusky blue complexion pop, and a sweater vest that showed off his hint of a paunch. Streaks of white threaded through long navy hair just like Xollen's, and lime green eyes swirled lazily with something that felt a lot like bored disdain. Both of his parents were crusted in jewelry, chains and charms dangling from their horns, woven through their intricate hairstyles, and twinkling from their throats, ears, and fingers. His mother even had cuffs on her tail.

"Darling, how *are* you?" his mother greeted him, standing and giving him a dispassionate kiss on the cheek. His father also stood, saying nothing, and only offering his son a respectful bow.

"Mother. Father. It's…good to see you again." His fingers tightened around my hand.

His parents finally noticed me, drawing back in shock and no little bit of disgust.

"What…is this?" his mother asked, not even trying to hide the curl of her lip.

"This is a person, and my name is Joss," I said sweetly, baring my teeth in an expression that I knew wasn't s smile. "I'm Xollen's mate and business partner." That had been another thing we'd decided to be clear on: I had wanted them to know that was all-in with Xollen, in every way.

"Xollen, you can't be serious," another female voice said from a distant corner of the room, the sound smoky and smooth. Beside me, Xollen froze, looking shocked, and my stomach sank and clenched with trepidation. Out of the corner of my eye, I saw someone slink closer, all emerald skin and a silky crimson dress. She was gorgeous, this woman who disapproved of me so thoroughly, even with the alien facial cleft making her look strange to me, and I immediately felt dumpy and plain and unworthy. Her bright silver eyes tracked over me slowly, taking in my every flaw and smirking, because she'd clearly come to the conclusion that I was worthless.

"Verilla," Xollen ground out, his voice tight and higher than it had been, "what brings you here?" Icy dread slithered down my spine. Verilla. Xollen's ex. And she was just as glamorous and sexy as I'd imagined.

"I ran into your parents at the health club this morning and they invited me. It's *so* good to see you again, Xoll. I've missed you."

I bristled at that, and to my relief so did Xollen. He dropped my hand to put that arm around my shoulders and pull me close against his side. His tail was wrapped tight around his leg already, but the tip of it flicked back and forth, like an irritated cat's. "It's good to see you, too," he said, then squeezed me and pressed a kiss to my temple. "As I said, this is my mate, Joss. She's also the creative force behind our success." His eyes were soft and full of pride as he looked down at me. He'd barely looked at Verilla, and that did make me feel a little better.

I inclined my head in the smallest bow I could manage while still technically being polite. "Verilla, so nice to meet you. I've heard a lot about you." I batted my eyelashes, making it as clear as I could that everything I'd heard had been bad. Which it had been: by all accounts she'd been abusive, using Xollen for everything she could and then dumping him like he was trash.

"Charmed," she said, her smoky voice dry and scathing.

Off to the side, a staff member rang a series of bells suspended from a long horizontal pole.

"Ah, that's dinner ready, then," Xollen's father announced, and I realized that neither of his parents had bothered to actually greet me or introduce themselves.

"You know, I didn't catch your names," I called over to his parents, making Xollen frown at my side.

"I am Tirri," his mother said, looking annoyed, "and this is my mate Faan." She hesitated, then added a slight bow of her head and a "nice to meet you." Jesus, these people.

We all settled into our seats at the table, staff scurrying around behind us with dishes, serving us the first course—some sort of soup—and then bowing and disappearing. It was so fucking creepy. Did Xollen's parents tell them to do that?

"So, Joss. Where are you from? How did you two meet?" Tirri asked, taking a delicate sip of her soup. I squirmed, my mind sticking on how people had often meant that question back home—"where are you from". But here on Billieu, no one would have known what Puerto Rico was, or why it would mean anything that some of someone's ancestors were from there instead of somewhere in Europe. No one cared that my skin produced a little more melanin, or that the Puerto Rican half of my family hadn't taught me any Spanish so that I didn't have an accent for all of the *gringos* to look down on. No one here would think I was too Latina for the white folks and too white for the Latinos.

"I'm from a planet called Earth, in restricted space. I'd been taken by th'rak slavers but luckily I was freed before they could do anything to me." Me and Xoll had decided that it was best to leave out the fact that Xollen had had a hand in my rescue, to avoid embarrassing him again. "Then I happened to meet Xollen and he offered to help me get on my feet, and the rest is history."

Tirri arched a brow delicately, looking incredulous. "Really? Xollen offered to help you, just like that?" Her purple eyes locked on her son's face in disbelief.

Xollen stiffened in his seat beside me. "Yes, mother," he ground out, and I slipped my hand onto his thigh, rubbing it soothingly. He relaxed, though I heard his teeth creak together in his mouth. "I think I could tell right away that she was special, and it was the best way I could think of to keep in contact with her." He grinned down at me. I'd actually propositioned him, of course, but he'd told me that he'd wanted to beg me to stay, and that he'd been too nervous to say anything, so it wasn't really a lie. Thank god I was such a horn dog.

"How nice," Verilla drawled, spearing us with a smile that didn't meet her silver eyes. "Xollen always was *so* sweet and romantic. He liked to draw me, said I was more lovely than any model he could have hired. Has he drawn you, yet?"

My face flamed hot, anger bubbling in my belly. "Yes, lots of times," I said through clenched teeth. I knew she was trying to get under my skin, and I hated that she was so fucking good at it.

Xollen put his hand on top of mine, still resting on his thigh but gripping it tight now. I unclenched my fingers and I let him hold my hand.

Faan leaned forward and studied us both, his soup bowl already empty. "So how do you two go about throwing together your little drawings, hm? Do you also like to draw, Joss?"

My god, I was going to have a rage stroke from all the patronizing.

"No, I write the outlines and the dialogue. Xollen does all the art." I looked up at his pretty face, smiling brightly. "He's so talented. He does all of that himself, and on a time crunch, too." Xollen returned my smile and squeezed my hand under the table. I wanted to kiss him, to show them all that he was mine and I was his, but even with a permit, PDA was frowned upon on Billieu.

"How nice," Tirri said blandly. The staff came back in and took our dishes away, a second set of people sweeping in with the next course: salad. I wished I wasn't so stressed out so I could appreciate all of this tasty food. Xollen's parents were clearly assholes, but damn was the food good. "And whose idea was it to post it on the nexus? That was a clever way to distribute." Tirri looked to her son, clearly expecting him to say he'd done it.

"That was me," I told her, lifting my chin. "It's how we do stuff like that on Earth, and I have a little experience with throwing together websites—that's what we call nexpages—so it wasn't too hard. It came out looking good, didn't it?"

"Yes, you could hardly tell it was the work of an amateur," Verilla interjected, smiling sweetly. "Very…easy to use."

I smiled back, anger making the crisp fruits and veggies in the salad taste sour.

"Have you registered your work anywhere?" Faan asked, shooting Verilla a sharp glance that set alarm bells off in my head. Were Verilla and his parents…working together, somehow? Why? To what end? Maybe he was just admonishing her for being rude.

Xollen shook his head, and I realized that that may have been a huge misstep on our part. I hadn't even looked into how copyright and intellectual property ownership worked here on Billieu; I'd just assumed that because we were publishing it it would belong to us. My heart sank, and I clutched at Xollen tighter under the table.

"Then it's a good thing we're all here talking now," Tirri said, spearing the last of her salad onto her utensil. "Me and your father can easily handle that for you. We can even have our security team comb the nexus for unauthorized usages and take legal action against them to set a precedent."

Xollen swallowed his mouthful of food. "You'd…you'd do that?"

"Of course, darling. You're my *son*. Do you really think I wouldn't take care of you?"

Xollen swallowed again, and I could practically hear how hard he was wishing that his mother meant that. I didn't believe her for a second, but I put aside my doubts and at least pretend I was falling for it. "That's so generous, Tirri. Thank you."

"We had our legal team draw up a contract before we left the office earlier," Faan slid in. "You can both sign it now and we'll get the process started."

The staff filtered back in, still perfectly silent and inconspicuous, replacing the salad with what I hoped was the main course.

"Well, we're not sure if we want to sign just yet," Xollen hedged, prodding at his dinner with his utensil. "We'd like to read through the contracts first." I squeezed his hand tight, proud of him for standing his ground. This was going to be where it started getting tough for him, I suspected, so I tried to pour all the love and strength into him that I could through our clasped hands.

"You don't trust us?" his mother asked, looking shocked and hurt. *Here we go,* I thought, my stomach gone too sour to keep eating. "We just want to take care of you, darling."

"I-it's not that. Mom—"

"Well, it feels like that's what it is. You know us. You know how we do business. I just don't see what there is to hesitate about, dear." I gritted my teeth together against the urge to start screaming at her.

"Well, you always told me to make sure I read over anything before I sign it, and this is important to us—"

"Yes, with *strangers*. You never know when someone will try to undercut you. But this is completely different."

"We've already given you the numbers," Faan added, nodding. "There's no surprises in there."

"Oh. Um. Well—" Xollen looked over at me, panic and uncertainty swirling in his eyes.

"I'm sure it's totally fine," I slid in, hoping I wasn't overstepping. "We just want to make doubly sure. Plus it's a good idea to get a feel for how things like that are supposed to look, so we can be smart about it in the future," I lied, impressed by my own smoothness. Like hell, this contract was on the up and up. I could practically smell the bullshit.

The smile Tirri shot me was stiff, more of a predatory baring of teeth than anything. Faan didn't even bother hiding the scowl. My sirens were going off at full blast. There was something super shady about this contract if they didn't want us reading over it beforehand.

"I read it over it while I was here waiting for you," Verilla slipped in, shooting a look at Tirri I couldn't read. "It looked airtight to me. Better than a lot of the contracts I get for the holos I star in." Okay, something was definitely fucky with that contract.

"We'll take a look at it after dinner, then," I said firmly, Xollen's tail winding around my calf even as his hand continued to squeeze mine.

"I'm sure it'll be fine," he added weakly, smiling at his parents. "Better than fine."

Chapter Thirty
It Was Not Fine

<u>XOLLEN</u>

It was not fine. I knew my parents, and I knew what the looks on their faces meant. Still more suspicious was Verilla's participation in whatever was happening here. But even so, without Joss here I would have caved to their pressure hours ago. But she *was* here, a solid and soothing presence at my side, holding me firm and giving me courage. It was easier to remember the things Dr. Vakkas had been telling me, had been helping me to see in the weeks that I'd been working with her, with Joss at my side.

The rest of dinner passed in tense silence, the only chatter Verilla's inane recounting of the social functions she'd been visiting lately. Seeing her again had been a shock, but I wanted to laugh at how silly I'd been, to think she was mature and interesting. How blind I'd been.

In the end, my parents didn't try to take us back to their home office to look at the contracts, and that told me everything I needed to know about what was in that contract. But even though I knew it wouldn't be good, I found that I needed to see it, to be faced with what my parents really thought of me, of this work that I was passionate about and managing to make a living off of.

"I'm ready to see that contract now," I told my mother as they tried to herd us into the sitting room for dessert and tea. "I'm too full for dessert anyway."

My father scowled at me, his deep facial cleft pulling at his lips and making it more severe. "Of course, dear," my mother trilled, her own smile tight and strained.

They led me out of the sitting room, and I looked around for Joss, panic squeezing my throat when I realized she wasn't there.

"Where's Jo—"

"In the hygiene room, dearest," my mother interjected. Verilla can bring her to us when she's done, can't you, Ver?"

"Oh, of course, Tirri. I'll bring her as soon as she gets back."

My parents nodded, as if it was decided, and since Joss wasn't there to be my backbone I nodded too, following them out without a fight.

Their office was painfully familiar, the place I'd always been most likely to find them when I was little, a room that made me feel lonely and small even when we'd all been in there together. My father strode over to his desk and picked up the charcoal-colored folder there, emblazoned with the firm's insignia, and I took it from him before settling into a chair to read.

Thanks to my business classes, I wasn't totally lost reading it, but I didn't entirely understand it, either. The first few pages seemed to be exactly what they had already outlined, as far as I could tell, and I was starting to feel sheepish, like I'd upset my parents and suspected them of foul play for nothing, but on the last two pages, I figured out what they'd been so cagey about.

On the second-to-last page, there was a section called "Rates and Figures in Perpetuity", where the percentages they'd quoted us earlier swung in a very different direction. It seemed to be saying that after a year the cut my parents would get, as the managing agents, would change, becoming higher than mine and Joss's portions of the revenue, and at that point they'd retain sole ownership of merchandising.

My parents were trying to screw me over. That last little part of me that had thought I could trust them shriveled with a sharp ache that took my breath away. To my eternal embarrassment, my eyes burned with the urge to shed tears. I was devastated, I was disappointed, but I was also furious. Had they ever actually loved me? Or had I always been a tool to them, rather than a person?

"You know how bad this is," I croaked, keeping my eyes locked on the paper in my hands. "This is—this is *insulting*. How could you?"

"What are you talking about, Xollen?" my father stepped in, crossing his arms over his chest and tucking his chin in. "It's a standard contract for representation, which you'd know if you'd bothered to give a *vrakaash* about your education."

I swallowed, forcing myself to sit up straight and stay calm, doing the breathing techniques I'd learned from Dr. Vakkas and practiced with Joss. "You know it's not, please just be honest with me. Both of you. This is—it's exploitive. After a year you control everything and me and Joss stop making money. But what I still don't understand is what Verilla has to do with it. Why have you roped her into this?"

"We've done no such thing," my father growled, while my mother did her best to look hurt.

"Xollen, how could you accuse us of something so ugly?" she cried, clutching at my father's arm. "After everything we've done for you, every opportunity we've handed to you on a platinum tray—" she broke off with a sob that might have been genuine, and I went hot and cold as I realized my parents were never going to see how they hurt me.

My mother and father weren't acting, not really—Verilla was the actor, not them. They genuinely believed the things they were telling me, and it didn't matter how hard I tried to show them why I was hurting; they'd always spin it so that I was wrong and they were right.

I sighed, clenching my fist around the contract so that it crumpled in my fist. "I'm going to leave now. If you genuinely can't understand why then that's on you, because I'm going to make it as clear as I can: you are obviously trying to use me. This contract confirms that you don't have my best interests at heart, and I think that unless you make significant changes I can't have a relationship with you. With either of you." I was so proud of myself at that moment, for how steady my voice was, how straight I was able to keep my shoulders, even if I couldn't quite stop the tears from falling. "I love you both but I can't have people in my life who would abuse my trust like this." I tossed the crumpled contract to the floor, then turned on my heel and walked out.

My father bellowed my name, ordering me to stop and come back and apologize for being disrespectful, while my mother started sobbing, but I didn't stop, didn't even let myself pause. I went in search of Joss, needing her sweet scent, her warm smile. I needed her to hold me and tell me I'd done the right thing, even though my heart was breaking into a million pieces.

But I couldn't find Joss. Instead, I found Verilla, lounging in the sitting room and sipping her tea. "How'd the meeting go?" she purred, setting the cup down on its saucer.

"Where's my mate?" I asked, too emotionally wrung out to deal with her right now. "Where's Joss?"

Verilla shrugged. "She left," she said, standing and slinking up to me. "Said she'd had enough." When Verilla reached me she trailed a perfectly manicured finger down the center of my chest, batting her eyes up at me. I grabbed her wrist and took a step back, putting more distance between us.

"What did you do?" I snapped at her.

"Nothing! She said she was done pretending she liked you and went off on her own." She yanked her hand back and placed it on her hip. "You know, I meant what I said. I really do miss you, Xoll. We had some pretty good times together and I regret not forcing myself to stick it out. I'd say it's obvious that we're meant to be together, you and I. We make such a lovely couple, don't we?"

I didn't even bother answering her; I just turned and left, leaving her to squawk in outrage.

I jogged through the familiar halls of my parents' house until I was outside and able to gulp in fresh air. It felt deliciously cool against my overhot face. I tried comming Joss, but it went straight to her mail; her comm was either off or she was already in a call. I kept walking, stomping over to the rented hover and sliding into the driver's seat. I'd just have to keep trying until I got through. Dread pooled low in my gut, making it clench, but I tried my best to ignore it and keep my dinner down.

Chapter Thirty-One
Uraka Like a Hurricane

<u>JOSS</u>

I used the hygiene room quickly so I could get back to Xollen and support him in this viper's nest. But when I slipped out only Verilla was waiting for me, her hip cocked and her long, slim arms crossed over her chest.

"Joss," she said, her voice distant and cold. "A word?"

I knew it was a bad idea, that Verilla was nothing but bad news wrapped up in an intimidatingly pretty package, but I nodded, crossing my own arms defensively. "Alright," I allowed, wary.

She smirked at me, slinking closer. "You seem like a nice enough female," she began, looking me up and down like she didn't believe that at all. "But do you really think you're worthy of being Xollen Me'Tirri Be'Faan's mate? Do you have any idea what power and influence his family carries? What sorts of expectations are set for a male of that caliber?"

"I have a pretty good idea," I hissed through clenched teeth. "He's told me a lot about it."

She snorted, rolling her striking silver eyes. "Clearly he's done a poor job of it if you're still all too happy to soil his name and reputation by agreeing to a mating." She stepped closer, looming over me. "You're clearly cut from a different and much more....budget-friendly cloth. You can't seriously mean to drag him down with you."

It hurt. It hurt to hear that, because a very loud part of myself had been saying exactly that for weeks now: that I couldn't land a hottie like Xollen. He was out of my league like crazy and I was doing him harm by letting him be with me. But at the end of the day, he was choosing me as much as I was choosing him. It was a deep and mutual thing that we were building, and I wasn't going to let Verilla make me forget that.

"You had your chance, Verilla," I ground out, keeping my shoulders back and my chin high. "He wants me. I want him. We care about each other. It's as simple as that, and I don't care what you and his parents are up to here, we're not going to fall for it."

Her silver eyes hardened to steel. Like a switch being flipped, all pretenses of civility and calm evaporated. "Listen here, you fat stupid bitch," she hissed, her hands curling into fists at her sides. "I put in *months* of time with that hideous loser, and I am not going to let you confuse him about what he really wants." She grabbed my arm in a vise grip. I tried yanking free, but her hold was surprisingly strong. "Xollen is going to sign that deal, I'm going to star in those holos and get my big break, and you are going to fucking *disappear*, do you hear me? How much do you want, hmm? 50,000 should be plenty of credits to suck all that fat off your body and fix that frizzy mess growing from your head."

I blinked, shocked at just how quickly she'd gotten this nasty. I hated that she'd been able to zero in on two of my biggest insecurities. How often had I wished for the money to get plastic surgery, so I could finally look acceptable to the rest of the world? How often had I dreamed of chopping off all the bleach-damaged hair, to start over fresh and get back to my beautiful natural hair?

Verilla was a seasoned bully.

"You can take your credits and shove them up your ass, Verilla," I shot back, taking a step away from her to reclaim my personal space but keeping my posture sure and confident so she didn't think I was backing down. "Xollen's a goddamn adult and makes his own decisions, now. And he chooses me."

Her jaw ticked with how hard she was clenching it, and then she was grabbing me, spinning me around and marching me out towards the front door. I kicked and struggled, trying to use what Uraka had taught me in that cell all those weeks ago, but she was much stronger than me and I was out of practice, so in the end, she managed to drag me out the door and put me in a hover, locking me in and sending me to coordinates I didn't recognize. I tried to stop the car from taking off, desperate to get out and beat Verilla's ass then go and rescue Xollen from what was clearly an attempt to take advantage of him, but none of the commands I tried worked. That asshole had managed to lock me out of the automated systems somehow.

I screamed and fumed, slamming myself against the door hard enough to make the cab sway and rock, but I was well and truly trapped, helpless but to let the hover take me where she'd sent it. I screamed, I cried, and then I took a deep breath and started making calls.

"Joss, my best friend, how are you?" Derris responded cheerily, Gesea just behind him and waving her own greeting.

"Not great, guys," I sighed, giving them a hurried explanation of what was happening. "Do you know how to get me out of here? I could also use your help getting Xollen away from his parents. He put his comm on silent for the dinner and I don't think it's back on yet. I tried calling him before you and it just rang and rang."

Derris and Gesea's faces were twin masks of fury. "We're leaving now," Gesea snarled, spinning on her heel to start grabbing her things. She was muttering furiously, too quiet for me to hear, though.

"You heard the boss," Derris chuckled, standing and looking much more serious. "I can't help you with the hover, unfortunately. But we will go to his parent's house to try and stop whatever awful thing they are doing. May the Goddess grace us all."

I agreed, then hung up, dialing Xollen's number a few more times and still not getting through. I tried Uraka next.

"Joss, my tiny warrior! It has been too long since I have heard from you!" Her three eyes narrowed, lips pulling into a scowl. "Has that cursed idiot harmed you? How shall I kill him? I have thought it would be fun to rip his spine out while he still lives."

"Jesus, Uraka!" I blanched, my gorge rising. "Don't you dare, I love that idiot!" I wouldn't necessarily grieve it if that had happened to Verilla, though. In fact... "I am in trouble though. Xollen's ex has me trapped in a hover, going someplace. I don't know where and I'm locked out of the controls somehow. Do you know what I can do?"

Fury hardened her already stern features. "My love!" she barked, "please ready our hover. We are needed!"

From "off-screen" I heard a yelp, and then Djelani was skidding around a corner, her tawny fur puffed like a scared cat's. "What is it, what's wrong?" She spotted me, her delicate feline features settling into a frown. "Joss? What's happening?"

"No time to explain, sweet flower!" Uraka shouted, surging to her feet. "Joss, ping your location and send it to me. Then repeat this every thirty seconds so we can plot your trajectory. Worry not, little Joss." Fire blazed in her golden eyes, Djelani still looking confused in the background, though she was at least de-poofing. "You have the might of an yvrenii vanguard captain behind you."

"Uraka, what in the name of creation is happening—" Djelani protested, but the comm cut out before I could hear more. I did as Uraka asked, wondering what on earth that crazy orc was up to now, then settled in to wait. I kept trying Xollen's comm, tried to pull up a nexpage on how to get myself out of this damn hover, but nothing worked. According to what I was reading, Verilla shouldn't have even been able to lock me out like this, meaning the car might be employing illegal tech. I had a feeling I *really* didn't want to see where this hover was taking me.

It was perhaps ten or fifteen minutes later when I realized another hover had pulled up alongside mine. I looked over, and there was Djelani's familiar furred face smiling at me and waving shyly, the control for her hover clutched tight in her hands. And Uraka…

Uraka was opening the back door of their hover, in full combat gear, her lips pulled tight against her tusks in a grimace filled with rage. She shouted something I couldn't hear, motioning that I should get on the floor of the cab, and I obeyed, flattening myself as best I could.

I didn't hear anything for a little bit, my heart pounding in my ears, but then a loud, heavy thud sounded on the roof of the hover, and in the next breath a las knife was punching through the metal and plastic, molten material dribbling onto the seat. The knife dragged, slicing into the top of the vehicle until three sides of a square had been cut. Then two knives punched into the top in the center of the incomplete square, about a foot apart and angled towards each other, and then the top of the car was peeling up, plastic cracking and metal groaning.

Uraka's insane laughter trickled in, not even the howl of the wind loud enough to drown her out. Then she was crouching by the hole and offering me her hand.

I took it, terrified about what might have been happening but willing to trust Uraka with my life. She hauled me up onto the roof of the hover, bringing me up to stand beside her. She leaned in close to shout in my ear. "We will have to jump back." She gently honked my boob, like back in the crate all those weeks ago, making me jump and squeak. "Djelani will get as close as she can," she continued, "and then you must move quickly. Ready?"

I shook my head, eyes wide, as Djelani swerved closer, bringing the open side door within five feet of me, and I froze, knowing there was no way I'd ever be able to get my body to make that leap.

Uraka seemed to realize this at the same time I did; before my brain could process what was happening I was being hauled up and flung through the air, my breath leaving me in a shrill scream. *Please,*

please, please, don't let me die, I begged, my eyes stuck open wide, weeping from the wind and my terror, but Uraka's aim had been perfect. I sailed through the opening and landed with a bounce and a shriek inside their hover. Then Uraka's muscles were bunching, and she, too, was sailing through the air. Her hands caught the edge of the door, and she hauled herself inside, closing the door behind herself.

I was panting, so freaked out I couldn't manage to do anything else.

"You did great, *pra'ja*!" Djelani called over her shoulder, making Uraka grin. "Hello again, Joss!"

"H-hi…" I managed. Then I blacked out.

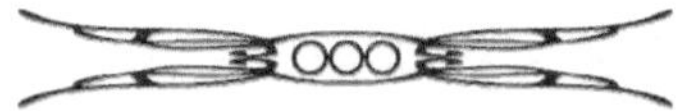

I came-to to the sounds of two voices murmuring, one deep and husky and the other light and lilting. My eyes snapped open, and I saw I was lying in the back seat of a hover, and just like that, everything was flooding back in, making me gasp and try to sit up.

"Easy, little one," Uraka crooned, placing a big warm hand on my shoulder. "You have been through a lot. We will be back at our home soon, and then we can talk and try to sort out our next move."

I turned my head, taking in Uraka and Djelani's familiar faces. "Thanks for helping me, guys," I croaked. "Have either of you tried calling Xollen?"

Uraka snorted, rolling her eyes—something that looked a lot more impressive with three of them.

"No, we haven't," Djelani cut in, shooting a hard look at Uraka, who smiled sheepishly. "Ura, why don't you try?"

Uraka looked like she wanted to protest, but she swallowed her complaints and flicked through her wristcom until she'd pulled up her contacts and dialed Xollen's number, which he'd given to everyone he'd rescued.

He picked up almost immediately, looking tense. "Uraka? What's going on?"

"We have Joss. If you want to see her again you will meet us at our home." She rattled off the address, then cut the call and leaned forward between the two front seats to place a smacking kiss on Djelani's cheek. "See, my love? I can be nice."

"That sounded like you were holding me hostage, Uraka!" I protested. I went to flick on my own comm, now that my head had cleared some and I was able to sit up, but when I tried to turn it on it was unresponsive. It didn't look damaged, so I must have forgotten to charge the damn thing. I sighed, hoping Xollen wouldn't have a panic attack. "Could you please tell him I'm not in danger? My comm's not working and I don't want him to worry."

Uraka sighed and rolled her eyes but opened up her text comm menu and typed a message, hopefully to do as I asked.

"Thank you, Uraka!" I said sweetly, giving her a bright smile. "Have I told you lately how you're one of my best friends and I missed you?" The annoyance on Uraka's face melted away, replaced by something more tender.

"Ah, I have missed you as well, little one. Why have you been hiding from your friend all these long weeks?"

I sighed, feeling guilty for a minute, then sat back and launched into telling her all about what I'd been up to since I'd last talked to her: helping Xollen move and get back on his feet, realizing we had feelings for each other and getting the paperwork for that taken care of, meeting his friends and the fight that led to him getting a new emoreg, then how we started our comic and it took off, finally recounting the disaster of a dinner. In no time at all we were touching down in their parking spot in front of their apartment building, which was a cute structure, smaller than I was used to at only four stories, with red brick and white trim.

"Then I called you. So now you're all caught up. I'm sorry I didn't reach out more, Uraka, Djelani. I really have missed you guys. As terrifying as the rescue was I'm glad it's forced me to get out of my little bubble and see you again." I sipped at the fragrant and spicy tea Djelani had made for me once we'd settled in to wait for Xollen.

Uraka waved her hand dismissively, her other arm wrapped around Djelani's shoulders. The delicate felican was sitting beside Uraka on their couch, tucked tight into her side and with her legs and tail draped over Uraka's lap. "Pah. I understand, little one. The important thing is that we keep the threads of friendship strong from here on out." She flushed, her free hand settling on Djelani's leg and squeezing. "I…hmm. I suppose I can forgive the billieuan male for his hand in slavery if he means that much to you. It…" she sighed heavily, and Djelani squeezed the hand that Uraka was still resting on her thigh. They shared a small, sweet smile. "It seems like perhaps I was hasty in my judgment of him."

My heart melted. "Aww, Uraka, you almost said a nice thing about Xollen!" I teased.

"Pah! You and Djelani should start a club. I am nice! I say nice things!"

I laughed. "I know you do, I've just never seen you be nice to

Xollen before. But he really does mean a lot to me," I said, my voice going softer. "I love him, and I think we might get married—er, I mean mated."

Uraka's face sank into an uncharacteristically gentle expression. "*Tch*, little one…I am happy that such a bad start to your life here has born such a delicious fruit." She gazed lovingly at her own mate, dipping her head to give her a kiss. When she pulled away she sighed heavily and opened her comm, flicking through menus until the little device started beeping and chirping like mad.

"*Uraka!*" Djelani scolded, slapping at the much bigger woman's arm.

I narrowed my eyes at my friend. "What did you do?"

"I may have…forgotten to hit 'send' on that text comm. And then accidentally silenced all of my notifications."

Wild pounding on the door interrupted before me or Djelani could start yelling at the crazy orc, and I heard Xollen's voice wailing out in the hall.

Djelani got to her feet with a sigh and jogged to the door, letting a frantic and pale Xollen into their apartment. His wide eyes darted all over, searching for me, and when he saw me he sprinted to my side and launched himself at me, sweeping me up into a bear hug and clinging tight. I could feel him shaking against me, and when he spoke into my neck his voice was raw and tight. "Joss, sweet merciful Goddess, you're alright. I was so worried, I thought you'd been hurt, I thought I'd never see you again…" He shuddered, falling silent. I held him tight, glaring at Uraka from over his shoulder.

Eventually, I coaxed him to sit in the armchair I'd been occupying, though he insisted on pulling me onto his lap and holding onto me tight. I told him what had happened with Verilla and how Uraka and Djelani had rescued me from whatever it was that his ex had been up to. Then he told me about the contract and how his parents were going to screw us over. How after he'd walked out and found me missing they'd tried to convince him to get back together with Verilla and get mated to her, because being with me was a disgrace and if he proceeded with our relationship then they'd cut him out and disinherit him. Derris and Gesea had pulled up while he was fighting with everyone out front, and they'd helped defuse the situation so that he could get away, then told him what had happened to me. "So, um…when we have our mating ceremony we will be using your name, sweetness," he added, his expression unreadable.

He'd chosen me. He'd been handed everything he'd wanted back when I'd met him on a silver platter and he'd still chosen me. My eyes burned, filling quickly with tears, and I sniffled even as I smiled. It silenced that last part of myself that had been insisting that this wasn't real, that there was no way I'd met the guy of my dreams and found happiness with him, that I'd actually managed to find someone who loved me for me, rolls and all. He wasn't faking, and he'd proved it to me once and for all by cutting himself away from his parents and Verilla.

Seeing I was crying, Xollen made a noise of distress and started patting me down like he was looking for an injury. "You're upset? Why are you upset?"

I beamed at him, cupping his beautiful face in my hands. "I'm not upset. I just love you so much, Xoll." I sniffled, blinking the tears out of my eyes and hoping it hadn't made my makeup run too bad. "I'm sorry this happened with your parents. I know it's got to be hard on you."

He leaned in and pressed his forehead to mine, breathing deep. "Yes," he whispered, pain thick in his throat. "But it is also…good. To know where I stand with them at last. And I still have you, my star. That is all I need."

I kissed him, pouring all of the love I felt for him into it, wishing I could make myself actually melt into his arms. Dimly, I heard Uraka make a noise of disgust behind me, followed by a light slap and a hissed admonishment from Djelani. But I don't think Xollen even noticed—he was too busy kissing me for all he was worth, holding me tight like he wasn't ever planning on letting me go.

When I finally pried my mouth off of his to catch my breath the room was spinning around me pleasantly. He tried to pull me back in but I stopped him with my fingertips and a grin. "Easy there, tiger. Uraka and Djelani have better things to do than watch us make out all day."

His eyes darted over my shoulder, and he grinned against my fingers. "I don't think they mind," he said, his voice sly. "They seem busy."

I looked behind me and made a strangled noise of surprise. Djelani had climbed into Uraka's lap to straddle it, and the two of them were kissing passionately, hips grinding together and completely oblivious to what me and Xollen were up to. "Should we leave?" I whispered to Xollen, turning back to face him. He nodded, standing up and carrying me bridal-style. I squeaked, clinging tight, sure he would drop me, but he was stronger than he looked, my Xollen.

"Thanks again for your help, you guys!" I called as we reached the front door. "I'll call you later about hanging out!" Then we were out the door and taking the elevator down to the first floor.

"I can walk, you know. You don't have to carry me, babe."

"I know. You think I'm doing this for you?" He snorted, tossing his head haughtily and making the simple silver chains decorating his horns tinkle. "This is for me. I want to be greedy with you and never let you out of my sight again."

I giggled. "Next thing you should talk about with Dr. Vakkas is this separation anxiety," I teased, kissing the tip of his nose.

"You love it," he rumbled, his eyes heavy-lidded. I gulped, my nipples prickling to attention. He was right: I did love it. I loved being needed like that by someone, wanted so completely that they weren't happy unless I was there beside them. I'd never been that to someone before, and it was addictive. Heady.

"Maybe," I murmured, my voice husky. Just then, the elevator stopped and opened up on the lobby, and Xollen continued carrying me to his hover, parked illegally out front.

Chapter Thirty-Two
No Contact

<u>XOLLEN</u>

"So now I am no longer talking to either of my parents, and have blocked them in all of the ways that I can. They will be furious, but I think it is for the best."

Dr. Vakkas blinked at me, looking stunned about what had happened since last week. "Wow, that is quite a lot, Xollen. I'm so glad no one was hurt, that sounds like it was very stressful for both of you." I nodded, thinking back to how me and Joss had torn at each other like wild animals on the hover ride back to our apartment, putting it on autopilot so that we could pleasure each other without worrying about causing an accident. "How do you feel about going no contact with your parents?" she asked me, cutting into my reminiscing.

I pursed my lips, my fingers playing with the tuft of hair at the end of my tail. "Sad," I admitted. "Angry, that they made me make that choice. Fearful of what they might do in retaliation. But I think sadness is the one that I'm struggling with the most."

"Of course. Can you tell me more about what things are making you sad?"

"I'm sad…that they tried to take advantage of me. That they didn't care about me enough to put me before their business interests. I'm sad that I may never be able to see them again, to talk to them, because even though they have been awful to me my whole life they…they're still my parents. And it's…hard. For them to be gone so suddenly."

Tears gathered in my eyes, and because this was Dr. Vakkas, I let them fall. "In some ways, it feels like they've died. Is that wrong to say?"

Dr. Vakkas shook her head firmly, "Not at all, Xollen. In a way, there has been a death, even if both of your parents are still alive. The relationship that you had is gone, and because of what *they've* done, it can't come back. It might be that they can realize what they've done and change for the better, and then you'll have a new relationship with them, but the one you had is gone, and it is perfectly valid to mourn that."

Tears flowed faster now, and I couldn't speak around the lump in my throat. I pulled up my comm menu and sent a text comm to Joss, then swallowed a few times and took a deep breath, wiping at my face with the backs of my fingers. "I miss them, but I miss the version of them that I always craved growing up. The version of them that I saw in brief flashes when I was very little. I—"

The door to my room flew open behind me and Joss burst in, looking frantic. "What's wrong, I thought you had your session?!"

I turned and held my arms out to her, beckoning her closer. "I need a hug," I told her, letting her see my tears. Joss was my mate, my partner. She could see my tears, too.

"Oh, honey…" she murmured, coming to me and wrapping her arms around me and kissing my cheek. That was when she saw Dr. Vakkas, watching us calmly on the monitor. "Oh! Um, hello. I'm Joss. Dr. Vakkas, I assume?"

The older felican female inclined her head. "It's so good to meet you, Joss. Xollen has told me many wonderful things about you."

My Joss blushed, her golden skin going rosy. "I'm sorry to interrupt, he just sent me a comm that said 'help I need you now' and I thought it was an emergency."

"It is," I grumbled, nuzzling my face into the side of her head. "I needed a hug very badly." Then I pulled her into my lap and cuddled her close, breathing in her scent and basking in her warmth and her softness. "I am finishing my session like this."

"But don't you want your privacy, Xoll? I'm right outsi—"

"No. I want you here. I'm only talking about things that you already know, or would want you to know, since we are to be mated."

"Xollen, you hadn't mentioned that! Congratulations, you two!" Dr. Vakkas exclaimed, clapping her hands and smiling brightly. I may have puffed out my chest just the littlest bit with pride, for managing to convince such a beautiful and perfect person to join me as one.

"It's still early yet, but we are hoping the process goes smoothly and we can be officially mated. Joss's people call it a weeding."

"*Wedding*," Joss interjected. "Close though, babe."

"But yes, it is very good and exciting that that is happening. It makes what has happened with my parents easier to bear." I rested my chin on Joss's shoulder.

"Certainly. There's nothing like something beginning to make losing something else a little easier. Did you want to speak more on what you feel sad about?"

I twisted my mouth, thinking. "I am also sad that they could not be happy for me and Joss. They tried to get me to abandon her and join with Verilla instead. They had met her, seen her and talked to her, and they were so blinded by their greed that they didn't see how wonderful she is, how perfect she is for me. It makes me realize that they do not really see people, or only see what they want to see. It must mean that they are very bitter and lonely, behind closed doors."

Joss's hand came up and cupped the side of my face, her cheek pressing into the top of my head. I held her tighter. She was my star, my miracle, the other half of my soul, and my parents thought I would ever be content with Verilla? They were fools.

True to my word, I finished up the last twenty minutes of my session with Joss in my lap, my arms wrapped tight around her.

"Thank you for trusting me to be present for that," Joss said softly once it was over. She twisted to be able to look at me. "You've come so far in the last couple of months, you know that?" She cupped my face in both her hands, looking me in the eyes. "I'm so proud of you, Xollen. You're doing so well."

At her words, something melted deep in my chest. My throat got thick again, but this time I didn't let the tears fall. This time I pulled my female in close and claimed her mouth in a searing kiss. I had learned much about kissing in the months since Joss had introduced it to me, and I tried to throw everything I'd learned at her in that moment. I stroked my tongue slowly over hers, letting her feel me, dance with me, then sped up my movements, my mouth hungry and hot against hers. She moaned, pressing closer to me, her sweet taste on my tongue and sinking into my pores.

I lifted her in my arms, taking the handful of steps in between my desk chair and the bed in a flash, and laid her down gently on her back. I crawled in until I was on top of her, balancing on my elbows as my hands wandered over her body, making her shiver and gasp into my mouth. I drank her sounds down greedily, my hands going bolder so I could wring more out of her. My palm found the peak of one of her breasts, my fingers curling around the meat of her until I was gently squeezing the whole thing in my hand, making her arch up into my touch and moan. I played with the heft of her for a moment, mesmerized at how soft and pliant this part of her was, before releasing her to rub my thumb back and forth over the hard little nipple I could feel through her clothes. She nipped at my lower lip, her breaths panting and her body trembling with her need. She'd begun grinding her pelvis into me, and I didn't think she was aware that she was doing it.

I released her breast and turned my attention to the other one, giving it the same treatment. Soon she was whimpering beneath me, begging me to touch her more, to go to where she needed me, and how could I not, when she asked so prettily?

With one last sweeping kiss, I pulled away and began to trail kisses down her body, removing her clothes slowly and worshipping every inch of flesh that was revealed. Soon she was naked beneath me, her golden skin gleaming in the light from the window. My eyes were immediately drawn to the damp curls clinging to her sex, and because I was an impatient male I grabbed her by one thigh and spread her wide, my cock aching and tje front of my pants damp with precum at the sight of her like this.

I settled myself between her legs, nuzzling the impossibly soft skin of her inner thighs and pressing kisses there. But I could not stop myself from devouring her for long—I never could. I spread her lower lips with my fingers, breathless at the sight of all that flushed and glistening flesh, then dove in, using the textured flat of my tongue to lap at the swollen bud of her clit. She cried out immediately, so sensitized and eager for me, making my cock throb hard where it was trapped between the bed and my body. My own desire was urging me to go faster, harder, but I knew my Joss liked a slow build, so I kept my tongue firm and steady against her sopping flesh.

Her cries filled the room like the sweetest music, the trembling of her thighs on my shoulders and against my head telling me she was getting close. Now I increased my pressure, laving my tongue against her sensitive clit faster, before taking it between my lips and starting to suck her gently.

It wasn't long before she was coming against my mouth, her thighs clamped so tight against my head that I could barely hear her screams of pleasure. I slowed my movements, gentling them, but I didn't let up, coaxing more orgasms out of her. I released her folds and used that hand to circle the slick, throbbing entrance to her core, then sank two fingers into her sucking heat. I curled my fingers up, stroking until I felt that spongy area she called a g-spot. I kept up the pressure there, sliding my fingers over it firmly, keeping my mouth glued to her sweet pussy as she began to cry and shake at a higher intensity again.

"X-xollennnn," she moaned, her voice hoarse from how much noise she had been making. "Fuck, baby. F-f-f-fuuuuuck." I moved my fingers faster, the wet sounds of them plunging into her delicious and filthy, as I suckled at her clit once again.

She came again with a keening cry, her whole body arching up off the bed and pressing her pelvis harder against my mouth. I pulled back in time to stop my teeth from connecting with her delicate flesh. I slipped my fingers from her fluttering channel, the spasming muscles reluctant to let me go, then licked them clean, groaning at her flavor—I had been drinking her down this whole time, but every taste was one to be relished. I stroked up and down her quivering thighs, pressing more kisses to them, to her curl-covered mound, before sitting up and beginning to strip my own clothes off.

Joss struggled up onto her elbows, watching me undress with a gaze that was equal parts dazed and hungry. "How about you now?" she rasped, her eyes widening as my cock sprang free from my pants to bob in the air.

I loved it when Joss used her mouth on me, but as incredible as that felt it wasn't what I wanted right now. I shook my head, kicking my pants to the floor and crawling over her so that my body was over hers again, my hips resting in the cradle of hers. "I want to be inside you too badly, my love," I murmured into her ear, my lips trailing down the line of her throat, breathing the smell of her skin in deep. She was a feast for all my senses, my Joss.

I kissed her again, my lips a hungry press against hers, even as I reached between our bodies and guided my cockhead to her entrance. I notched myself there, my heart racing in anticipation, then sank into her in one smooth motion, making both of us groan at the sweetness of our joining. One of her legs hitched up around my waist, the heel of her foot pressing into my backside and urging me to move. I curled my tail around that foot, anchoring her to me more securely.

"So eager for me, my mate?" I asked her as I drew my hips back and pushed back into her with agonizing slowness.

"You're in a very t-teasing mood today, huh?" she asked me breathlessly, a small smile tugging at the corners of her mouth. "Do you want me to beg for it?"

I froze, my cock surging into her at the idea. "Yes," I blurted, resuming my slow pumps in and out of her sweet heat. "I think I do."

She licked her lips, a wicked grin curling them as she gazed up at me. Her hands gripped my biceps hard, almost enough to hurt, both of her heels digging into my ass and urging me faster. "Fuck me, Xollen. Please, I need you so bad. Can't you feel how much I need you?" She rolled her hips, making my eyes roll back into my head. "My pussy is aching for you. Please, baby. Please."

Something in me snapped at her words, and suddenly being slow and teasing was the last thing I wanted; I snapped my hips forward, grinding into her so that my thatch could caress her clit and make her whimper in pleasure. Her eyes went dazed and unfocused. "Yes, just like that," she gasped, her teeth worrying at her plump lip again. "God yes, I need that beautiful cock so bad, Xolllen. Give it to me."

I snarled, pressing my face into her throat and doing as she asked, my hips pistoning in and out of her, obscene wet sounds fighting for dominance with the sounds of our breaths and our cries in the cool air of the room. She was already so sensitized that it felt like no time at all before I felt her clenching and fluttering around me with the beginnings of another orgasm. I kept my thrusts shallower, but no less hard, concentrating on keeping the tentacles of my thatch poised over her clit, flicking and stroking it even as I pounded into her. She had to drop one of her hands from its death grip on my shoulder to brace herself against the headboard, to stop her from sliding with the power of my thrusts.

Her eyes screwed shut in concentration, her cries reaching a fever pitch before she went almost eerily silent, too focused on her mounting pleasure, and I knew that meant a big one was coming. She only got quiet for the big ones. I felt my own orgasm begin boiling down my spine. My sac was pulled up tight against my shaft, ready to pump her full of my seed as soon as I let go. I refused to let up until she reached her peak, knowing these bigger ones were rarer for her.

Just before she snapped, her eyes flew open, meeting mine with amazed wonder, then everything in her clenched tight, her cunt clamping onto my aching cock like a fist, wrestling my control away from me and making me tumble over my own edge. I kept moving though, even though I was coming so hard I thought my legs might cramp, to make sure she saw the entirety of her peak.

Once I was spent, I collapsed on top of her, burying my face in her sweaty hair. She held me close, encouraging me to put my full weight on her. She said she liked it, but I didn't want to hurt her, so I kept myself propped on one leg and an elbow.

She was giggling and petting me, feeling the curious effects of my seed on her body.

"*Ave María,* that was some good shit," she said dreamily. I chuckled, rolling us onto our sides and maneuvering her so I was curled around her in a position she called "spooning". An Earth device, apparently.

"I am glad you approve, my mate. I aim to please."

She patted the arm I had slung over her middle. "Well, then good job. No, *great* job. No, *amaaazing* job. I feel like I'm flying."

I squeezed her tighter, burying my face in the crook of her neck as much as my horns would let me. "I am glad I can make you fly, my star. You make me feel the same. With you, I feel…free. Alive. Happier than I ever thought I could feel." My chest felt tight from all of the love I felt for her.

She spun in my arms to face me, her pupils blown wide but eyes warm. She kissed me softly, sweetly, her lips a soft caress against mine. "I love you so much," she whispered into my mouth.

"I love you, too," I whispered back. I nuzzled her nose with my own, flatter one. "Let's get mated right now. Today. I want you forever."

She barked a laugh. "We already applied for it, goof," she reminded me. "We're just waiting on the certs."

I growled, grabbing her comically small hands and nipping at the fingers playfully, making her giggle and squirm. "How dare you remind me," I grumbled, rolling her on top of me. "I am utterly devastated now. I'm dying from heartache. Some incredibly gorgeous physical manifestation of the Goddess herself is going to have to find a way to revive me." I clutched at my hearts, groaning and flailing under her dramatically, before slumping back into the bed, eyes closed. I stuck my tongue out and exhaled loudly for added effect. Which I may have ruined by cracking my eye open to watch Joss.

She was struggling not to laugh, but she pressed her lips into a firm line and then started wiggling down my body. "Oh no!" she said, her voice sly. "I've got to do CPR *right now!*" She slid the rest of the way down my body, crouching between my spread legs, and licked a bold stripe down the middle of my spent cock, making it reinflate with new life.

Her brilliant mouth made quick work of rousing me, re-awakening my hunger impossibly fast. When I started groaning and panting she released me with a wet pop, smirking up at me. "It worked! The patient lives!" She then proceeded to do her best to remove my soul from my body.

Epilogue

<u>JOSS</u>

"Close your eyes, okay?" I smoothed the flowing crimson skirts down against my thighs and patted the short hair at the back of my head. I was still getting used to the pixie cut, but it didn't look too bad on me. I'd decided it was time to get rid of the frizzy bleach-fried mess and go back to how I liked my hair: *au naturale.* I'd been nervous that Xollen wouldn't like it, because guys back on Earth had hangups about short hair on femmes for some reason, but he loved it. Said it let him see my face that much better.

"Besides, my sweet mate," he'd said, tucking one of the longer pieces behind my ear, "I have been worried that one of these days we will wake up with our long hair knotted together and unable to free ourselves. So this soothes me." I hadn't been able to tell if he was joking or not.

My insanely handsome soon-to-be-offically-mine mate shuffled into the room, arms outstretched but eyes dutifully closed. "I don't know why you are insisting on keeping this a secret," he grumbled, coming to a stop once he'd cleared the doorway. "I have helped you pick all of this out. I have already seen it."

"It's an Earth thing," I told him, grinning at his pout. "It's supposed to be bad luck for the groom to see the bride before the wedding."

"Groom? Bride?"

"The two people getting married."

"Gah, there are so many terms for that one ceremony! It is a marriage and you get married but it is also a wedding, and then you have the two people getting married, who are the newlyweds, or spouses, and now you tell me they are also a bride and groom? I like our words better. You get mated. You are mates. Simple."

I laughed; this was not the first time I was hearing this particular rant, but I still found his grumpy huffing adorable. And I knew he didn't mean it; he'd told me he was just teasing the first time.

"Alright, you lunatic. Open your eyes, then. We have to head down to the room soon anyway."

He did as I said, opening his eyes and taking me in in my full "mating day" getup.

Since I wasn't a virgin (and we weren't on Earth anyway) I'd gone with a gauzy bright red dress with a sweetheart neckline and off-the-shoulder sleeves. Layers of tulle floated around me, wrapping around the bodice of the dress so that it showcased my waist and bust but flowed out to hide my tummy—I was getting less insecure about it all the time, but it was a work in progress. I'd borrowed one of Xollen's horn chains and worn it around my neck, and had a hair comb carved from something pearlescent and glowy in a spray of flowers. More flowers carved from the same material dangled off of it by delicate chains. It had been a gift from Gesea, before she knew I'd cut my hair, but I was making it work with a lot of really clever hair pinning and styling gel. I'd kept my makeup light but couldn't resist painting my lips a bold red that matched my dress. I felt like a princess, and I hoped Xollen would like it.

I was not prepared for him to start crying.

"You are stunning, Joss," he croaked, producing a silk handkerchief from thin air and dabbing at his eyes. "I cannot believe the Goddess has blessed me with such a perfect mate."

My own eyes started prickling with tears, and I waved my hands in front of my face to try and stop them from falling. "Goddammit Xoll, you're going to make me cry and ruin my makeup."

He handed me his hankie and I used it to carefully dab away the tears. "I'm sorry, but one could argue that this is your fault for being so beautiful at a time like this."

We both laughed, and then I couldn't resist taking this smudge-proof lipstick for a test run, kissing my man silly.

Uraka burst into the room, making us both jump and separate.

"They are ready, Joss!" she exclaimed, panting like she'd run here. She looked very dashing in her suit, her long hair pulled back into an elaborate tangle of braids that Djelani has done for her this morning. "What are you still doing here?" she howled, spotting Xollen. "Leave this place at once and get into position!"

I shared a look with Xollen. You'd think *she* was the one getting mated today, instead of just giving me away in the Earth tradition. "Ura, calm yourself. The room is right down the hall. The justice of the peace isn't going anywhere. It's fine. Better go though before she picks you up and throws you there," I added to Xollen, giving him one last peck.

"I think you are *too* calm, little one," she grumbled once he'd left, crossing her arms and showing off how her biceps bulged against the fabric of the suit. "This is a momentous occasion. You reach into the aether of the universe as one and declare your bond for all to see. Veldar themself could not rip you apart after this day."

I smiled at my friend, patting her cheek, where the traditional yvrenii mating tattoo had been inked after her and Djelani's joining last month. "I know, but I'm worried you're going to hurt yourself if you stay worked up like this."

She chuckled, gold eyes flashing, then offered me her arm to begin leading me down the hall to the small auditorium where mating ceremonies were held.

I hadn't been interested in doing a whole other ceremony just to get the things I wanted from an American-style wedding, but I had wanted to involve all my new friends and family in the ceremony, so I'd convinced Uraka, Djelani, and Gesea to be my wedding party, while Derris acted as Xollen's best man.

We'd invited Hellum, the yvrenii security guard, after all, as well as Ghena and Wren, so while I thought it was an incredibly small wedding, it was a huge collection of people for a mating ceremony according to everyone else. We'd gotten a lot of looks from the officials in this wing of the building, and even though we'd told them what to expect, Justice Hollstis still seemed shocked and a little overwhelmed.

Other than that the process was very official and dry: the justice read over the mating agreement, we signed all the necessary paperwork, and then spoke our vows. I had added the kiss and the ring exchange, and then that was it: me and Xollen were officially mates. He was mine and I was his, and there was nothing his parents or Verilla could do about it.

"Let me get another picture of the happy couple!" Gesea called, urging us together. "Let's see a kiss!"

We obliged, and everyone cheered like dorks. "That one's going on the nexpage!" Derris called, making us laugh. They'd convinced us to announce our mating on the comic's nexpage, as a reason for why there'd be two weeks with no updates, and the outpouring of support and affection from our readers was almost overwhelming. So many had asked for pictures and updates, and who was I to deny those wonderful people anything?

"We should head over to the restaurant," Djelani pointed out, flicking the tasseled end of her lavender garment—I forgot what it was called, but it resembled a sari back on Earth—over her shoulder and threading her arm through her own mate's. Uraka was a wreck, sobbing and gasping with emotion, and Djelani tugged her out the doors to help her calm down.

"You are so beautiful, little one!" Uraka hiccuped over her shoulder. "I am so happy for you!"

"We're moving to the restaurant!" Derris bellowed from between cupped hands. "Everyone out!" They'd have to start setting up the room for the next couple's ceremony soon, anyway.

Hellum strolled up to us, beaming and looking a little misty-eyed. "I'm so happy for you two. Congratulations, my friends!" He clapped us both on the shoulder. "I hope I can find something half as beautiful as what you have." I noticed that his eyes darted over to Ghena, who was helping Wren clear away the few decorations we'd bothered with. Hellum congratulated us once more, sweeping us into a tight hug this time, then said his goodbyes and left to make his way to where we'd have a nice dinner together to celebrate.

"Come, my bride," Xollen said, wrapping an arm around my waist. "I'm starving."

"I'm actually your wife now that the ceremony's over," I told him, suppressing my laughter.

As expected he squawked and turned his head to look at me. "That's it, I give up. I can't handle all these Earth words. You are my *mate*, and that is good enough."

I laughed, tilting my head back to look at his beautiful face, grinning down at me with love.

"Yeah, it is." I agreed.

¿Cómo se dice?

<u>Pronunciation Guide</u>

<u>Cast</u>
    Josslyn Aceveda/Joss (J*OZZ-lynn ah-seh-VAY-duh)/ (J*AWSE) *as in "jam"
    Xollen Me'Tirri Be'Faan (ZAHL-len MAY-teer-ee BAY-fahn)
    Uraka (oo-ROCK-uh)
    Djelani (gel-AHN-ee)
    Derris (DEHR-iss)
    Gesea (g*eh-SAY-uh) *hard g sound, as in "game"
    Wren (REN)
    Ghena (G*EN-uh) *hard g sound, as in "game"
    Hellum (HELL-uhm)
    Tirri (TEER-ee)
    Faan (FAHN)
    Verilla (vur-ILL-uh)
    Dr. Shiya Vakkas (SHEE-yuh VAH-kuss)

<u>Places</u>
    Billieu (bill-YOO)
    Escheva (eh-SHAY-vuh)
    Quellor (KELL-or)
    Tunnalah (too-nah-LAH)
    Mon II (MAHN two)

<u>Alien Races</u>
    Billieuan (bill-YOO-uhn)
    Yvrenii (i*hv-REN-ee) *short i sound, as in "in"
    Felican (fell-EE-can)

213

Myauanni (myow-AHN-ee)
Th'rak (THRAK)/Th'rakkan (THRAK-ahn)

<u>Miscellaneous</u>
Vrakaash (vrah-KAHSH)/vrakaashaad (vrah-kah-SHAHD)
Pra'ja (prah-ZSA*) *as in the name Zsa Zsa Gabor

El mundo

<u>Worldbuilding Fun* Facts</u>

<u>Billieu</u>

- Naming conventions: the surname is compounded, with "Me" prefix denoting the birth-giver and the "Be" prefix denoting the secondary parent. The suffix is always the given name of that parent. Xollen's mother's given name is Tirri, and his father's given name is Faan, which is why Xollen's last name is Me'Tirri Be'Faan. The shorthand is the neuter "Se" prefix plus an elision of the parent's names. This is why Xollen's parents' business is called Se'Tirraan Entertainment.
- Billieu's thorny relationship with illness and sanitation began two generations prior, when back-to-back pandemics ravaged the population. Some instances were airborne, others sexually transmitted, and still others genetic in nature, and the desire to avoid further damage to the population has resulted in strict laws and regulations surrounding hygiene. Clearance (with permits) must be given to live with anyone who is not immediate family. Courtships must be registered and all parties involved must be listed and given complete physicals prior to engagement in the relationship. When courtships wish to progress into matings, additional certification obtained via genetic testing must be done, unless all parties are sterilized. Since enacting these strict measures Billieu's population and economy are recovering and experiencing fresh growth.
- Billieuans refer to months as lunars (because a month is one lunar cycle) and years as orbits (because it is that amount of time for their planet to complete its orbit around their sun. Their sky is green.
- The most common religion worships an unnamed goddess, thought to protect their people and guide their lives. She does not have a name because it is believed that it is untranslatable into mortal speech.

* * *

The Intergalactic Collective
- The Intergalactic Collective, also called simply "The Collective" or "IG", is the planetary alliance between the space-faring populations of known space. Contact with primitive (i.e., not yet space-faring) planets is strictly forbidden so as not to influence the evolution of primitive peoples.
- Several species in the Collective are known to form lifelong mate bonds. Of the species mentioned in *All or Nothing* Billieuans, felicans, and yvrenii form these bonds. It isn't common for the bonds to occur interspecially, but it can happen.

Random Shit
- Most Billieuans are born with a deep cleft that goes from their hairline all the way down to their chin. They also have horns, prehensile tails, and are born with two hearts. They tend to be very tall and willowy in build compared to humans. Their eyes have no sclera, and are swirls of different tones of one color, and their sexual fluids are the same color. The swirling is affected by mood and exertion.
- During sexual intercourse, semen and vaginal secretions mix and react to induce a feeling of relaxation in the impregnable partner. The reaction in a Billieuan and human coupling is much, much stronger, leading to an intense but short-lived high for the human woman.
- The Pokemon Mew is totally based off of a myauanni alien seen by a designer at Gamefreak while on vacation in 1992.

**fun is a subjective experience and thus cannot be guaranteed by the author of this list. Please note that she is a gigantic nerd who thinks things like the workings of an extraterrestrial government are the height of entertainment.*

Delirios de una loca

I know these things are supposed to be all formal and talk about what's going on next so I can market my books, but I just like chatting with you guys, so that's how I'm doing it.

All or Nothing was my attempt at NaNoWriMo 2022, and marks the first win in over a decade of haphazardly attempting it. This bad boy is kicking off my much more chill and laid-back *Interstellar Attraction* series, which is meant to be more casual and fun, as well as being sci-fi instead of fantasy or paranormal. I have at least three books planned for the main series, plus a couple of associated books that aren't directly related but that take place in the same universe. The one I'm working on right now, *Not Even the Stars Are Alone*, is an offshoot where some minor characters make another appearance but it's a separate storyline, if that makes sense to y'all. I'm hoping to publish that one in late April or May! My pitch for it is that it's like *Spy X Family* meets *Claimed By the Alien Bodyguard* by Tiffany Roberts. Sephyr, the MMC for that one, is probably the hottest guy I've written so far. He intimidates me, despite my being the one to spawn him into existence, but fret not—he is still a certifiable cinnamon roll. I absolutely love him and Eva, and hope you guys will too!

Uraka and Djelani are going to get a book, obviously—Uraka exploded off the page and has not given me a moment of peace since, but I love that crazy orc and her mega mommy vibes. Ghena and Hellum also will get a book, but they're going to be much further out in my schedule, I think. I'm contemplating a book for Wren (who, in my headcannon, absolutely inspired Mew, even if she acts more like Mewtwo) but I think I'd make her ace and possibly aro if I did, which means hecking research! I'm demisexual personally—which is on the ace spectrum—but I like to find books written by the folx I'm trying to convey to get the inside scoop, so…research!

I sincerely hope that my very Americanized Latina Joss isn't problematic; I wrote her that way with the intent of representing people like my husband and his siblings. For those who don't already know, he's Latino, but was purposely raised to be as "white" as possible (my mother-in-law has said this outright) because of the stigma and racism that his parents and so many people of Latinx descent face here in the US (really though it's a lot of different ethnic groups that suffer with this. It's kind of a big problem). Hubby has said on multiple occasions that he feels "too Hispanic for white people but too white for Hispanic people", and that's the experience that I wanted to speak to with Joss. But I wasn't able to get a sensitivity reader for this one in the time I had allotted (due to some life stuff that exploded) so if you come from this background and feel like I bungled it then 1) I wholeheartedly and sincerely apologize for my ignorance and problematic depiction and 2) I would eternally appreciate such feedback (via email) so that I can learn from my mistakes and do better in the future! I *do* have another still-untitled book I'm planning with a much less Americanized Latina FMC—so I'll add that if you'd be interested in sensitivity reading for that down the line then to please let me know, also via email: MirandaSapphireWrites@gmail.com

Now I know what you're thinking: "hey, where are all the sequels? You just keep writing the starts of new things, dummy!" and yes, yes I do. It's one of the things I struggle with as a writer, and it's a weakness that I didn't discover until *after* I started publishing. Yippee! But this year I *will* get to *Out of the Dark,* the sequel to *A Light in the Dark*, even if it kills me. I've been trying to outline it for like, three months and it's just *refusing* to place nice and let me wrangle it, so I'm going to rawdog it like I did ALITD and see what happens. Sam and Claire just haven't felt like cooperating and telling me what they're interested in getting up to and *it is driving me crazy*! I have some scenes written already, it's just the overall narrative that eludes me *grump grump grump*. I'd also like to get another *Star-Crossed Cryptid* novella out this year, and *at least* one more *Interstellar Attraction* book besides AoN and NETSAA, but we shall see. I'm still figuring this all out and getting my feet under me, and I appreciate how kind and understanding people have been thus far! <3

I know I've said this before, but my website is coming! My husband is building it for me from the ground up, but he's doing it in his limited free time, and the poor guy is doing the best he can! In the meantime, I have a temporary website at: mirandasapphirewrites.carrd.co

If you sign up for my newsletter (the sign-up link is at the temp site!) that'll be one of the first places I'll send out notice that things are up and running! I'll also be giving access to little freebies through my newsletter, like bonus and deleted scenes, so while it's not much right now it's going to be a very happening scene in like…AN amount of time.

A huge freaking thanks to my amazing beta babes Mattie (I'm so sorry I spelled your name wrong last time >.<), Amanda, and Catrina! Your feedback was, simply put, the tits <3

Thanks a million to Tainah Ferreira/@taylaedraws for the cover! You brought my adorable dweebs to life so beautifully!

—Miranda Sapphire, February 2023

* * *

PS: Bonus internet points for anyone who knows what real-life book Joss is reading in the first chapter :3